ALSO BY GLENN BECK

Cowards: What Politicians, Radicals, and the Media Refuse to Say

Being George Washington

Snow Angel

The Original Argument

The 7

Broke: The Plan to Restore Our Trust, Truth and Treasure

The Overton Window

Idiots Unplugged: Truth for Those Who Care to Listen (audiobook)

The Christmas Sweater: A Picture Book

Arguing with Idiots: How to Stop Small Minds and Big Government

Glenn Beck's Common Sense:
The Case Against an Out-of-Control Government, Inspired by Thomas Paine

America's March to Socialism:
Why We're One Step Closer to Giant Missile Parades (audiobook)

The Christmas Sweater

An Inconvenient Book: Real Solutions to the World's Biggest Problems

The Real America: Early Writings from the Heart and Heartland

AGENDA 21

GLENN BECK

WITH HARRIET PARKE

THRESHOLD EDITIONS · MERCURY RADIO ARTS

New York   London   Toronto   Sydney   New Delhi

Threshold Editions/Mercury Radio Arts
A Division of Simon & Schuster, Inc.
1230 Avenue of the Americas
New York, NY 10020

First Threshold Editions/Mercury Radio Arts hardcover edition November 2012

THRESHOLD EDITIONS and colophon are trademarks of Simon & Schuster, Inc.

GLENN BECK is a trademark of Mercury Radio Arts, Inc.

For information about special discounts for bulk purchases, please contact Simon & Schuster Special Sales at 1-866-506-1949 or business@simonandschuster.com.

The Simon & Schuster Speakers Bureau can bring authors to your live event. For more information or to book an event, contact the Simon & Schuster Speakers Bureau at 866-248-3049 or visit our website at www.simonspeakers.com.

Designed by Joy O'Meara

Manufactured in the United States of America

10 9 8 7 6 5 4 3 2 1

ISBN 978-1-4767-1669-5
ISBN 978-1-4767-1700-5 (ebook)

*To all those who hold fast
to the spirit of the American Dream Labs;
the storytellers like Harriet who seek the hard facts
and then find new ways to expose, enlighten, inspire
and spread courage across the entire world.*

Humanity stands at a defining moment in history. We are confronted with a perpetuation of disparities between and within nations, a worsening of poverty, hunger, ill health and illiteracy, and the continuing deterioration of the ecosystems on which we depend for our well-being.

The developmental and environmental objectives of Agenda 21 will require a substantial flow of new and additional financial resources to developing countries.... Financial resources are also required for strengthening the capacity of international institutions for the implementation of Agenda 21.

This process marks the beginning of a new global partnership for sustainable development.

—PREAMBLE, AGENDA 21,

UNITED NATIONS CONFERENCE, RIO DE JANEIRO, JUNE 1992

[The purpose of Agenda 21 is] to promote patterns of consumption and production that reduce environmental stress and meet the basic needs of society.

—AGENDA 21, CHAPTER 4, OBJECTIVE 7.A

CHAPTER ONE

They took Mother away today.

I was on my energy board when they came. They didn't knock. They just came in, men in black uniforms. Enforcers. I shut off my board and stumbled, hitting my hip against the metal sidebar. They didn't say anything but held up their hands in a way that told me to stop and not come any closer. My meter was only halfway to the finish point. Mother had gotten off her sleeping mat when she heard them at the door and stood there, head down. How tangled her hair looked, gray and lifeless.

They asked which sleeping mat was hers. She pointed to mine. I started to say, "No that's mine," but she gave a little shake of her head so I kept quiet. One of them rolled up the mat and put it under his arm. The other one tied short, dirty ropes to Mother's wrists. I knew not to cry in front of the Enforcers but tears burned hot behind my eyes.

Mother hadn't done her duty walking since I was paired with Jeremy two days ago. She had stayed curled up on her sleeping mat, her face to the wall, her back a row of bony knobs. I had walked both my board and hers those two days so our meters would register at Central Authority for two people. That was the only way to get food for both of us.

Maybe they could tell one person was doing two different meters because the meters registered at different times. Who knows? I've seen too many things over the almost eighteen years I've spent on this Earth to ever doubt the Authority's power.

Mother went quietly, shuffling her feet across the rough concrete floor. She looked back at me and said, "I'm sorry I didn't teach you enough. . . . I love you." There was a scratchy sound to her voice as though the words were stuck inside her. "I'm sorry, Emmeline." I didn't know what she meant and I didn't have time to ask. The Enforcers, one on each side of her, tugged on the ropes. She looked weak and shrunken between them.

I watched through the window slit as they pulled Mother up the steps of the bus-box. How trapped she looked sitting between them. Six other men, large and muscular in orange uniforms, stood in their harnesses. The Transport Team. The bus-box lurched forward as the men began walking in unison. I watched until it disappeared around the curve past our Compound.

Then I ran after her. The Gatekeeper didn't see me; he was making rounds at the far end. I ran as fast and as hard as I could along the ridge between the ruts in the dirt road, the muscles in my legs clenching and unclenching like fists, until I could see the bus-box.

I slipped to the side of the road, crouching down, creeping closer. The bus-box turned onto a narrower road, hidden by trees. I never knew that road was there.

The green flag marking the area was barely visible. Beyond it was a building I had never seen before. Bigger than any Living Space and a deeper, darker gray than the other buildings. No window slits, just blank, forbidding walls.

The bus-box stopped in front of the building's only door. Through the trees I could see the Enforcers walk Mother to the door. Dust swirled around her ankles as she shuffled. The odor here seemed familiar but was much more potent.

Mother still had the ropes on her wrists and the Enforcers were holding them tightly. She turned, looked at me as though she knew I'd been following her the whole time, and somehow was able to raise one hand to touch her chest, her heart. That motion lasted only a second. I'll remember it for a lifetime.

A hand reached out and pulled Mother inside. The door slammed shut.

While the Enforcers got back on the bus-box, I hid behind a tree and watched until they disappeared. Then I leaned my head against the tree and beat my fists against the rough bark until they bled.

* * *

Alone.

I had never been alone before. Mother never allowed that. Never. Jeremy was not yet back from work. Around me was only gray. Gray walls, gray floor. A cold concrete square. One window slit on each of the four walls and the single wooden door that led outside to the Compound's common area, a packed dirt space with a gate, guarded by a Gatekeeper. Inside, the space was divided into three areas. To one side of the door was the eating space with a counter to place our nourishment cubes and water bottles on. On the other side, the washing-up room with its limp privacy curtain. In the back was the sleeping area, with our mats on the floor and hooks on the wall to hang our uniforms. Along the wall on the right was the energy output area. This is where our boards stood, side by side.

These were all the spaces where Mother used to be.

I walked into the sleeping area. Mother's mat, just long enough and wide enough for one person, covered with the same frayed fabric as the privacy curtain, was stretched over a foam mattress four inches thick on the cold concrete floor. Her blanket had fallen onto the floor. I picked it up and held it to my face, breathing deeply. The fabric was rough and cold, but it smelled of Mother, her skin, her hair. I could see the imprint of her body on the mat. Where her head had been, her shoulders, her hips. I ran my fingertips over the mat, feeling those spaces. Then I curled up in the imprint and pulled her blanket over me. It was safe to cry now.

* * *

There was nothing to do but get back on my board and walk. Create energy. Create energy. Create energy. Get my meter to finish. The sound of my feet pounding on the board and another sound, a low hiss, as the friction and heat of the board is siphoned away through a small hose connected to an outlet in the wall and then into the energy download bar in front of our space. Every Space has a download bar like ours, but the bars belong to the Central Authority. They own everything. They use the energy to supply our needs. Our nourishment cubes, our clothing, everything. They call it the Energy Neutral Policy. I hate their big titles.

Mother once told me that producing energy was one of the two things the Republic cared about most. The other thing was producing healthy babies. Being productive and being reproductive. The most valuable Citizens were both. Mother said I was one of the most valuable. I didn't know what she meant at the time.

The half-hour-till-dusk bell tolled. Jeremy would be home after dusk. We'd eat our nourishment cubes together, drink our water rations. I didn't think I'd be hungry, but I was already thirsty. I noticed that the needle of my energy meter had moved past halfway.

When they had paired me with Jeremy, Mother refused to get off her sleeping mat to meet him. Men with mustaches from Central Authority got off the bus-box first and walked in lockstep to our door, legs moving straight and stiff as though they had no knees. They had a new headscarf for me, white trimmed in black, and they turned their backs as I removed my black headscarf, my widow scarf, and put this one on. Then Jeremy, escorted by an Enforcer, got off the bus-box. He was thin, scrawny, and his skin was pale.

They did the pairing ceremony, the exchange of vows, in front of our Living Space: *I will honor the Republic. I will produce energy for the Republic. I will produce Citizens for the Republic. Praise be to the Republic.* Then we all made the circle sign, with our thumb and forefinger held against our foreheads, to salute the Republic.

The men went back to the bus-box and left. Jeremy and I were officially paired. We went into our Living Space. He looked around as though he had never seen one before. He pulled the privacy curtain aside and glanced into the washing-up area. He looked out of the window slits, going from one to the other, pacing back and forth with nervous little steps. Finally he stopped pacing and leaned against the counter.

"I wanted a virgin. And what did I get?" He glanced at me. "You. And an old lady." He glanced at Mother.

She sat up slowly and pointed her finger at him. I noticed for the first time how old her hands looked, how her finger curved like a claw. She looked sad and started to say something but didn't.

Jeremy said nothing else, but his eyes narrowed and his lips pinched together. Mother lay back down and never did speak to him.

That was two days ago.

I didn't teach you enough. What did she mean? What didn't I know?

Sometimes she talked a lot. Her voice had been like a metronome. Tick, talk, tick, talk. It filled our space. She scratched at her skin as she talked. Fingernails digging into her arms, her ankles. Making little sore spots bigger, crusted with blood.

"It wasn't always like this," she would say.

"Tell me."

"We had our own farm once. Land. Rolling hills. Green fields. We raised animals, crops. We owned property. It was ours."

"What happened to it? Where was it?"

"Far away. It was far away. Laws changed. The Authority owns all the property now."

Why, I wanted to ask, did the laws change? But I didn't ask her, didn't interrupt the stories. If I did, she would shut down and turn her face to the wall. That would be the end of her talking.

"We kept animals on the farm," she said.

Imagine that! Keeping animals! At every Social Update Meeting they remind us that animals are sacred and belong to the Earth, not to people. Animals are protected. We have to recite, in unison, the Pledge of Animals.

I pledge allegiance to the Earth and to the sacred rights of the Earth and to the Animals of the Earth.

Just last month a man was dragged by the Enforcers to the front of the Social Update Meeting and made to kneel before the Authorities. They accused him of running over a snake with his energy bicycle. I think he tried to say it was an accident, but his voice was shaking and hard to hear. His head was down, his chin almost on his chest. He looked small and old, kneeling that way. They put the ropes on his wrists and led him away.

Everyone at the meeting kept their eyes on their shoes. They looked tired and pale and wilted. I think every single person watching knew that could just as well have been them on any given day, for any given reason.

Mother said taking him away was wrong, just wrong. But she didn't say it very loudly.

CHAPTER TWO

Just past dusk.

Jeremy was home. I could hear him attaching his energy bicycle to the download bar, the low hiss becoming steady as energy transferred from his bicycle into the storage cell. Then I heard the metallic squeak of the nourishment box lid as he got our rations.

He came in and sat the rations down in the eating space. Didn't look at me. Didn't say hello. Just went into the washing-up area. I could smell the sanitizing solution and hear the splash of it on his skin. But there was another smell hanging in the air, something unpleasant.

"They took your mother away today," he said when he came back to the eating space.

I nodded and felt the tears behind my eyes again.

"I knew they would," he said.

"How did you know that?"

He smiled unkindly but didn't answer.

The unpleasant smell was stronger as he stood near me. It was the smell of the Recycle Center where he worked. We stood in silence, there in the eating space, facing the window slit, not looking at each other. The day had faded into dusky gray.

I drank my water rations first. The wetness felt good on my lips and tongue. Mother used to share her water with me when I was really thirsty. Would Jeremy do the same?

I wasn't really hungry but I had to eat. You can't recycle or save your nourishment cubes and you aren't allowed to waste them. I unwrapped the perfectly square, three-by-three-inch cube and ate the wrapper first. This one was fish-flavored soy, rice, and parsley.

Mother told me she used to go fishing when she was a little girl. Went with her father to a stream on the farm. They caught real fish together. She described it so vividly: running water, tumbling over stones. Other times they fished in a big round lake with crystal blue water. I loved when she talked about the past.

After we ate our cubes Jeremy went to his sleeping mat, stretched out, and immediately fell asleep. He looked tired and faded, the color of dusty stone. Even his lips were pale. He was too skinny and scrawny to do hard work.

I still felt alone, even though Jeremy was here. The Living Space was so quiet without Mother's voice. She said it was wrong how they just assigned people to each other. She said in her day, when she was young, boys and girls did something called going out on dates. I can't remember her exact words, but the whole time she talked, she scratched. Every time I had a chance, I would place my hand over hers and ask her to stop scratching at her skin.

What else had Mother said?

"We lived in the middle of the nation." That's one of the things she told me. She didn't say Republic. She said nation.

"A new law started on the East Coast," she said, "because that's where laws were made. They gave it a fancy-sounding name. Agenda 21." She walked a while on her board before going on. The rubber mat on her board and mine moved at the same speed as we stepped in unison.

"The West Coast people were the first to be moved into the Planned Communities. We found out later that there were a lot more of these communities than anyone expected. No one seems to know the exact number, or where they are all located, but we do know that each of them contains a cluster of Compounds, just like ours. Oh, such perfect organization by the Authorities!" She gave a little laugh. "Some really believed all the stuff about this new law being for the good of everyone. Life would be easy because the Authority would take care of all of us. Give us food, houses. Money would not be necessary. There would be no more poverty. They promised Paradise."

Mother said that things from that point went so fast that most of the people in the middle of the nation didn't even know what was happening. She told me that they were the last to be relocated to Planned Communities.

"We used to be able to listen to the radio, the televisions. Comedy shows. Sitcoms. News programs. Talk radio shows. We had so much to choose from.

"For a while after the new laws took hold the only thing on the radio or television were speeches by the Authority or music, patriotic music. Marching band music. But eventually even the marching band music stopped. It wasn't my favorite music but at least it was something," she said. "Something is better than nothing. Most times."

"What's a marching band?" I had asked her.

"We are. You and me, marching along on our boards."

"But there's no music. What made the music?"

"Drums and tubas and trumpets. We'll be different. We'll be a marching band without music."

We walked in silence for a while, our feet moving in matching rhythm. Then she started talking again.

"Everyone thought it changed in a blink of an eye. But not in a blink of *my* eye," she went on. "I knew."

* * *

I was just a baby when we were relocated and I don't remember much of what she was talking about. Everybody has that black hole at the beginning of their life. That time you can't remember. Your first step. Your first taste of table food. My real memories begin in our assigned living area in Compound 14. I learned the color gray from the color of our Living Space. I learned the other colors by the uniforms that people wore for their different duties. Orange uniforms for the Transport Team. Dull green for Recycle. Gray for Gatekeepers. Pink and blue for Children's Village workers. Yellow for Nourishment Cube makers. White for Chaperones. Vibrant green for Managers of Nature. Black for Enforcers. And, most important, black with gold trim for the Authorities. The all-powerful Authorities.

Our Living Space was a square building, small and squat, on a path used by bus-boxes and bicycles, in Compound 14, the Transport Compound. Men in our Compound spent their day providing transportation by pulling wooden bus-boxes. These boxes could transport up to six people at a time, one in the forward seat, one in the back, and two on each side. These existed because all transportation had to be approved by the Authority. No Citizen could walk freely because that was an expense of energy that could not be afforded. Our daily energy was, of course, to be used walking our boards or performing our assigned tasks for the betterment of the Community.

The Transporters worked in teams of six. Father had muscles on his back that bulged, hard and round, under his orange uniform. Mother said the only good thing about Compound 14 was that everybody assigned there came from the middle part of the old nation. Common, hardworking folks.

"They're just like us," she said. "And that gives me comfort."

Mother stayed at home with me and walked the energy board. Back then I had a toy energy board I had to walk every day. Not as many hours as Mother, of course, because I was a child. Children had some privileges then, but they still had to be trained. Sometimes Mother would get off her board long enough to give me a hug or teach me a song. *"I'm a little teapot, short and stout"* and she showed me how to pretend someone was going to *"tip me over and pour me out."* Other times she taught me *"The itsy bitsy spider crawled up the water-spout. . . ."* but I had to stop her and ask what a waterspout was.

"A waterspout is a pipe that allows rain to drain from a roof of a building into a container. There are no more waterspouts anymore. No more collecting rain."

I thought about this for a minute then asked her: "Why can't we collect rain? Why can't we drink the rain?" Rain was water, after all, wasn't it?

"Rain," she said, "belongs to the Earth, and the Authority controls everything that belongs to the Earth." She stopped singing and talking for the rest of that day.

I am one of the last children to have been allowed to stay at home with parents. That was my biggest privilege. Mother told me so. She said it was her biggest privilege, too. She explained to me what happened at one of the Social Update Meetings. The only thing I remember about going to those meetings when I was little was that I had to stand very quietly in the row with Mother and Father and not fidget or Mother would pinch me on the arm. It's hard for a four-year-old to stand still for so long, but she didn't want anyone to notice me. At the end of this particular meeting, when we were outside on the bicycle path, she bent down and hugged me hard and tight. And she was crying. I felt her wet cheek and touched it with my hand. When I put my fingers in my mouth, they tasted salty.

"I'm allowed to keep you," she said. "I'm allowed to keep you." I didn't know why that would make her cry or why she thought she couldn't keep me. I was her daughter. Father hugged me, too, but he kept looking around nervously, and shuffling his feet as though he wanted to run somewhere.

"Let's go home, Elsa," he'd said to Mother. "Let's go now. Not everyone is as lucky."

CHAPTER THREE

About four years ago I reached reproductive age. It was scary to see blood on my underwear. I thought I was dying. I tried to hide the underwear by rolling them up in a ball and shoving them under my clean clothes, but I couldn't fool Mother. She found them. She gave me a folded cloth to catch the blood and said it was time we had a talk.

By then I had a real energy board with a rolling black mat, metal side arms, and the little, round meter with a red needle. Mother and I walked side by side on our boards. I've forgotten lots of things Mother told me, but I will never forget what she said about the Children's Enhancement Laws.

"The Authority," she said, her words in rhythm with her steps, "decided they could do a better job of raising the children than us. Make them more productive. Train them better than their parents could."

As she talked, I put my fingers in my mouth, tasting the salt in my sweat. I needed her to explain the blood on my underwear. Why was she talking about this? But I knew she would just shut down if I tried to change the topic.

She gave me a sideways look, as if trying to figure out how much information I could hold, like I was an empty cup that needed to be filled a little bit at a time, and only with what she wanted to tell me.

"I don't know how long they had been planning this. They never announce plans. Or ideas. They just proclaim." She scratched at her left forearm with her right hand without breaking the rhythm of her walking. When she talked about the Authority, her words came out like spit.

"Quit scratching," I said.

"Quit sucking your fingers," she answered. "You're not a child anymore, you're fourteen and a half."

We walked for a few minutes in silence, with just the low rumble of our rotating mats and the occasional hiss of the energy being sucked into the download bar.

"Your father saw them putting up some buildings. I think he knew what was going on. The Transport Team always knows at least a little bit—"

"What buildings?"

"The Children's Village. A new Compound. New flags. Pink and blue."

Everything, it seemed, had an assigned color. Colors to define rank. Colors to define purpose. Citizens could only wear their assigned colors. You could tell at a glance what someone did or if someone was important. Mother and I wore the same orange as Father. Our colors marked the boundaries of where we could go.

"But he didn't tell you?" I asked. "He didn't tell you about the new buildings?"

"No. He didn't." Mother pursed her lips.

"Why not?" Mother and Father must have had secrets from each other as well as secrets from me. And those secrets must be about bad things. Why else wouldn't Father have mentioned the new buildings?

She glanced at me again. "He had his reasons."

Through the window slit, we could hear the rumble of a bus-box going past and the shuffling footsteps of the Gatekeeper making rounds. We didn't talk until he passed our space.

Then, in her metronome voice, she told me what the Authority had announced at that Social Update meeting over a decade ago. They were concerned about the decreasing birthrates in various Compounds as well as the way the older kids were maturing. They said children didn't reach their full potential because parents were not properly raising their children. They said that they could do it better.

"I told your father that maybe they should consider blaming the decreasing birthrate on the increasing demands for all Citizens to create energy. There's no energy left to create babies." She actually gave a little laugh when she told me that. She could be sarcastic, almost funny, on the days she felt good. Other days she was just quiet, her voice flat.

But the most important thing she told me that day, important as anything I ever heard, important enough to make breathing hurt all the way from my ribs to my feet, was that I had had my fourth birthday a week *before* that meeting. It was there that it was announced that all future babies and all existing children under the age of four were being assigned to a new Compound. Compound 2. The Children's Village. As a result, I am one of only a few Citizens to actually be raised by a natural parent.

We were about halfway done on our boards. I had already drunk my morning ration of water and my lips were dry, my tongue furry. The folded cloth in my underwear felt sticky and wet. I thought she had forgotten about my bloody underwear. But she hadn't.

"You're old enough now to have to undergo testing. To get your reproductive-ability score. They'll schedule it when your father tells them about it."

"About what?"

"You got your first monthly. The bleeding. It's normal. Your father will tell them, they'll schedule the test, and the Transport Team will take you to the Human Health Services."

"It's normal?"

"It's normal. It means you're old enough to be paired with a man. It means you may be moved to a different Compound." Her voice was sad but, at the same time, had the abruptness of a door slamming shut. She was done talking.

CHAPTER FOUR

Jeremy was still sleeping, but he was moving restlessly from one side to another. Even though he had done his washing up, I could still smell that rank odor. My heart began to race, fluttering like bird wings in my chest and high in my throat. That smell! The smell from the building I saw this morning, the one they took Mother to. The Recycle building.

Feeling dizzy, I sat on my sleeping mat and held Mother's blanket against my face. I don't know how long I sat there, breathing in the smell of Mother from her blanket, trying to shut out that other odor, trying not to remember seeing Mother pulled into that building, hearing the door slam behind her. I heard Jeremy whimpering in his sleep. A whiny, childlike whimpering. I wanted to escape his smell and that sound. I wanted to run away from him but there was no place to go.

Useless to try to sleep. My mind was racing with questions, with memories. Images and conversations as vivid as if they had just happened.

Like the day I heard my parents talking while I was in the washing-up area. Father's whisper had come slow and deep out of his throat like the growl of a crouching animal, while Mother's was higher, faster, like a bird, chirping and swirling.

They were arguing about something being scheduled, and Father was angry that Mother hadn't told me about something else. She said she just wanted to keep me safe. And then Mother said something strange. "If I tell her *everything* she'll never feel safe again."

Jeremy moaned, sat up, then went to the washing-up area, interrupting my thoughts. As he walked past me, the smell got stronger. I wondered what he did at Re-Cy. I wondered if he had seen Mother with those ropes on her wrists. I sat still and small when he went back to his mat. When I could hear him snore, I went back to thinking, back to that day Mother and Father had argued.

I remembered rubbing sanitizing solution on my hands. It burned around the places where I bit my fingernails. Mother was always after me about putting my fingers in my mouth. I pulled aside the privacy curtain and they immediately stopped talking. I remember the dead silence. It seemed to last forever.

Then Father told me I was scheduled for reproductive-ability testing the next day. He said they would examine me all over. I didn't like the sound of that. He didn't look at me when he said it. Mother didn't say anything. I said I didn't want to go because I didn't know what it meant to be examined. He told me the Authority required it, and I shouted that I didn't care.

That's when he grabbed both of my shoulders. His fingers were so strong that they dug in. He seemed like he was about to shake me, but instead he just looked straight into my eyes. How dark his eyes were, the whites tracked with little red veins. I had never seen him so angry.

"Whatever you do, Emmeline, whatever you do, don't fight them. Do you hear me? Don't ever fight them."

I pulled away and stared at him. "I'm not going!"

He let his hands drop to his sides, his fingers still curled into a grip.

"Yes, Emmeline, you are. I mean it. Promise me you won't fight them. Do whatever they ask. Promise me." He sounded like he might cry. I had never seen my father cry.

"Emmeline," Mother said, her voice thick, "listen to your father. Promise."

Sitting here now in the dark, I realized Father wasn't angry that day, he was frightened. I dug through my memories, trying to remember every detail for any clue I might have missed. Every conversation, the way people looked and talked and what they did. The night dragged on while Jeremy slept. It was long, and my memories pressed in on me like the walls of our tiny Living Space.

I remembered the morning after Mother and Father had argued; Mother gave me a headscarf. She brought it in with the nourishment cubes. The Gatekeeper must have left it. It was white. How did the Gatekeeper know to leave it? So many mysteries.

Her fingers were shaking as she helped me tie the scarf. "You only have to wear this when you're outside of our Living Space. Inside you don't have to."

I reached up and felt the smooth coolness of the fabric.

"Why is my scarf white but yours is white with black around the edges?"

"Because."

"Because why?"

She clicked her tongue, and a little puff of air pushed through her lips. That meant she didn't want to answer. But I asked again, pushing against the wall of her nonanswers. "Because why?"

"White means you're of reproductive age. They add a black band when you're paired. Enough with the questions."

We both heard the rumble of the bus-box at the gate.

Mother looked at me with a sadness that made her appear older. "Go now," she said, nodding toward the door.

"Come with me."

"I can't. You'll have a chaperone."

"Just to the gate, then?" I asked.

"All right. Just to the gate."

She stood at the gate as I got on the bus-box. As we pulled away, she put her hand on her chest, on her heart.

The Gatekeeper made a notation on his clipboard. The bus-box was a square wooden thing with wooden bench seats. I don't know what the wheels were made of, but they were big and the bus-box was high enough off the ground that I had to use a step to get on. When the Transport Team started pulling, it lurched forward and I almost fell over. There were no backrests on the side benches.

A woman was already on the bus-box. The chaperone. And she was paired. Her headscarf was like Mother's, white with a black band. It felt good, figuring that out by myself. She sat on a bench in the front of the box, facing me. Her bench had a backrest. We left Compound 14. Past the great flag, the same orange as Father's uniform. The same orange as Mother's and my clothes. It hung limp and lifeless.

The trees grew close to the bicycle path, the branches arching over-head so that as we moved, the sun and shadows flickered over my face. I pulled my headscarf back to feel the sun on my head. The chaperone frowned and shook her head. Her headscarf was wrapped so that even her forehead was covered. I wasn't used to a headscarf. I fumbled with it until I made it look like hers.

The bus-box was wider than the bicycle path and lurched over the uneven ground. I held on to the side and swayed with the movement. I could hear the Transport Team breathing hard, grunting. Father was not on this team. I heard him tell Mother last night that he hoped he would not be one of the men who took me for testing.

We entered another gate. Here, two flags were hanging side by side from one pole. A pink flag and a blue flag. This had to be the Children's Village. We turned toward the largest building. I didn't see individual Living Spaces. Instead there was a fenced-in play yard with practice energy boards lined up very neatly and evenly spaced against the fence.

The work of children is play. Mother told me that a famous person had said that. There was nothing else in the play yard, not even grass. Just hard dirt. Most of the window slits on this building were lower than the ones in our home.

Waiting by the main doorway were two girls about my age, both in pink uniforms. Pink is such a pretty color. The tall woman standing with them was gently adjusting their headscarves, tucking their hair under the fabric, but the girls looked bored, scuffing their shoes against the dirt and sending little poofs of dust into the breeze.

When the girls got on the bus-box, they sat together across from me.

"Ever been on a bus-box before?" one of them asked. She had thick eyebrows, like caterpillars that grew almost across her nose.

"You got your monthlies?" the other one asked me. "How old are you anyhow?"

"Fourteen and a half."

"Fourteen and a half?" the girl with the eyebrows said. "We're thirteen and a half and we already got our monthlies. And not a day too soon. I can't wait to be paired." I was pretty sure the chaperone couldn't hear her.

We passed an animal feeding station where wooden boxes were filled with some kind of grain. And something else. Lumpy things, maybe nuts. Fat gray animals with furry, curled tails jumped from tray to tray, eating the grain and the nuts. Squirrels. I had never seen so many in one place. Hundreds of them, a swirling mass of gray fur and curled tails. So many it seemed like a great gray thunderstorm, right there by the bus-box. They chattered and scolded each other, and the bigger ones chased the smaller ones off the trays.

"Why are there so many squirrels?" I asked.

"What are you, stupid? Don't you know anything?" said the girl with the eyebrows. She turned to the other girl. "I pity the man she gets paired with."

There was that word again. *Paired.*

"Praise the squirrels," one girl said.

"Praise those who feed the squirrels," said the other one. Each formed the circle sign with the thumb and forefinger of her right hand and held it to her forehead as they gave their praises. They said it loud enough for the chaperone to hear. She nodded her head and gave them a tight smile. As if her face might break if her smile was too big.

It seemed strange to me that the squirrels were so free, free to go anywhere. Why didn't I feel free?

"Never saw you in the Village. You must be one of them," the girl with the eyebrows said.

"One of what?" I didn't like the way she said "them." It was like a snarl.

"One of the home-raised. Homeschooled. You know. Not one of us. If you were one of us, you'd know there are so many squirrels because the Authority makes sure they get lots of food. That's what the Managers of Nature do. They take care of nature. You would know that if you were one of us."

She said "us" like it was special. They smiled at each other. The second girl was small and pale like the waxy paper on nourishment cubes. Her lips and fingernails were kind of blue, and she worked hard at breathing. I could see her shoulders pulling up with each breath like she needed more air.

I didn't answer her. I didn't know much about the Managers of Nature. I didn't want to talk about being different. We turned off the main bicycle path at a gate with a white flag and stopped in front of another large cement building.

The chaperone stood up. "We're here, girls. Human Health Services. I'll walk you one by one to the intake officer. I'll take you first"—she looked down at one of the folders she was holding—"Remy." The girl with the thick eyebrows stood up. "You two wait here until I come back. Don't get off the bus-box."

They looked clumsy as they dismounted. Remy almost fell but caught herself at the last minute.

The Transport Team stood silently in their harnesses. The leather straps were tight across their shoulders, with a wet line of sweat along the edges. They didn't look at each other or talk, but stood strong and still.

As Remy and the chaperone stepped into the building, the waxy pale girl turned to me.

"So what's it like having a mother? I don't even remember mine."

I looked at the Human Health Services building, so gray and square, and the quiet, sweaty Transport Team. I glanced up at the deep green of the tree branches against the sky. White clouds, faraway blueness. I looked at the pale girl. She didn't even remember her mother? I fought the urge to put my finger in my mouth, like a child. Instead, I put my hand to my chest, my heart, remembering how Mother did that while she stood at the gate and watched the bus-box pull away.

What's it like having a mother? I thought about how to answer such a question. Mother is always there for me. If I wake with a bad dream, she wakes, too, and sits with her arm around me until I'm not afraid anymore. She doesn't go back to sleep until after I go back to sleep. She shares her water when I'm thirsty. On good days, she laughs and sings and tells funny stories. She smiles at me. Even on bad days, quiet days, she's still with me. I am never alone. That's what it's like. I didn't say all that. I didn't want to cry thinking about what it would be like to not remember your mother.

Instead, I just said: "I guess it's normal. It's normal for me." I didn't know what else to say that she might understand. What can you say to someone who doesn't remember her mother?

She just looked at me blankly, then said, "Here comes the chaperone. I'm sorry you were home-raised. But I'm glad you got your monthlies. The Republic is depending on you." She made the circle with her thumb and forefinger and held it to her forehead.

I did the same. It made me feel closer to her.

She stood up. "We could have been friends, you know. If you were raised in the Village. My name is Marina."

"Mine is Emmeline," I replied.

She got off the bus-box and smiled at me over her shoulder before she went into the big building with the chaperone.

I sat alone. It was the first time I almost had a friend. It felt good to be out of my Compound and to meet someone. An almost-friend named Marina.

CHAPTER FIVE

The intake officer was a thin man with a narrow, rough-looking black mustache. A crumb of soy from his breakfast was trapped in the bristles.

"No folder?" he asked the chaperone.

"No."

"Not many no-folder kids left, are there?" He picked up an empty folder on his desk.

"No, not many. Her name is Emmeline. Compound 14. Over fourteen years old. Confirmed monthlies."

He wrote in the folder as she talked. I stared at his pencil and papers. I must have been about six years old when the Enforcers took everybody's books and pencils and paper away. I wanted to hold that pencil, touch that paper.

"What else?"

"Her father's Transport. Her mother has antagonistic tendencies but, so far, has not violated any rules or regulations."

The way she said that sounded bad. Mother wasn't bad. Why did she say that about Mother? I turned the word *antagonistic* over in my head, trying to feel out its meaning.

"But her monthlies are definitely confirmed?"

"Yes."

He kept writing. "Too bad the other two weren't actually fertile," he mumbled. "Waste of time and resources. Using precious medication to jump-start them but not getting results."

The woman looked at him with a frown. "It wasn't my idea to bring them in for testing. I only do what I'm told. I'm just a chaperone." She sniffed loudly and looked away.

"I'm not blaming you. Waste of time and resources is a specialty of . . ." His voice faded away, as if he was afraid to say any more.

"I know, I know. It's just that there don't seem to be many reproductive females. So they push, you know, push the limits, push for testing. But what do I know? I'm just a chaperone."

"And I'm just an intake officer. We all have our titles, don't we?" They nodded at each other as though agreeing they were no more than their titles.

"Odd, though, don't you think, that we aren't having more babies, healthier babies?" she said.

"Why odd?" He looked puzzled.

"Well, one of the reasons for all of this—the whole relocation, everything—was that there were supposedly too many people for the Earth. But now they're pushing for *more* babies. There aren't enough. And so few are healthy."

"I don't think that's odd at all."

"Why not?"

"Because," he said, "it's all about unintended consequences. They think they can mandate things. Create this much energy every day. Have this many babies every year. But it just doesn't work like that. The more new laws and rules and regulations they issue, the worse the results are."

I had no idea what they were talking about. They seemed to have forgotten I was even there.

Finally they took me into a room with lights—how bright they were! If only our living space could have lights like these! Is this where the energy we make goes? Who else has lights this bright? Authorities? Probably. All those hours of walking the board so somebody else can have bright lights? That didn't seem right to me.

I had to undress. They gave me some sort of backward sleeping robe to put on, which felt silly. The intake officer left the room, but the chaperone stayed with me. She told me to sit on a high metal table. I had to use a stool to get on it.

Then a man came in and explained that he was the reproductive specialist. Draped around his neck was a set of black tubes connected at the end with a round black disk. Another man came in with a metal basket that rattled with some other kind of tubes. He said he was going to take blood, which sounded dangerous.

First the man with the metal basket tied a rubbery brown thing around the top of my arm. It was tight and pinched my skin.

"Make a fist," he said. My heart beat harder. "A fist, like you're punching."

He tapped his fingers against the inside of my elbow and I could see a vein bulging out like a worm, but big and blue. Then he reached into his basket and got a tube and a pointy thing. Sharp and shiny.

"Don't move."

It was a surprise pain and I bit my lip. Blood flowed into the tube. He was taking my blood out of me. He pulled out the pointy tool, took the tight rubbery thing off my arm. It made a snapping sound. Then he handed me a little white cloth.

"Hold this tight against your arm."

He left the room, my blood in a tube rattling around in his basket.

Then I had to lie down on the table. It was so cold and hard. There was no sleeping mat to cushion my skin against my bones, and my spine and shoulder blades began to ache. The chaperone put my feet into some kind of holders so they were up in the air. I could see my toes, higher than my head. I knew I couldn't run. She spread my knees apart. Her fingernails were sharp and dug into my skin. I felt dirty and helpless. The only thing I could do was stare at the ceiling and wish the bright lights would melt me away.

The reproductive specialist examined me all over with his hands. They were cold and smooth. I didn't like the way he looked at me. His pupils were big, and he stared at me while he touched my body and tried to put his fingers inside me.

"Forget the speculum," he said to the chaperone. "No entry here."

I tried to pull my knees together but the chaperone held them apart. Then he pushed in on my belly, which hurt less than when he had put his fingers between my legs.

When he felt my breasts, I felt so ashamed. No one had ever touched my breasts. It felt wrong.

I didn't fight. I felt hot tears building behind my eyes, but I didn't cry. I did what Mother always did. I turned my face away from them.

The chaperone surprised me by patting my shoulder gently. Then she looked out the window slit, relieving me of her gaze.

The blood results came back while I was getting dressed. The reproductive specialist read them and smiled. "She's good," he said to the chaperone. "Quite ripe, in fact. Reproductive and productive. Finally, a reproductive female. *Praise be to the Republic.* I'll forward her folder to the Pairing Committee. At least the day was not a total waste."

"What does that mean?" I asked.

The chaperone and the reproductive specialist looked startled, as if they had forgotten I could speak.

"What does what mean?" he repeated.

"Ripe," I said, louder. "What does ripe mean?"

"Ready to be picked," he said, laughing. The chaperone looked at him as though she didn't think what he said was funny. She came closer to me and put her hand on my shoulder again. It felt warm.

I still didn't know what being ripe meant. But I wasn't going to ask again.

The intake officer and the chaperone made the circle sign to each other as we were leaving. I didn't make the circle sign. I didn't want to be like them.

CHAPTER SIX

The bus-box stopped at the Compound 14 gate. My Compound, my gate. The chaperone smiled at me. "You can walk to your space from here, Emmeline. Congratulations on passing the reproductive-ability test. The Republic thanks you." She made the finger circle sign on her forehead, smiled, and nodded. She acted like she was proud of me and maybe even liked me a little. Was it just because I was reproductive? Was that going to be my title?

I stood at the gate and watched the bus-box pull away, the six men leaning forward in their harnesses, the chaperone swaying on her seat, and I realized then that I knew nothing.

The Gatekeeper glanced at my headscarf and lowered his eyes. He fumbled with his clipboard, made a notation, and finally opened the gate for me. The Living Spaces, identical in size and shape, were arranged in a semicircle, up against the chain link fence. The common ground in front of each was dirt packed hard and smooth. No animal would be tempted to try to come through the fence into this barren area. All of the Living Space Compounds were the same. At least that's what Mother told me. She said if you could look down from the sky, it would look like a big round lacy doily—she had used a little stick to draw a circle in the dirt outside our door—and the important buildings like Human Health Services and the Central Authority buildings were in an entirely separate area.

I stopped outside of our door because I could hear Mother and Father talking inside. Father was home already? That wasn't right. In fact it was terribly, terribly wrong. He was supposed to work until dusk. The work rules were very strict. I moved closer to the window slit to try and hear them.

"Already? They assigned her already? How is that possible?" Mother's voice was loud and angry.

"Elsa, you knew it was coming. You knew. Why do you fight everything?" I could hear Father pacing back and forth on the rough floor. "You know what happens when—"

"Enough with the 'you knew, you know, you knew.' I'm sick of it. How did we let all of this happen? God damn it. God damn it to hell and back."

"Stop it, Elsa. Stop it right now."

"God damn it. God damn it. God damn it. There. I said it!" She was yelling, too. I looked over at the Gatekeeper, wondering if he could hear them. I think he was too far away and besides, he was leaning against the fence with his eyes closed. Probably sleeping even though that was against the rules.

"Shut up!" Father's voice, harsh.

"Don't you tell me to shut up."

"Don't use that word again. You know it's forbidden."

"God. God. God. There! What are you going to do about it?"

"Elsa, please. Please. We have to survive. Don't make us destroy each other. Do you want to end up like—" He sounded like he was crying.

"I don't care. I just don't care," Mother said, but she wasn't shouting. Her voice was muffled.

They were quiet for a while after that. My face felt warm in the sun, but inside I felt cold. I started toward the door, but then they started talking again.

"Who? Who did they pair her with?"

"George."

"George? Oh my God, George? Our old neighbor? Oh my God."

"Elsa, don't use that word. I'm begging you." He paused. "Yes, that George."

"But George is too old. He's what, over thirty already? And he's married. Married!"

"His wife was never productive. Then she got sick. Couldn't walk her board. Some chronic condition, maybe kidney failure. I don't know what. Something about chronic and the criteria for allocation of resources. Some kind of a futility thing. That's all I know."

"I know all about chronic and all about allocation of resources. I know all about futility. I know all about *Praise be*. I went to the Social Reorientation Programs just like you did. Those damned sessions. Brainwashing."

A soft breeze rustled the trees on the other side of the fence.

"But the fact remains, George is still married."

"They took her away. That's all I know." His voice was so low I had trouble hearing him clearly.

"Dear sweet Jesus," Mother said in the same low whisper. "She was a good person. She was my student." I heard her sniff, like she was crying.

The sun was shining. The sky was blue. I remember it vividly.

"Well," Mother said, in a tone that sounded like she was squaring her shoulders, "at least he is one of us. One of us who remembers how it used to be."

The edge of my headscarf caught on the rough cement wall, slid off my head, and fell onto the dirt. I picked it up and tried to shake the dirt off but a smudge remained. The Gatekeeper saw me without my headscarf and looked at me the same way the reproduction specialist had looked at me. I quickly put the scarf back on. I wished it hadn't gotten dirty.

"So when do they . . . ? " Mother's voice trailed off.

"In two days."

"Two days? That's not enough time to teach her."

The concrete felt hot against my back. I saw something moving beside me. A bug crawling up the wall. A round, red ladybug with black dots on its back. *"Ladybug, ladybug, fly away home. Your house is on fire and your children will burn,"* I whispered. Mother had taught me that.

"Elsa, for crying out loud, you had ten years to teach her—"

"I did teach her. I taught her how it used to be."

"You were supposed to teach her how it is now. You were supposed to prepare her. Reproduction . . ."

I picked the ladybug off the wall and watched it walk along my finger. I blew on it and watched it fly away. Then I put my finger in my mouth. It tasted bitter.

"How it used to be is over, Elsa. You need to tell her the truth."

"You'll have to do it. I can't. I don't have the courage. Or the strength." I heard Mother turn on her energy board. The conversation was over.

CHAPTER SEVEN

Father came out of our space and slammed the door behind him. He looked surprised to see me there. He stared with his eyes wide and his mouth open.

"Hello, Father," I said.

"How long have you been out here?"

I shrugged.

"Did you hear . . . did you hear us talking?"

"Yes."

"Well, then. Well." He looked up at the sky as though trying to figure out what to say. I looked up at the sky, too. Still clear blue, no clouds. Some birds flew high above us, little specks of brown against the blue.

"You look very pretty in your headscarf," he said finally.

"I dropped it. It got smudged."

"Sanitizing solution will take care of that. Let's not go inside just yet. Let's talk. Over there." I followed him past the Living Spaces. Some of the doors were open and we could hear the low rumbling of energy boards as we walked by. Once we were past the Living Spaces, Father stopped. We stood there at the edge of our Compound, by the fence, with trees on the other side. Sunshine and shadow seemed to dance about on the packed brown dirt. The main path ran along the other side of the fence. How long ago was I on that very path in the bus-box going for my tests? An hour ago? Two hours ago? A childhood ago? And now here I was, in my headscarf, outside with Father. We had never talked much. He worked the dawn-to-dusk shift on Transport and was always so tired when he got home. And now we were together and he wanted to talk. Everything about the day seemed strange, like it wasn't really happening because it didn't fit with what I was used to.

"It's nice right here, isn't it? Near the trees."

"Yes."

"How did the testing go?"

"I hated it."

"But you didn't fight it?"

"No."

"Good girl."

He didn't ask me any more about the testing. I was glad he didn't. I didn't want to talk about it.

"So tell me more about how you and your mother spend your days together." He paused and rubbed his shoulder. I could see where the leather straps had made deep wrinkles in his uniform.

"We walk our boards."

"And what do you talk about? While you walk, you must talk."

"Some days she talks a lot. Other days, not so much."

A tired-looking woman with sweat stains under her arms stepped out of her Living Space, glanced over at us, then went back inside and closed her door. How strange it must have seemed to her, seeing Father home early and us outside talking.

"Well, when she feels like talking, what does she talk about?"

"The farm, mostly."

"Oh, yes, the farm. We both loved the farm. It was a good place."

He bent down, reached through the fence, and pulled up a little bit of grass. I hoped the Gatekeeper didn't see him do that. "She can't let go of the farm."

He rubbed the grass between his thumb and forefinger. "Smell that," he said. "The smell of green, the smell of growing. How I miss the smell of a green, living thing!" He held the grass near my nose and I could smell it and the salty sweat of his hand. His thumb had swirly green circles on the skin. "I can still see you, little Emmie, learning to walk. Toddling back and forth on the grass. And when you fell, you would laugh and pull up handfuls of grass and try to put it in your mouth."

Then he brushed his hands together and bits of grass fell onto the dirt.

"Did your mother tell you about the Relocations?"

"Yes, yes, she did. About Agenda 21, the new laws, and the Authority. It sounded complicated."

"It was."

"And Mother didn't like it."

The Gatekeeper started making his rounds. He walked slowly past each Living Space, carrying his clipboard. He walked past Father and me, glancing at us with curiosity, and making a notation on his clipboard. Father stood silently until the Gatekeeper was back at the gate.

"Guess he's not used to me being home so soon."

"Guess he's not used to me being outside."

We smiled at each other like we were sharing a secret. A warm little secret between us, out here near a tree.

"What else did your mother tell you about the Relocations?"

I thought for a moment before I answered. "She never told me *why*. Why it happened."

He rubbed his hand across his forehead and sighed. "Oh, there's so much, too much, to teach you in one day. Too much history."

"Mother was a history teacher, wasn't she?"

"Yes, and a good one at that. Except when it counted the most. With her own child." He rubbed his shoulders again. "Look, Emmie, learning all of this is going to take time. Let me just go over it with, I don't know, a kind of a big-picture overview. That'll be a start."

"Why didn't she teach me?"

"Well, I guess it upsets her to even think about." He frowned, making deep up-and-down lines between his eyebrows. "Do you want my big picture overview?"

I nodded.

"People didn't trust the government, not the way things were going. The economy was bad. There were wars with other nations. Of course, people were worried. So they elected new officials. Officials who made big promises."

I tucked the unfamiliar words into my memory and vowed to learn to understand them as soon as possible. Elected. Officials. Not knowing the meaning of the words was like being thirsty and not having water.

"And these new officials got right to work. Started passing new laws. Little laws at first." He shrugged his shoulders. "None of them seemed important enough to worry about."

He paused, looked up at the sky, then turned back to me.

"Then the laws got more strict. More broad. Almost impossible to comply with."

He pulled a leaf off a tree branch close to the fence. He crushed it in his fingers and smelled it. He kept rubbing the leaf between his thumb and his finger.

"Can I touch it?"

"Touch what?"

"The leaf. Can I touch it?"

"I'll do better than that." He pulled off another leaf and handed it to me. "Your very own leaf," he said. It was cool and smooth in my fingers. I tucked it into my pocket. My very own leaf.

"What kind of laws? Laws about what?"

"Emmeline, I can't explain all of it, not in one day. There's just too much! Let me do the big picture, please." He sounded impatient, but I was impatient, too. Impatient for more. I saw the tree, the fence, the Gatekeeper clearly, as though they were outlined against a blank page and I made up my mind that from that moment forward I would learn and learn and learn. I had so much to learn. Somebody, somewhere could answer my questions.

"Your mother was limited on what she could teach. Absolutely no history. At least no accurate history. History was being changed, rewritten by the officials. That was very difficult for her. I think that's why she spends so much time telling you how things used to be. That's her history, the *real* version, and she wants to share it with you." He smiled at me. "Does that make sense to you?"

I nodded. The headscarf felt smooth and silky on my cheek.

"Okay then. I'll tell you some of the good history I remember. Just for a change of pace."

He told me about the wonderful soup Mother used to make at harvest time. Fresh vegetables. Vegetable soup. Chicken. Applesauce. He said the kitchen smelled like Paradise and Mother cooked like an angel. Then he stopped abruptly.

"I guess I'm doing what she does, aren't I? Talking about what was. And now we eat nourishment cubes." He paused and stared out past the fence for a few moments before continuing.

"It's hard, looking back, to know what started all the changes," Father said. "I wish I had been more vigilant, more aware. But I wasn't. Your mother was."

"Aware of what?" I asked.

"Policies. Politics. What was happening." He shrugged his shoulders. "Once everyone became aware, it was too late." I waited for him to continue. Dusk would soon be approaching.

He said the laws kept changing and got harder and harder to obey. Soon there were no more elections because the officials felt that people kept making the wrong decisions. That word again, *elections*. "Those in power stayed in power. They sucked the power and will out of the people. Money became worthless. Churches were converted to community centers and then eventually torn down." His voice was low and sad. More new words. *Money. Church.*

"Mother never told me about churches. What are churches?"

"Churches were special buildings for the people." His voice dropped down to a whisper. "Places where people could worship God." I strained to hear him so he bent down, his mouth now right next to my ear. "But the Authority made all worship punishable unless it was worship of them or of the Republic. I shouldn't be talking about it now, it's forbidden. Mother didn't tell you because she wanted to protect you from accidentally talking about something that could get you in a lot of trouble. Everything she did was to protect you."

I thought back to my ride on the bus-box. I wished I had told Marina that having a mother was having somebody who did everything they could to protect you.

Father started to talk again as if to himself, staring off into the distance, as though I weren't there. As if he were reciting a strange tale, something he had read about in disbelief. His voice was flat, a straight line of words, not one word more important than another, until they all sounded meaningless.

"And the people were taken from their homes, their farms, their towns and put on trains. Relocated to Planned Communities like ours and assigned work. They had to produce energy. They had to attend Social Reorientation Sessions. There are probably a lot of communities like ours, but they're all far away from each other. There's no way to know, no way to communicate."

A tear slid down his cheek. I reached out and touched his hand, then tugged on it, to reconnect, to make him look at me. Finally, he took my hand in both of his and held it. He didn't wipe the tear away. We stood connected like that, quiet, touching each other. Our hands together. He looked down at me for a moment, solemn. One shiny tear curving down his cheek.

"She hated those sessions. Hated them. She changed. Became bitter. Bitter and angry and clinging to the past." He put a hand on my shoulder and it felt warm. "She clung to you. She wanted to keep you in that past, in the happy times. That's when she started scratching at her skin. Like she was trying to shred herself."

I saw the deep lines on his face. The back-and-forth wrinkles on his forehead, dark with dirt and sweat. A couple of stiff gray hairs in his eyebrows, like mistakes or afterthoughts. Curved creases descended on both sides of his face from his nose to his mouth, and his mouth was pinched, surrounded with feathery lines. With clarity, I now knew he had worked as hard as Mother to protect me from knowing exactly what happened. Even now, he was withholding things from me, things he didn't want me to know.

Birds were beginning to roost in the trees, twittering, shifting from branch to branch as they sought the safest one. I wanted to learn more but I knew that it would take time. More time than we had right now. And, with a chill, I realized that, by protecting me from knowing what had happened, Mother and Father had actually put me in danger. I felt vulnerable and solitary because if they didn't teach me, no one else would. Nobody at all.

"One more thing before we go in," he said. He dropped the squashed leaf. It fluttered, spinning to the ground. His voice dropped to a whisper. "Some folks say there are people out there. People who slipped away in time. People who are free." He motioned beyond the road, beyond the fence, beyond the trees. When he moved his arm, there was a smell—something musty and afraid, like a dark bit of breeze. He ground his foot over the leaf, shredding it.

I felt the smell of fear move to me, wrap around and encase me. That one more thing, that bit of whispered information, coming from Father, made me so cold I shivered.

"Almost dusk," he said. "Time to go in."

And so it began. Learning things to be afraid of.

CHAPTER EIGHT

Later that evening Mother told me about George. He worked on the Transport Team with Father, but before the relocation he had lived on a nearby farm. They had all worked together at harvest time.

"The only good thing," Mother said, "is that he was my student once and I remember how much I liked him. Back then, before the changes. He was a good boy. If you have to be paired, he is a good choice. Not that you really have a choice," she added.

She told me other things, too. Like what being paired meant. It wasn't what I thought. It wasn't like paring the skin off an apple. It wasn't like anything I had ever heard of.

"Do you have any questions?" she asked.

I shook my head no.

"Good. Now take your fingers out of your mouth." I didn't even realize they were there.

And so we were paired. The bus-box brought the man named George to our Living Space. Two Enforcers in dark uniforms walked beside him to our door. He was taller than either of them, and stronger-looking. But the Enforcers had mustaches, like all the men in power. He had on the same orange uniform as Father. Father was at work. Mother stood beside me right outside of our door. At first I kept my head down; I didn't know where to look. One of the Enforcers said some words about the Republic, *Praise be to the Republic,* and some words about *Reproduction, Praise be to reproduction.* Then he made the circle with his fingers on his forehead. George did the same. So I did, too. My white headscarf, still dirty, was exchanged for a white scarf trimmed in black. That meant I was officially paired.

Color marked boundaries. Color marked occupation. Color marked Compounds.

Flags and headscarves and uniforms.

The language of the colors of the Republic.

Living with George was like moving from being a child to being an adult. They assigned us a Living Space next to Mother and Father, and while Mother said that was just a lucky accident, I thought it was a wonderful accident. Our window slits faced each other so Mother and I could talk while we walked our energy boards. We could still be connected.

George didn't try to touch me for over a year, which I didn't mind. He said he still missed his wife and that made him sad. Instead of pairing with me, he sat and talked with me after he came home from work. He had the same strong back and leg muscles as Father from pulling the bus-box. He was older than me but younger than Mother and Father. He was like a bridge between what they knew and what I needed to know. Those were comfortable, peaceful years with Mother right next door and George by my side.

He told me what it was like pulling the bus-box. Hard, hard work. No wonder Father always seemed so tired in the evening. The bus-boxes were used to take people to Human Health Services for testing or to drive the Authorities and Enforcers around.

"You'd think going uphill would be the hardest," George said. "Those things are heavy enough even when they're not loaded with anything. But downhill is even worse."

"Why? I'd think downhill would be easier."

"Oh, would you now! We have to use our backs and legs and feet to slow it down or it will run over us. If an Enforcer is riding, he'll sometimes help using a wide wooden beam against a wheel as a kind of brake. But if we're just hauling supplies from the farm co-op to the train depot, well, our bodies are the only brakes."

"Train depot?" I had seen pictures of trains in one of the books we used to have. "Where are the train depots?"

"The depot is far enough away from the Compounds that nobody can see or hear the train. Not many people know about the depot. We're not allowed to talk about it."

"You're telling me about it."

"Guess that means I trust you." He touched my cheek with his finger. "I hate it when the train isn't running. Then we have to go all the way to the co-op. I don't much like going out there," he said.

"Why not?" It was so easy asking him questions.

"I feel sorry for the people that work there. They're not real bright. And they aren't near their families and don't have their own Living Spaces."

"Where do they sleep?"

"In tents. Tents are cheaper than Living Spaces."

"What's a tent?"

He walked to the doorway and drew something in the dirt. I liked seeing him standing in the sunlight, strong and tall. I liked knowing he trusted me enough to tell me about the train depot and tents and bus-boxes. He never turned away from me when I asked questions.

"Oh, it looks like a triangle," I said.

"Exactly."

"Mother taught me the names of shapes. Circle, triangle, square. Back when we still were allowed to have paper."

"Did you know I was a student of your mother in school?" he asked.

"She told me."

"She was a brilliant teacher, you know. Just brilliant."

"How so?" I asked.

"She taught us so much. Starting with the history of our nation. The Founding Fathers. All of that. I'm ashamed to admit sometimes I doodled and daydreamed while she talked. I wish now that I'd paid more attention." He smiled when he said that. "She liked bright colors and wore long dresses and she would make cookies and bring them to share with the students. We all loved her for that. Did you know that she wrote poetry?"

"No."

He looked at me and went on. "I know she changed after all the upheaval. After the Social Reorientation Sessions. That was a difficult time for everyone. Bad things happened. It was especially hard for your mother."

"Why?"

For the first time he looked away from me before answering.

"Imagine, Emmeline, living on your own land, free to go wherever you want, whenever you want, and then having to move here. A big circle of land, divided into work Compounds. A fence all around the outside right up against the back wall of the Living Spaces. Not an ordinary fence, but a great tall fence of heavy metal mesh embedded in thick concrete at its base."

He took my hand and we went back into the Living Space. It was dim compared to the bright sun outside and my eyes took a minute to adjust.

George went on. "Not only is there an outer fence, but there are also fences between each Compound. And, of course, a Gatekeeper for each Compound."

He let go of my hand and rubbed his forehead. "I think it made your mother feel like a bird in a cage. She couldn't fly."

I had a sense that, for the first time, he wasn't telling me everything.

* * *

When George finally touched me, it wasn't like when the reproduction specialist touched me. It was different somehow, gentle and kind. And then he paired with me.

We pulled our sleeping mats together each night, and it was good to feel the warmth of another person in the darkness. It was good to feel his breath on my neck. It was good to be paired with George. Another year passed before I missed my monthly.

* * *

"I missed my monthly," I told Mother through the window slit. I could see her scratching. "Quit scratching your face. Did you hear what I said?"

"I heard you. And I'll quit scratching my face when you quit putting your fingers in your mouth."

Our energy boards creaked and hummed as we walked, creating energy.

"What does that mean? Why did I miss my monthly?"

Walk, walk, walk. The red needle crept around the dial as the day warmed. I was hot and sweaty. I ran my finger across my forehead and put my finger in my mouth, tasting the salt. I wondered if it was ever this hot back on the farm.

"It means," Mother said in a flat voice, "that I am going to have a grandchild I will never see and you are going to have a child that you will never see. That's what it means. *Praise be to the Republic? No! Republic be damned.*"

She turned off her energy board and went to her sleeping mat. I kept on walking, afraid to stop.

There were rules to follow.

CHAPTER NINE

George was sympathetic when I told him I missed my monthly. He rubbed my feet in the evening and tried to remember some poetry that Mother had told him about.

"The quality of mercy is not strained," he said, "but falleth as a gentle rain from Heaven and sitteth at the right hand—" He stopped abruptly.

"What does that mean?" I asked.

"I don't know. I don't think I have it quite right. Let me try another one, one we used to say at school. *I pledge allegiance.*" He stopped again and there was an awkward silence. He looked like he was remembering something that hurt, something sharp and pointed.

I wanted to help him past that hurt; I ran my hand across the back of his head, feeling the smoothness of his hair, across the back of his neck, and rested it on his shoulder.

I broke the silence. "Mother taught me: *I'm a little teapot, short and stout, so tip me over and pour me out.* Does that work for poetry?"

"It'll do for now," he said, smiling. He put his hand over mine and gave it a gentle squeeze. "Time for bed."

The baby grew and kicked and squirmed within me.

"Mother," I asked the next morning, through the window slit, "what's it like, having a baby?"

She didn't answer right away. I could hear her walking her board.

I asked again.

"It's hard to explain. It hurts. Except after it's over and you hold the baby, you don't remember the hurt."

"How does it hurt? How do you know it's time to have the baby?"

"You just know."

My needle was a little past halfway. Outside it was raining. A Social Update Meeting was scheduled for this evening. Everything in the Living Space looked gray and damp. The baby hung heavy in me. Like a rock. Like an anchor.

"Does it hurt like a knife? Like, sharp?"

"All I remember about having a baby is that it was like I suddenly had to push you out so bad that I didn't care who saw me, didn't care who was watching, didn't care about anything except pushing and pushing."

That didn't sound like something to look forward to.

"Is there any other way to do it?" I asked.

"No."

"What else do you remember?"

"I remember seeing you for the first time. You were pink and red and wet and slippery. Your face was the most beautiful thing I had ever seen. Your fingers were small and perfect, and your fingernails were small and perfect, and your toes were small and perfect. You were curled up and you fit into the crook of my arms. Your father kissed my forehead." She sounded like she was crying. I couldn't see her face. I could just see her arms holding the sides of the energy board.

"Are you crying?" I asked. "Why are you crying?"

She didn't answer me. I saw one of her arms move as though she were reaching up to wipe her face with her hand.

"Why won't you answer me? Why are you crying?"

There was a long pause. "Because," she finally said, "because all you will have is the pain. You will never see your baby. You will never have the joy."

It was still raining.

We kept walking, Mother and I, in silence.

CHAPTER TEN

My nourishment cubes were now bigger than George's because of the baby. But I wasn't very hungry that evening. My arms and legs were sore, and my heart was heavy. I gave what I couldn't eat to George. I didn't care if it was against the rules.

"You're not hungry?" he asked.

I shook my head. He put his arms around me. "Okay, little teapot. Pour it out."

"I talked to Mother today. About what it's like. What it's like having a baby."

His arms felt strong and safe around me.

"She told me I will never see the baby."

He stepped away and looked out the window slit. I could see the stains on his uniform from the harness straps. The rain had picked up and the packed dirt in the common area was beginning to soften. Small puddles formed where the ground was uneven.

"Emmeline, you already knew that, didn't you?"

"No, I didn't know it! How would I know?" I wondered whether he was right. Did I know but hadn't cared until now, now that something was going to be taken away from me? Something that was precious and valuable and should've been mine forever?

"Emmeline, you had to know it. Do you ever see any other women with their babies? Of course not, but you didn't want to think about it."

He was right; I just didn't want to think about it. I turned away from him, arms folded across my chest, hugging myself. "Don't talk to me. Don't. Unless you can tell me how they got this power."

I turned back to him. He had his head down, not looking at me. "Father said they got it a little bit at a time. Nothing very important. Nothing to fret about. But that's not true at all; this *was* important. Why didn't anybody stop them?"

I lay on the sleeping mat, trying to curl up like I imagined I had as a newborn in Mother's arms, but my belly was too big. George was right. I should have known they would take my baby. Maybe I thought it wouldn't happen to me. Never again would I think that way. Anything could happen to me.

* * *

George didn't wake me to go to the Social Update Meeting. The Republic gives special permissions to pregnant women. Extra food. Extra sleep. *Praise be to the Republic.* When I woke up, it was dark outside. I could see a few stars through the window slit and I heard the Gatekeeper walking by, making his rounds. The rain had stopped. Whispers came from Mother's Living Space, and I knew they were home from the meeting. George must be with them.

They didn't hear me enter. Father was saying something about being on next week's schedule with George to pick up grain for feeding stations.

"I don't know," Mother said. She scratched at a spot above her elbow. "No one knows for sure what's out there."

"There might be armies. We know there are animals, like wolves, and community farm co-ops. Our best shot is the train depot, if the train is running," George said. "The farm co-ops are pretty far out. The less time it takes, the better."

"What are you talking about?" I asked. They all looked up, startled.

"Did you have a good nap?" George asked. "How do you feel?"

"What about the depot and the co-op?" I asked again and sat down. I would keep asking until someone answered me.

Father put his finger up to his mouth, saying *shhh*. We stopped and listened. I didn't hear anything except an owl, far away. A lonely, mournful sound coming out of the dark. George and Mother sat on either side of me like protective pillars. The baby, my baby, was stretching in me, moving in me. I put my hands on my belly. George and Mother put their hands on top of mine.

Father went to the window slit and looked out. Then he came back and sat down facing us. He began talking softly and urgently.

"Maybe, just maybe, there's a way for you to keep the baby. George and I are assigned to pick up grain two days from now." He went back to the window slit and looked to both sides. "We're thinking maybe we could hide you under the empty grain bags."

I watched his lips move, how they stretched wide with some words, curled into an O-shape with others. I watched his eyes. Dark, darting. He had sweat above his lip.

They hadn't worked out all of the details. How to get me under the empty grain bags. How to avoid the army and whatever else might be out there. How to allow George and me to slip away. Maybe we could find a worker at the farm co-op who would help us. We would have to avoid Enforcers. How to explain George's absence when Father returned?

"But where would we go? How would we get our nourishment cubes?"

"Emmie, if it works, you could keep your baby," Mother whispered.

"But isn't it dangerous?"

"Yes," Mother said. "Very." She lowered her eyes then looked back up at me. "But most things worth doing are."

Father went back to the window slit and watched for a while, then came back to us.

"Enough for tonight," he whispered. "We have time to think this through."

George walked me back toward our Living Space. The moon was big, round, silvery, and stars were strewn across the sky. I eased onto my sleeping mat and he covered me with my blanket, tucked it around my feet, and whispered softly. I couldn't hear what he said.

I had restless dreams that night. I dreamt of grain in my mouth, of squirrels running across my legs, and of the baby in my belly. I dreamt of her deep inside me making a circle of her tiny thumb and forefinger and holding it to her forehead.

CHAPTER ELEVEN

The next morning, Mother and I walked our boards just like every other day, her in her Living Space and me in mine. It was almost as if last night hadn't happened. We didn't dare talk through our window slits about it. The air was fresh and cool after the rain, but still I felt hot and couldn't walk as fast with my belly as big as it was. Mother slowed her walking pace to match mine and we finished about the same time. Not quite dusk. The half-hour-to-dusk warning bell rang, signaling the time when Father and George should arrive at home.

The Gatekeeper was bringing around the nourishment cubes. A metallic screech echoed across the Compound as one nourishment box lid after another was opened. The dull thud of the cubes being dropped in. His footsteps, approaching, receding.

Eager for more fresh air, I went to my nourishment box and found only one cube and one water bottle. "Wait," I called to the Gatekeeper, "you made a mistake." He kept walking away as though he hadn't heard me.

Mother was at her nourishment box, too. She was holding up one cube, one water bottle. Her hands were shaking, her face pale.

Something was terribly wrong.

A bus-box pulled up to the gate. Two men in all-black uniforms—Enforcers, then—approached the Gatekeeper. I couldn't hear what they were saying, but the Gatekeeper was nodding his head like he was agreeing with them. Then they went to Mother's door. She cried out, like the mournful call of the owl I had heard the night before. I stepped back inside my space, trembling. Then they came with Mother to my door. Her headscarf was black.

"We regret to inform you," one said to me, "that we must take your headscarf and replace it with this." He held out a black headscarf like the one Mother had on. Her hands were shaking as she finished tying it in place.

"There's been an accident," the taller of the two said. He was a man of authority, power. A man with a mustache. "Your partner and father were traveling back to the Central Authority from an outpost, going down a hill. They were going too fast, couldn't control the bus-box, and it overcame them. Both died instantly, we regret to inform you." The way he spoke, the way he stood there stiff and straight, made it easy for me to hate him, but it also made it hard for me to believe what he was telling us.

Just last night George had covered me with a blanket. And I could see Father's face when we stood outside talking. I could see him pick up a leaf, hand it to me.

They couldn't be dead. I turned to Mother. Her face was buried in her hands.

A bird flew overhead, then another and another.

The shorter man stepped forward. "You will both be relocated to Compound 18, the Recycle Compound, and assigned a Living Space together. The Republic will use your Living Spaces here for Transport Team replacements. No space can be used by a single individual. You will be living together until further decisions are made. Be prepared to move in one hour."

This couldn't be true. They had to have made a mistake.

"I want to see their bodies."

"No. A statement will be read at the next Social Update Meeting recognizing their service to the Republic. That is the protocol."

I was stunned. *That is the protocol?*

They made the circle sign on their foreheads, turned, and walked away in lockstep. The Gatekeeper nodded, let them pass, and made a notation on his clipboard.

* * *

Mother and I didn't talk after the men left. We just sat in my Living Space with our arms around each other, silent and frightened. Mother was sobbing, but I couldn't. I was having enough trouble just breathing. The baby was strangely motionless in my womb. No kicking, no turning. We just sat, still and heavy as stones. *I don't believe they're dead.*

Within an hour, the Transport Team arrived. I rolled up my sleeping mat and went with Mother to her space. She had trouble rolling her mat. It seemed stiff, or maybe she was just distraught. There was nothing else to pack. Our uniforms in Compound 18 would be a different color.

The Transport Team took us to our community's Authority building. A file clerk was looking at charts for available housing, and available partners. I was, after all, of reproductive age. I would require an appropriate partner to pair with. After this baby was born, I would have to make another and another and another. The Republic required it. I had learned that much, but I still knew so little. Mother stood beside me, this woman who had once loved poetry, wearing her black headscarf like a shroud.

The Central Authority building had a smell like moss, old shoes, and wet grass. The light was dim and the workers looked pale and dull.

The file clerk working on our case was about Mother's age. She leaned forward across the counter that separated us and whispered, "I am so sorry for your loss."

I felt a rush of love for this stranger. She touched my hand, then quickly pulled away. A warmth lingered where she had made contact.

"Compound 18, Recycling," she said. "Available housing. Available partner. Youth recently turned adult named Jeremy." She studied the forms in front of her carefully, reading them slowly, her lips moving as she read. "Youth recently turned adult?" She shrugged as if she didn't agree. I wondered what she was thinking.

She laid the forms down on the counter and went to another file cabinet. Mother tilted her head sideways at the abandoned forms, reading them. She frowned and shook her head as she read. When the file clerk came back and saw Mother studying the papers, she snatched them up and gave her a severe look.

"For now your mother can stay with you. Just until Central Authority makes a disposition decision. Until Jeremy can be relocated from the Village to the Compound. The final paperwork and reproductive-ability testing for Jeremy will take a few days." She handed the paperwork to the Transport Team leader, made the circle sign on her forehead, and turned away.

"Wait," I said. She turned back to me. I made the circle on my forehead and said, "Thank you." I hoped she knew why.

CHAPTER TWELVE

The Living Space that Mother and I were relocated to in Compound 18 was identical to the one in Compound 14. The arrangement of Living Spaces along the fence was the same, too. The sameness added to the dullness. The only differences were the dull green color of the flag and the heavy, putrid smell in the air. The smell of recycling.

Father was gone.

George was gone.

I was over seventeen years old, but I felt as helpless as a baby. I felt like someone had reached in and pulled out part of me and left a hole so big that no amount of tears could ever fill it. The edges so jagged that no matter which way I turned or sat, it ripped at me. A hole invisible to Enforcers and Gatekeepers and the Authority but nevertheless all-consuming.

I thought about what Father had told me last night. The grain bags. The escape. Was he serious? Could Mother and I still try it ourselves? Impossible. There was no one to help, no one to care. And even if we succeeded, then what? I dismissed the idea just as quickly as it had come to me.

After we moved into our new Living Space, Mother stopped walking on her energy board. She stayed on her mat all day, curled up on her side, facing the wall. Father was gone and it felt like I was losing Mother, too. I tried to get her to talk. "Tell me one of your poems." "How do you make vegetable soup?" "How old was I when I learned to walk?" "What kind of cookies did you make for your students?"

She didn't answer. She never did. She just lay there. Silent, unmoving. I finished walking my board, then I walked hers. I had to produce enough energy to justify our very being.

The Gatekeeper brought our nourishment cubes that evening. He looked exactly like the Gatekeeper from Compound 14. Did they move him here to watch us? He gave me a banner to hang out of our window slit when I went into labor. It was a bright red triangle with the image of a newborn in the center. The newborn had a hand to its forehead, fingers curled in a circle. "Praise be to the Republic," he said, when he handed me the banner. Mother wouldn't look at it.

"Praise be to the Republic," I replied, and made the circle salute.

* * *

I had trouble getting comfortable on my sleeping mat. How dark the little bit of sky beyond the window slit seemed. Even the moonlight seemed dull. I laid the red banner beside me and stroked it. Suddenly I felt a wet rush of hot liquid on my legs, spreading up my back. So much liquid. Even the edges of the banner got wet.

"Mother," I said. "Mother, I'm all wet. Everywhere."

I heard her turn over. "Oh, Lord," she said. "It's time."

She shuffled over to me, lifted the banner, and hung it out the window slit.

I heard the clanging of the bell; the Gatekeeper signaled for the Transport Team. Then he was at our door.

"Put your headscarf on," he said. "They're coming."

* * *

They wouldn't let Mother come with me. I wanted her with me more than I ever wanted anything. I held on to her and she held on to me. We clung to each other's arms tightly. But the Gatekeeper and the Transport Team separated us. They handled Mother roughly, pushing her aside. "Stay here, lady," one of them said. "You are not welcome."

In the bus-box they let me sit on the seat that had a backrest.

* * *

I don't remember having the baby. As soon as we got inside the Human Health Services building a technician gave me a shot. She said it would make labor easier. She said it was an amnesiac, and I wouldn't remember the pain. I didn't know what that meant, I just remember feeling like I had to push.

The next thing I remembered was the Transport Team coming to take me home.

The technician was helping me with my black widowhood scarf.

"My baby?" I asked her. "Can I see my baby?"

"Don't be ridiculous," she said.

I didn't think I was being ridiculous.

"Where is my baby?"

She didn't answer.

"Where is my baby?"

She didn't answer again. I grabbed her shoulder. "Answer me!"

Two men from the Transport Team grabbed my arms but I pulled away and whirled back at the technician, sobbing. "My baby. My baby."

She ignored my pleas. "Take this." She handed me a pill and a glass of water.

I threw the pill on the floor. She picked it up and handed it to me again.

"Take this, now." Her voice was firm.

I took the pill. The glass of water was only half full, but it was generous compared to what we were usually allowed to drink. The Authority knew how much water the citizens needed to keep them hydrated and that's exactly what we got. No more, no less.

She nodded to the Transport Team. They took me by my arms again and started to walk me out of the building. My legs felt weak and trembly. "I want to see my baby!" I shouted over my shoulder. "Please!"

"You're stable. Your vital signs are good. We have no reason to keep you; you can rest in your own Living Space. And we'll tend to the baby."

"But I have to see my baby." I couldn't stop crying.

"Quiet, do what she says," the man on my right whispered into my ear. He was a big man, muscular and tall. "Wait till we get outside."

It was still dark. Labor must have been quick. My belly still felt big but softer.

"I knew your father," he said when we got outside. "He was a good man. His farm was next to mine. I knew George, too. Whatever happened to them, whatever the Authorities told you, was wrong." He was still whispering. "My name is John."

He helped me up into the bus-box. "Give me a minute here," he said to the other men on the Transport Team. They stood, silent and still in their harnesses, and he turned back toward me. "I overheard the technician tell the Village staff that your baby passed initial functional testing," he said, talking fast and low. "I saw her hand the baby to the Village worker. The baby was in a pink blanket. That's all I know."

He got into his harness and the bus-box lurched forward. I was on my way back to our Living Space.

The bus-box stopped at the gate. I stood up but felt a swirling sensation in my head. I had to hold on to the side of the bus-box to keep from falling. The wood was rough and splintered under my hand. John slipped out of his harness, ran to the step of the bus-box, and helped me down the step, holding me tightly around the waist. I could smell the leather of his harness on his shirt.

The Gatekeeper stepped forward, frowning. "Stop right there," he said. "Transport Team members aren't permitted to enter the Compounds." He put his hand on the top of a wooden club hanging from his belt as he spoke. The wood was smooth, shiny, and very dark.

John didn't release his arm from around my waist. He was bigger and taller than the Gatekeeper. "She doesn't feel well. I'm just helping her. I'm Transport. Gatekeepers aren't permitted to transport people. You know the rules."

The feeling in my head got worse. The fence, the flag, the buildings, the trees on the other side of the fence all swirled, twisting, fading. I felt myself slipping down.

John picked me up. "I'll carry her to her space. That's transport, don't you agree?"

"What is your name?" the Gatekeeper asked.

"My name is my name. I don't need to give it to you. It's one of the few things I have left." His voice sounded foggy, far away but confident.

He carried me to the door of our space. The Gatekeeper followed, a few steps behind us. John whispered in my ear; I had trouble hearing him but his breath was warm on my face. I think he said he would try to find out more about my baby. Or maybe that's just what I wanted him to say.

Mother stood at the door, her hands on her cheeks.

"Emmie, let me help you." She reached out for me. Then she looked at the man carrying me. "John, is that you?" she said.

"Yes, it's me. I've brought your girl home."

"Can you stand, now?" John asked me. I nodded, and he put me down.

"Oh, Emmie, honey, are you all right?" I went to Mother, letting her wrap her arms around me like a safe blanket.

"Far from the farms, aren't we, Elsa? They transferred Joan and me from farm co-op supervisors. Assigned Joan to the Children's Village and me to Transport."

The Gatekeeper edged closer.

"Praise be to the Republic," John said to my mother and made the finger circle on his forehead. He nodded briskly at the Gatekeeper and went back to the bus-box.

* * *

A pink blanket. The baby must have been a girl.

I wanted to see her, as Mother had seen me for the first time. Pink and red and wet and slippery. Fingers, fingernails, toes, all small and perfect. Curled up, fitting into my arms. I wanted George to kiss me on my forehead.

"I think I had a baby girl," I told Mother.

"Sweet Jesus," she said. "Dear sweet Jesus."

Footsteps crunched outside our window—the Gatekeeper, taking down the red triangular banner.

Mother and I curled up together on her sleeping mat. We were all that was left of real family. The room felt empty. Something was missing.

I wish I had held Mother even more tightly than I did that night. I didn't know at the time that she was about to be taken from me as well.

CHAPTER THIRTEEN

After Mother was taken away, just Jeremy and I were left. We settled into a sullen relationship. Nothing like the way George and I had been with each other. I tried asking him questions, to find out more information, to learn all the things that everyone had kept from me.

"What was it like, growing up in the Children's Village?"

"I guess it was okay. Better than here," he said.

"What did you learn?"

"Stuff," he said.

"How old are you?"

"What's it to you?" He wiped his nose on his forearm, childlike.

And so it went. Questions. Short answers. "What do you do at Re-Cy?"

"Sweep the floor. Burn stuff. That's it."

"What kind of stuff?"

"Stuff."

He never asked me anything. Nor had we ever paired. I was still bleeding from having the baby and he had made no effort to touch me. His mat was against one wall, mine against the other, and the arrangement suited us both. I couldn't bear the thought of him pairing with me. I wouldn't let that happen. Republic be damned.

Every day was spent walking, creating energy. At the end of the day, I was hot and tired, and my muscles burned. My thighs were getting bigger and more defined.

Father used to tease Mother about her legs. "Nothing better than a woman with thighs," he used to say, and they would both laugh. It's been so long since I've heard anyone laugh.

I'd never felt so tired. Mother was gone, and her absence left a big hole in our Living Space. I wished I could step into that hole and disappear as she had. The only thing of hers still with me was her sleeping mat. It was hard and lumpy but I wanted to spend all day, every day, lying on it, smelling her, and pretending she was still here. That's all it was. Pretending. But that's all I had.

Falling asleep and staying asleep grew difficult. Often I would wake before sunrise. I started dragging Mother's sleeping mat near the doorway and would sit on it, looking out, watching the stars fade, waiting for the sun to rise. The stars were a mystery to me, scattered across the sky. The way they sparkled some nights more than others. The way they faded away when dawn came. Where do they go? I would cry, too. Missing Mother, missing Father, missing George. And missing my baby. How you can miss something that you never really had? I finally understood how much Mother missed what she once had, what was taken away from her. I wished I had understood this kind of grief better, when it still would have counted. Too late, now. That's what brought the tears—understanding doesn't matter when it comes too late.

From my doorway I saw the dusk-shift Gatekeeper making his rounds, delivering the breakfast cubes. They gave us cubes in the morning to fuel us up, so to speak, for a full day of producing energy. We had to earn our evening nourishment. The Gatekeeper put the breakfast cubes and water rations in the nourishment box outside each doorway. I watched him from the shadow of my doorway as he walked the perimeter, bending at each Living Space, lifting the box lid, putting in the cubes, moving on. The metal lids on the boxes creaked and screeched. The stars had almost faded. Streaks of gray light appeared beyond the fence, above the trees.

He came closer. He was taller than the day-shift Gatekeeper. I couldn't quite see his face. He bent and opened our box. The screech hurt my ears.

"Good morning," he whispered.

"Oh!" I didn't have my headscarf on. My hands flew to my neck for it, but it wasn't there. "Good morning. I didn't think you could see me."

"The little bit of light through the window slit. That's how I saw you. Praise be to the Republic."

"Praise be to the Republic." We both made the circle sign.

I watched him as he walked away. I watched the way he walked, strong strides, arms swinging only slightly but with rhythm, head up, alert, back straight, shoulders wide.

And then it was morning.

CHAPTER FOURTEEN

One morning, as I pulled Mother's mat across the concrete floor to the door, I heard a ripping sound. I turned it over to see how much damage I had done.

There was a small tear in the gray fabric. In the dim dawn light I could see something white inside the tear. Something that looked as though it did not belong. I put one finger into the void. Whatever it was felt smooth, like paper, which was odd since we hadn't been allowed paper for a long, long time.

The day the paper was taken was still vivid in my mind. I think I was about seven. Mother had taught me to read, but we didn't have many books. *Huckleberry Finn,* I think, and *Little House on the Prairie,* and my favorite, *The Little Prince.* I couldn't picture the worlds in *Huckleberry Finn* or *Little House,* but the pictures in *The Little Prince* were as barren as our Compound. We had a few schoolbooks too, early readers, and a children's picture dictionary. Mother went over the books, word by word, teaching me to read.

Central Authority sent workers to each Living Space. Mother had stood beside her energy board, arms crossed over her chest. "As was announced at the Social Update Meeting, we are authorized to remove all paper products including, but not limited to, books, photographs, maps, and letters." That's what the worker said. He had a mustache, but it was a mousy kind of mustache. Thin, brown, and wispy. He didn't look important.

"I heard the announcement," Mother said. "But I don't suppose you can help me understand the reason, can you?"

"The reasons were announced. Paper is to be recycled. There is no need for private ownership of paper. All communications will come directly from the Central Authority to the Citizens." He was frowning and tapping his fingers on the sidebars of my board. "You were to have all your papers gathered together and ready for pickup."

She turned her back on him. "I put all I had on the counter. Take it and leave."

"And you verify that is everything."

"I verify."

"But you can't take what is in my head," she muttered when he was out of earshot.

So the few books we had were taken. I was sad because I liked the feel of them. Hardbacks, some with pictures, and the pages marching forward, numbered. The paper, smooth between my fingers. The musty smell. But most of all, I liked sitting next to Mother, her arm around me as she read. The smell of the books, the smell of Mother. Sun through the window slit.

After they left with our books and little packet of paper, mostly old letters from friends long ago, Mother got right back on her energy board.

"Get on," she said to me. "Some things you have to do. The things that are monitored. So get on your board. Start walking." She walked heavily, stamping her feet against her board with anger. "But not everything can be monitored. Free will can't." She stopped talking.

* * *

That's what I remembered. And now, early morning, the next day, with Jeremy sleeping, I found paper in Mother's sleeping mat. I wanted to pull it out immediately, touch it, smell it, read it. But the light was dim and Jeremy would be awake soon. I sat in the doorway waiting for full dawn, my arms around Mother's sleeping mat. It was good to have something to hug.

The Gatekeeper started his morning rounds, bringing breakfast. I watched him step, bend, deposit, straighten up, step, bend, deposit. The wooden club on his belt swung forward each time he bent over.

He arrived at my doorway.

"Good morning," he whispered.

"Good morning," I answered. Should I have put on my headscarf? That was twice now, and he could report me for sitting in the doorway without my headscarf. I needed to be more careful, but it was so hard to be careful when you were tired, missing Mother and Father, having a child you had never seen, and living with the smell and sullenness of Jeremy.

"An egg, tomorrow," he said, and moved on. Odd. We hadn't had eggs for a long, long time. I pulled Mother's sleeping mat inside and put it against the wall, torn side down.

After Jeremy ate his breakfast cube, he left for Re-Cy on his energy bicycle. He didn't talk much. He never smiled. He was so different from Mother and Father and George. So different from me, too. I never would have picked him as a partner. But, of course, those were not my decisions to make.

I wanted so badly to pry open Mother's sleeping mat again but instead I decided to get started on my board, move that needle, move it as quickly as I could, so no one would be suspicious.

What was it Mother had said? *If it's monitored, you have to do it.*

And so I walked. And walked. And with every step I took, I thought of what might be on the paper in Mother's sleeping mat. My mind ran wild with possibilities. It must have been something important for her to take the risk to save it.

When my needle was a little past halfway, my legs were burning hot and heavy and I needed a break. A little breeze came through the window slit and the open doorway. I could smell the trees and grass on the other side of the fence. A rich green smell, living and clean. The smell Father said he missed.

I turned off my board and glanced out the door. The day-shift Gate-keeper was at his station by the gate and there was no reason for him to be making rounds. Not at this time of day. The bus-box was at the gate; I didn't wait to see if they were taking someone away. Wouldn't make any difference anyway. Nothing to be done when they come for you.

I quietly closed the door and then pulled Mother's mat into a corner where it would be hard for anyone walking past the doorway to see me. I sat on the floor with it across my lap. There it was, the little tear with white showing through.

It was too small for me to pull the paper through so I tore it a little larger. Then a little larger. I saw a word. KODACHROME. I didn't know what that was. The paper was still too big to pull out.

One more tear. It was very quiet outside except for some birdsong.

I slid the paper out carefully, slowly, and turned it over.

A picture on shiny paper, in color. A little girl in a pink dress, white shoes, and white socks with ruffles around the top. A lady holding her and smiling at her. They were standing outside of a big house with big windows. The little girl grinning at the lady. She had one hand in her mouth and the other hand on the lady's cheek.

The lady was Mother. Her skin was smooth, without scars or blotches.

The little girl must be me.

I put my hand inside the torn mat. I felt more papers, but I could tell from the sun through the window slit that I didn't have much time left to get my needle to finish. I had to get back on the board. I had to do what they can monitor.

I slid the picture back into the mat, flipped the mat torn-side-down, and smoothed the wrinkles off the cover. She had saved that picture for me. Now it was almost like she was here with me. Like we were in this together.

CHAPTER FIFTEEN

That night it was as though the Kodachrome had come alive. In my dream the little girl kept patting Mother's cheek. And Mother kept smiling and nuzzling her face against the little girl. Against me. And then Mother put me down on the grass and I took a couple of steps, then toddled with my arms out to my sides. Then I tumbled down and pulled up a handful of grass and tried to put it in my mouth.

Just as Father had told me I had done.

I didn't wake before dawn this time. My sleep was good and deep and peaceful. I woke when Jeremy did. Our breakfast cubes and water were already in our box, along with two beautiful hard-boiled eggs in their shells and two packets of salt.

"Look," I said. "Eggs."

"Who cares?" he said. "In the Children's Village the food was better."

"Jeremy, the food is the same everywhere. You know that."

"Yeah, but I liked it better there. I didn't have to go to work."

"Here you have to. And we're lucky to have eggs."

"What's lucky about stupid old eggs? I hate it here. I hate the energy bicycle. I hate going to work every day. I want to go back to the Village." He looked like he was going to cry. Who thought this boy was ready for work and reproduction? He was just that. A boy. Skinny, unable to carry on a conversation, exhausted from the energy bicycle and Re-Cy work. As much as I disliked him, I felt sorry for him.

I reached out to touch his shoulder but he pulled away. "And I hate you," he said.

"Eat your food, then go to work."

He only ate his cube, then left, slamming the door behind him. After he bicycled away, I opened the door to let more fresh air in. Jeremy's rancid smell lingered in our space.

Today would be a good day. Two eggs, two packets of salt, and later, more paper from Mother's mat. But first, the energy board. I felt like I could walk faster and harder than ever. I finally had a reason. Feet pounding, making the mat turn as I marched in place.

I turned the energy board off with the needle a little past halfway and went to the open door. For some reason the daytime Gatekeeper was making rounds, pausing at each door. That was unusual and I felt uneasy, so I went back to my board. The sleeping mat with its secrets would have to wait. I knew I would have to be very careful searching in that mat. I would have to resist the urge to rip it open and shake it out to see what else might be hiding in there, because at any time, someone could be making rounds, watching or listening.

Then he was standing at my doorway. "You didn't have the early morning awakening today, did you?"

I shook my head no.

He made the circle sign and moved on.

How did he know about my early-morning wakeups? Did the night-shift Gatekeeper tell him? Do they keep reports in folders somewhere? I closed the door and went back to walk my board. My hands were sweating and the metal sidebars were wet.

Sometime later, while I was still walking, I thought I heard someone calling my name.

"Emmeline. Emmeline."

There it was again, a man's voice.

I stopped my board, went to the door, and opened it.

No one was there. I went to the right window slit. No one. Left window slit. No one. Back window slit, the one that faced the fence. There was John, from the Transport Team, on the other side of the fence, under a tree. He reminded me of Father—same age, same big muscles—and the feeling you got that this man could take care of you. Protect you until he couldn't anymore. Like Father did. Like George did. As long as they could until . . .

"John?"

"Yes, it's me. I promised I would find out about your baby. And I did."

"What about my baby?" I felt like I couldn't breathe. My legs were trembling. What if something happened to her?

"She's fine, Emmeline. She's healthy. Her name is Elsa."

"Elsa? But that was Mother's name. How did she get named Elsa?"

"My wife works at the Village. She knew your Mother, so she named your baby after her. I've got to go. I'll give you updates when I can. It's dangerous but important. Family is important."

"How did you get outside the fence? Away from the Transport Team?"

"Don't ask. I don't have time to explain that now."

Then he turned toward the shadows of the trees.

"Don't go," I called. "Please don't—" But he was gone. "Thank you, John, thank you," I whispered toward the trees, into the shadows.

Back to the board. With each footstep walking in rhythm to El-sa, El-sa, El-sa.

Tonight was a Social Update Meeting. The only bad thing about today was tonight. And the odd question about early morning awakenings from the Gatekeeper.

CHAPTER SIXTEEN

The Gatekeeper hung the official flag on the pole above the green flag of our Compound to signal that it was time to start walking to the Social Update Meeting. It was large and black, emblazoned with a brilliant blue-and-green Earth in the center. I wondered if the Earth was really that beautiful or if the flag was a lie. I saw none of its beauty inside our fenced Compound, and most often, the flag hung limp so that the globe folded in upon itself. Then he rang the bell, a clanging sound that was impossible to ignore.

"It's time to go, Jeremy," I said, tying on my headscarf.

"I don't want to," he mumbled. He had been on his sleeping mat since eating his nourishment cube.

"You don't have a choice. Come on, now."

"I'm tired." He did not look well. "And my stomach hurts."

"I know you're tired. But you have to go. These are not optional."

"Why do I have to go? In the Village they did Social Updates and we didn't have to walk anywhere. They came to us. They took care of us."

"Jeremy, in the Compounds, you have to do what they monitor. And they monitor attendance. So come on." I tapped his shoulder and thought I was starting to sound like Mother. The feeling of missing her washed over me. Such a hopeless feeling, like dead weight.

"What will happen if I don't go?"

His question startled me.

Don't fight them. Do whatever they ask. Lay quietly. Let them examine you. That's what Father had told me. I should have asked him what would happen if I had fought them. But he had seemed so frightened that I had been scared as well. Too scared to ask any questions. If only I hadn't been so young, too young to pick up on clues, push for answers. That was then, this was now. Now I knew they had the power to take Mother away.

"I don't know. Just come." I was getting tired of coaxing him.

"I won't know what to do."

"Didn't they teach you at the Village?"

"We never went to an Update Meeting. We just sat in the classrooms. And the teachers talked. That's all."

"Did you pay attention?"

He didn't answer me. That was answer enough.

"Follow me. Do what I do. Okay?"

He nodded, got up reluctantly, and we walked to the gate. The Gatekeeper checked our names off a list that was written on a broad swath of creamy paper.

Pairs from our Compound and the others within our Planned Community had already left their Living Spaces and walked ahead of us toward the Central Stage. We were all wearing the colors assigned to us.

The closer we got to the Central Stage, the more people converged in their assigned areas. Assembled in stalls cordoned off with rope at the base of the Central Stage, we were all defined by our singular purpose, all wearing uniforms the colors of our Compounds. A rainbow that had been pulled apart was reuniting. The Nourishment Cube Makers wore uniforms the color of egg yolks. Ahead of us, the Uniform Makers in deep brown. And to one side, the bright orange of the

Transport Team contrasted with black of the Enforcers. The gray of the Gatekeepers, the vibrant green of the Managers of Nature. Other Compounds, other colors. Ours were the dullest of all. The groups stood together, but divided, as commingling of the Compounds wasn't allowed. The only exceptions were the Children's Village workers, who worked shifts at the Village but lived in their partner's Compound. The peaceful and flowery colors of their pastel uniforms were sprinkled throughout the gathering.

And finally, escorted onto the stage by Enforcers, the two Central Authority Figures lined up in a perfect front, their black uniforms trimmed with gold at the collar, at the cuffs, along the shoulder seams. The color of power.

Everyone was quiet. The only sound was the shuffling of feet as people moved into position. The occasional cough. The groups fanned out before the Authority Figures like the tail of a peacock.

Two Enforcers remained on the stage; the others joined their Compound. A hush fell over the crowd as we waited for the rituals.

The tallest of the Authority Figures moved to the front of the stage. He made the circle sign. We did the same.

"Praise be to the Republic." His voice boomed loud, vibrant, almost with an echo.

"Praise be to the Republic," we all responded, making the circle sign.

"Praise be to the Earth we serve."

"Praise be to the Earth we serve." Again the circle sign. Jeremy watched me for clues. He was pale and shifted his weight from foot to foot.

"Praise be to the animals."

Praise, repeat, praise, repeat.

I saw John, over to my right, in the bright orange of the Transport Compound. He was smiling at me. Next to him was a woman in pink.

Was she the one who'd named Elsa?

She smiled at me, too.

"I pledge to produce more than I consume."

"I pledge to produce more than I consume." Monotone.

Jeremy fidgeted. "Be still," I whispered. "Or I will pinch you."

The second Authority Figure moved forward on the stage.

"I bring you news of our Republic."

"Praise be to the news of our Republic," we murmured.

"In the name of our Republic, I have the following news," he said. "First, our birthrate is not keeping pace with our enemies'."

A collective sigh of sorrow flowed across the group.

"We have had some good births. Some good, healthy births. But not enough to compete with our enemies. Fertile women and their partners in our Republic will undergo more reproductive-ability testing in the near future. Failure to reproduce is failure to the Republic."

I glanced again at John and the woman in pink. I had to find a way to talk to her. She may have actually held my little Elsa. She may have kissed her forehead.

"The second announcement."

I'd learned from so many Social Update Meetings that when they spoke of "news" it would be about something far away, like other republics or wars being fought somewhere else. But "announcements" were always about changes in the rules for living in this Republic. And changes were never good.

"The Central Authority has determined we must increase our energy production to compete with other republics. Other republics are growing larger armies than ours. We have news of increased strength in other republics. We must produce more energy."

I felt tired and drained listening to this man dressed in black, trimmed in gold, demanding we produce more energy.

"The friction on energy bicycles will be increased, starting tomorrow."

I heard Jeremy groan.

"The energy board requirements will be increased tomorrow, as well."

A collective hiss went around the Compounds. Stifled, but palpable.

"Indicate your understanding." His voice was loud, angry.

"We understand." The response was muted.

"Verify your participation." Again, loud and angry.

"We verify our participation." The response a little louder.

"All Citizens will be issued energy collection cells and thigh straps. The cells will store energy generated by your movements."

People glanced sideways at each other, confused.

"The collection cells are to be worn on your right thigh from dawn to dusk and downloaded each night into the download bars."

An Enforcer stepped forward on the stage and demonstrated fastening the energy cell on his thigh. People strained and stretched their necks to watch. Some stood on tiptoes, their hands on their partner's shoulders for balance.

"The cells will be placed in your nourishment boxes tomorrow. Praise be to the Republic."

"Praise be to the Republic." All around me came the rustling of cloth as hands were raised to foreheads to make the circle sign.

The meeting droned on and on. Statistics on current crops: Corn at only 90 percent of last year's crop. Root vegetables not yet harvested. Blight on 20 percent of apple trees. The Managers of Nature will handle the feeding of animals and any crop surplus. Statistics on the health of the forest: new seedlings planted to replace storm-damaged hardwoods. Statistics on the health of animals: wolves were reproducing well. Given supplemental feedings. More feeding stations placed in the woods.

My mind wandered. I looked over at the lady in pink. She nodded at me. I nodded back, ever so slightly.

Then I heard the Authority Figure say, "It has been reported that some in the Compounds have been experiencing early morning awakenings. This is a sign of depression and is of deep concern to the Central Authority. A depressed subject is not a productive subject. You are all reminded to respect the night darkness given to us by the Earth and remain on your sleeping mats until the half-hour warning bell of dawn."

Again, people gave each other sideways glances.

Jeremy shuffled his feet, nervously.

"Verify your understanding."

"We verify our understanding."

"We will close now with our Pledge of Dedication."

It was the same numbing cadence of words that I had heard for as long as I could remember people gathering to recite it:

We pledge our allegiance
To the wisdom of the Central Authority.
We pledge our dedication
To the Earth and to its preservation.

The Enforcers escorted the Authority Figures off the stage. They entered their decorated bus-box. It had high sides and a roof, unlike the common bus-boxes. It was painted glossy black and bore the blue-and-green globe on its side.

We were free to leave and obligated to return directly to our Compounds. I searched for John and his wife, but they had already disappeared. I tried pushing forward, but everyone was walking in the other direction, and the crowd pushed back. Jeremy tugged on my sleeve.

"Where are you going? What are you doing?"

I wouldn't be able to find her. Not tonight. But somehow, someday, I would.

"Never mind, Jeremy. Let's go home."

The day-shift Gatekeeper checked a box on his paper list as we filed back into our Compound.

Who, I wondered, reported my early morning awakenings to the Central Authority? And why?

CHAPTER SEVENTEEN

I slept poorly that night. I wanted to pull the picture of Mother and me from my sleeping mat but it was too dark, and besides, Jeremy was tossing and turning on his mat. I would have to wait for morning when he left for Re-Cy. I'd have to be more careful around the day-shift Gatekeeper. Wait. Watch. Worry.

Through the window slit I heard the night-shift Gatekeeper opening and closing the nourishment boxes outside the Living Spaces doors. As he got closer to ours, the sounds got a little louder. After he closed the lid to our box, I heard him whisper, "One egg, just for you. I wasn't able to barter for an extra egg this time."

I grabbed my headscarf and put it on. Dawn had begun bleeding pale colors of daylight above the trees and into the window slits. I went outside to the nourishment box and there, indeed, were two breakfast cubes, two water rations, and one egg with one packet of salt. Plus two energy cells with thigh straps.

When I reached into the box, I saw him standing in the shadow at the outside corner of our Living Space. Startled, I dropped everything back into the box.

"Don't be afraid," he whispered.

I kept my eyes down. I didn't want to look at him.

"You remind me of someone. She was about your age. You probably don't remember, but you used to play with her. Back at the farm. She liked hard-boiled eggs. She died when the illness came here, and I miss her."

He started to walk away.

"Wait," I said. "Who was she?"

He turned to face me. He was much taller than me. His shoulders were broad, his hips narrow. He looked, I don't know . . . he looked *solid*. A person of substance.

"My sister."

I wanted to say, "I'm sorry for your loss," maybe reach out and touch his hand. But I was stuck in place, and my hands were sweating even though it was a cool morning.

"Did you report me?"

"What?" He looked surprised.

"Did you report me?"

"Report you for what?"

"Early morning awakenings."

"Why would I do that?"

"I don't know. Someone did."

"It wasn't me. I wouldn't do that," he whispered. And he continued his rounds.

"Thank you for the egg," I said and went back inside. Jeremy was stirring on his sleeping mat. As he rose and fumbled about his morning tasks, he grumbled that his mat was too hard, that his cube was too dry, and that he didn't want to go to work. I handed him his new energy cell, the thigh straps dangling.

He stood in the doorway, his hands on his hips, facing me. "I thought you weren't allowed early morning awakenings. If I have to follow the rules, so do you. Don't think you're someone special. You're not. You're just home-raised stupid." Then he got on his energy bicycle. He hadn't put on his new energy cell. As he pushed off on his energy bicycle, he said over his shoulder, "So there."

The machine must have been harder to pedal today; he seemed to be struggling to force the pedals through their rotation and he wobbled through the gate. But I didn't feel sorry for him. I felt afraid. For him or of him, I wasn't sure which.

I ate my egg first, taking little bites to make it last longer. I ate the white part, smooth and cold, then the golden, crumbly yolk. When it was gone, I licked my fingers, savoring the yolk crumbs and salt.

Time to get dressed. I pulled the green sleeping shirt over my head, tossed it onto my mat, and quickly donned my ugly green uniform pants and top. I strapped the energy cell onto my right thigh as the Enforcer had demonstrated. It was tight and my pant leg puckered under the strap.

Then to the energy board. Later, the sleeping mat with its hidden secrets.

It took longer to get the meter to halfway. I don't know how they change the requirements during the night, but somehow they did. They have the power to change things. As they choose. As they decide.

I wanted to get off the energy board and go sit in the sun. I wanted to hold Elsa. That was all that mattered to me.

When I was finally able to take a break, I went to the door. The day-shift Gatekeeper was at his post. I pulled the mat to a corner of the sleeping area and carefully turned it over. I pulled out the picture first. Reaching through the torn opening, I could feel something else. It was slippery. I slowly pulled it through the tear. It was a little plastic bag with stiff cards inside. It had a kind of zipper closing. I opened it and, one by one, I pulled the cards out and turned them over.

They were yellowed, and some of the ink had smeared. They were in Mother's handwriting. Recipes. Vegetable beef soup. Bread pudding. Ham and potato casserole. Pumpkin pie. Chocolate chip cookies. There were about twenty. I ran my fingertips over the old food stains.

The very last card read: *Dear God, I pray that someday I can again make meals for my family. Amen.*

Someone was coming. I quickly turned the mat over, covering the picture and the recipes. I grabbed my headscarf and went to the door. A bus-box was parked by the gate, and two Enforcers and the Gate-keeper were coming toward my Living Space. The Transport Team stood stiff and silent in their harnesses. I recognized John.

"Citizen," one of the Enforcers said, "where is Jeremy?"

"At work," I answered. "At Re-Cy."

"No, he's not. His supervisor contacted us. Jeremy's not there."

"I saw him leave this morning. On his energy bicycle. See, it's not here. It's not connected to the download bar." I didn't know what else to say.

"We're going to enter your Living Space. We're required to find him."

I stepped aside to let them come in. The Gatekeeper stayed outside.

I went to my mat and sat on it to guard it. They mustn't find my treasures. They mustn't find what is in Mother's sleeping mat.

They opened the door to the washing-up area. They glanced into the eating space and the sleeping space. They checked the meter on my energy board. One of them glanced at the new energy cell on my thigh. When they were satisfied that Jeremy was not here, they stood in the doorway and frowned. One of them said, "This is a serious infraction."

And then they left.

My heart was racing so fast that I could feel my pulse in my throat and hear it in my ears. I would walk my board and think of Elsa. My feet pounded against the rotating mat. The thigh strap felt tight, constricting.

El-sa. El-sa. The marching band rhythm.

Finally, the needle hit finish and I turned off the board. It was quiet in the Compound. Men had not yet returned to their Living Spaces from work. I didn't know if Jeremy had been found.

I put my headscarf on and leaned against the doorway, drinking the last bit of my morning water. The Gatekeeper saw me, I know he did, but he didn't nod or smile or anything. Just stood by the gate as a bus-box pulled up with two Enforcers. John was still on Transport. Six men, three sets of two in harness, and he was on the right side, in the front. I wondered if the front row had more work than the back row, or if the middle row had the most work. They all looked hot and tired and miserable.

The Enforcers approached my Living Space. I think they were the same Enforcers who took Mother away, but I couldn't be sure. They're hard to tell apart, with their black uniforms and mustaches. They have the same look on their faces, grim and determined, the same way of walking—striding, really. The same way of looking taller than they really are. I stood as straight as I could, shoulders squared back. I would not let these men make me feel small.

I remained in my doorway as they approached. My hand fluttered to my headscarf, tugging it in place. I had fulfilled my energy quota. I had no reason to fear them. What else could they demand of me? What was left to give?

"Jeremy has been located," one of them said.

I just stared at him.

"May we come in?" Usually they didn't ask permission. Something different was going on.

"Yes. Come in."

The three of us stood in the eating space. I realized I was hungry.

"He was found trying to climb the fence into the Children's Village."

Stupid! He missed being taken care of. But to try to climb back in?

"That was an infraction. You realize that, don't you?"

"Yes, but it was Jeremy's infraction, not mine." My voice had the same sharp tone Mother used when questioned by Enforcers. I felt proud that I could talk like that, challenging them.

"Correct."

"What is expected of me?" I asked.

"At this time, nothing. Jeremy has been relocated to the farm co-op."

I raised my eyebrows. Or, at least, I think I raised my eyebrows. It's hard to know what you are doing when the Enforcers are watching you. "The farm co-op?"

"He can be a productive worker there," said the Enforcer who was doing all the talking. "The Human Health Services reevaluated him. They found him, after all, too young to be paired but capable of farm work. Would you agree?"

"I cannot disagree with the Human Health Services, can I?"

"The official who initially evaluated him and found him mature has been"—he looked sideways at his partner—"dealt with."

The other Enforcer looked as if he wanted to smile.

"In any event, Jeremy will not be returning. At the present time, there's no reproductive male available to be paired with you. The Authority will make decisions regarding your future assignments. In the meantime, the Gatekeepers will continue to supply your nourishment cubes. The Gatekeeper sent this for you." He handed me my evening cube and water ration.

I nodded. "Praise be to the Republic."

We all made the circle sign.

They asked which mat was Jeremy's. I pointed to it and they took it. He wouldn't be coming back and I wouldn't miss him.

Now there was just me and Mother's mat. I was completely alone and I wasn't sure how to feel about that. Was this loneliness? Or was it just the absolute silence, the total grayness of this space? I wouldn't miss Jeremy. Lonely or not, I had the things Mother had left for me. And there was enough daylight left for me to explore her treasures.

So I did.

CHAPTER EIGHTEEN

I propped the picture up against the wall so I could glance at it as often as I wanted. I left the recipe cards inside the mat and reached deeper, past them. My fingers probed back and forth until I felt something. Carefully, I pulled it out.

It was paper, folded many times. A map. I unfolded it carefully because it was thin and fragile along the fold lines. One side was a map of the United States of America. All of the states were different colors. Maine. New Jersey. Florida. California. And more. A circle on top with the word *north* at the top, *south* on the bottom, *east* on one side, *west* on the other.

I traced my finger along the line of the East Coast. Its dips and curves. That long piece of land at the bottom that hung down like a finger. Mother said that's where the Relocations Laws were written, somewhere on the East Coast. Then I traced along the line of the West Coast. That's where the first Relocations were done. The great vast blueness on either side of the coasts. Beautiful blue water. So much water. And we had lived somewhere in the middle. I scanned the center of the map but I didn't know exactly where our farm had been.

It made me sad to think like that. Where our farm *had* been. Maybe the farm is still there but it isn't ours.

I turned the map over carefully. On the other side was a map of a state called Kansas. Someone had drawn a circle around an area in the middle of the state near a lake named Wilson. Maybe that's where we lived. Maybe that's where Mother used to fish. I turned the map back over and found Kansas in the middle of the nation. Lake Wilson was just a tiny, tiny dot on this side of the map. How big the nation was!

I looked up at the picture of Mother and me. Was it taken in front of our house in Kansas? Is that what the green grass looks like in Kansas? How close to the lake did we live? Had they ever taken me to the lake? I closed my eyes and tried to picture Mother and me sitting on the grass by a lake, looking out at the water, watching Father standing nearby, fishing.

I was glad that no one could see me crying.

I refolded the map carefully but it took me a couple of times to get it just right. I slipped it into the underside of the mat and then slipped the picture back in, too. The sun had dipped below the tops of the trees and the Living Space was dim. I went and sat in the doorway, looking out at the packed brown common area. Where did I live now? Where, in this large country, was this Planned Community? Who would know? Who could I ask? The day-shift Gatekeeper was reporting off and starting the same ritual the Gatekeepers did at every change of shift. I have no idea what it involved, but I am sure it ended like all other rituals, with *Praise be to the Republic* and the circle sign.

"Emmeline," a voice said.

John. I scrambled to my feet and went to the back window slit.

"I'm here," I said.

"Good. I heard about Jeremy. I just wanted to make sure you're okay. Are you?"

"I guess. Jeremy was pretty stupid to try a stunt like that."

"He should have never been paired with you. Never. My wife knew him from the Children's Village. She said he wasn't mature or stable enough, that the Central Authority is pushing the children to reproduce and be productive before they are ready. She sent me to check on you."

"I'm okay. How's Elsa?"

"Growing."

"How big?"

"Don't know exactly. Just know that she's growing. Do you need anything?"

"I don't think so. I'm getting my cubes and my water. The board is harder." I could barely see John in the evening shadows.

"I know your night-shift Gatekeeper. Let him know if you need anything. He promised to keep an eye on you to make sure you're okay." I remembered how John had helped me from the bus-box after Elsa was born and how glad Mother was to see him. I felt I could talk to him.

"What about the day-shift Gatekeeper? Do you know him?"

"No. And if I don't know somebody, I don't trust them. You'd be wise to do the same."

"John," I asked, "did we used to live in Kansas?"

"Why do you ask? Didn't your mother tell you where we used to live?"

"She told me some things but not everything. But I found a map."

"You found a what?"

"A map."

"Where in heaven's name did you get a map?" His eyes widened. He looked startled, maybe even frightened.

"Mother had it hidden. But I found it."

"That's contraband. What a find! Leave it to your mother!" He leaned his face even closer to the window slit. I felt the warmth of his breath.

"But did we live in Kansas?"

"Sure did."

"And where do we live now?"

"That's a good question. We were relocated without specifics. That's what we were told. On trains with the windows painted black. Where's the map now?"

"Hidden."

"Can I see it? Maybe I can figure out where we are. I don't know. Maybe Joan and I can figure it out."

"If I give you the map, can you bring Elsa to me so I can see her? Or take me to her?"

"Emmeline, you really are your mother's child. Your mother would be so proud of you." He sounded proud of me, too.

"I will give you the map. You figure out where we are. You bring Elsa so I can see her. Or, like I said, take me to her. Your wife works there. She should be able to arrange something, anything. And I get the map back." I knew he could hear the impatience in my voice. I knew that what I was asking for was impossible, but I was desperate.

He sighed. "Do you have any idea what you are asking for? How dangerous that would be?"

"Do you want the map?"

"Of course, but—"

"No buts. Elsa is all that is left of my family. As you said, family is important."

"So is staying alive, Emmeline."

I didn't say anything. A chill ran down my spine like cold fingers. I stood there on my tiptoes, looking out of the window slit. It was getting darker.

"Give me the map. I'll try to figure something out. But I can't promise anything."

I pulled the map out of the sleeping mat and held it through the window slit. My arm was shaking. He took it and squeezed my hand, steadying my tremors. How warm and strong his grip felt.

And then he was gone.

I slid the picture of Mother and me back into the sleeping mat and lay down on it. The smell of her was fading and I buried my face against the fabric, trying to keep it alive.

A sound pulled my thoughts back to the present—that shuffling sound of shoes on dirt. The Gatekeeper making rounds. The footsteps paused by my doorway, and I bolted from the mat and went to the door, opening it just a bit.

"Hello?" I whispered. John said I could trust him, but, still, this was unexpected.

"Hello," he whispered back. "It's very unusual for the Central Authority to allow a female to live alone. Very unusual. They weren't prepared for the move what's-his-name pulled."

"Jeremy?"

"Yes, him. He was a brat, wasn't he?"

"What do you mean?" The way he said it, though, described Jeremy perfectly.

"He was always mouthing off to me. Always saying he was going to report me for this, that, or the other. It would have all been lies. Anyway, you say you're okay?"

I opened the door wider and stepped out into the cool night. "I'm fine. Really I am. And thank you for the egg."

"My pleasure. Dusk-to-dawn shift workers get a hard-boiled egg for middle-of-the-night nourishment. But I thought you needed it more than I did." His voice had a kind sound, gentle and smooth.

"What's your name?"

"David. I know yours, Emmeline. Nice name. I bet they move you somewhere else soon as they figure out what to do. But I hope not." He touched my shoulder as he passed by and said, "Sleep well, Emmeline."

The second human touch in one day. And for a brief moment I was not alone. Then he was gone, making rounds, disappearing into the darkness of the night. I laid my hand where he had touched it and let my fingers linger there before I turned and went back into my empty Living Space.

CHAPTER NINETEEN

The next day was long. It had rained hard all morning, making the common area muddy and dank. Even inside, everything felt damp. The sidebars of my energy board were cold and slippery.

The day-shift Gatekeeper didn't make rounds but stood huddled in his rain poncho by the gate. No bus-box went by, probably too muddy for the Transport Team to make it over the path.

I wished I had one of the books Mother used to read to me. If I had one, I could prop it up on the front bar of the energy board and read while I walked to make the time go faster. With no one to talk to, I wished John would call out to me from beyond the fence. But no fool would be out under the trees in this storm.

Afternoon was even worse. Thunder rolled in, ominous and loud, with dark clouds ripped open by lightning. I got off my board, afraid that a bolt would zip through the metal and send its unimaginable surge of energy through my body. Mother had always warned me about lightning striking metal with more energy than we could produce in lifetimes of walking the board.

I curled up on Mother's sleeping mat, waiting for the storm to pass.

I slept a bit, and when I woke, the clouds had brightened from iron to silver. Sun filtered through the window slit onto my face. It felt so good, so warm, so . . . I don't know, *hopeful.*

I went to the doorway to feel the sun on me. Above the trees was a double rainbow, crystal clear, with strong colors. The inner rainbow, red, orange, yellow, green, blue, indigo, violet. Mother taught me "Roy G. Biv" to remember the colors and she made up a rhyme:

A rainbow is named Roy G. Biv
To remember the colors and the joy they give.

The colors in the outer rainbow were reversed. I didn't have a poem for that.

I still had to finish my board. So I did. Do what they can monitor. The needle moved slowly to finish. Crept, really.

The Gatekeeper put my nourishment cube and water in the box and left. I was certain, now, that he was the Gatekeeper when we lived in the Transport Compound. I also knew that John was right when he said not to trust him. I would wait until the change of shifts before going back to Mother's sleeping mat to look for more treasures.

It was almost dusk when David arrived at the post and spoke to the day-shift Gatekeeper, who pointed to my Living Space. Finally, they made the circle sign and David took over.

It was time to explore deeper, reach deeper, into Mother's mat. I pulled out the picture and propped it against the wall. I was developing my own little ritual, and it gave me comfort. Reached past the packet of recipes, deeper into the mat, as far as my arm would go without tearing it any more.

Something firm.

Smooth.

A book. *The Little Prince.* My favorite of all the ones Mother used to read to me. I remembered that the author's name was strange. Antoine de Saint-Exupéry. Mother said he was French. I liked that book the best because of the pictures. When we still had paper, I tried to copy them—and there, when I opened the cover, I found a picture I had drawn tucked inside. The one of the Little Prince looking up at a star. Underneath I had copied the words from the book: *He fell as gently as a tree falls. There was not even any sound.*

Mother had saved this for me. There had to be a reason. Perhaps she believed that someday I would be free to read it again.

It was too dark inside to read anymore. I slipped everything back into the mat and went to the doorway. David was by the gate. So tall, with broad shoulders, narrow hips, long legs. His dark hair dipped over his forehead and perfectly framed his firm jaw. He gave a little wave without raising his arm, moving only his fingers. I smiled and gave the same secret wave. Perhaps later, when he made rounds, we could talk briefly. Or when he brought my breakfast cube. The thought gave me comfort.

I had trouble falling asleep because of my earlier nap. And Mother's mat was getting lumpier as I moved the hidden treasures around. Over the years they must have formed their own little places, molded into the mat, but I had changed that, rearranged everything.

"Emmeline." A whisper filed in through one of the window slits. "It's me. David. I'm outside your door."

I could feel the pulse on the side of my neck, fast, fluttery. I got up, tightened the belt on my sleeping robe, and went to the door. He seemed even taller now. And so solid, his shirt was taut against his chest. A person of substance.

"John asked me to check in on you. You don't mind, do you?"

I felt my face getting hot. I hoped he couldn't see that.

"No, I don't mind. Not at all. I haven't really talked to anybody all day."

"They'll change that as soon as they can. They don't approve of solitary living. It's not efficient use of space."

"Do you want to come in?"

"That's forbidden." He paused. "But I wish I could."

"Maybe no one would know." I couldn't believe how bold I was being.

He stepped closer to me. Touched my cheek. Smiled.

"I'll try to after I make rounds. If the Compound is asleep."

He turned to leave, and then turned back. "Maybe we can pretend we're going out on a date."

With that he was gone.

I smoothed the wrinkles on Mother's mat. Earlier, I had tossed my uniform shirt and pants on the sidebars of my board. Now I folded them neatly and put them on the shelf in the washing-up area. Glancing around in the dim light I decided that my Living Space looked neat.

Then I sat down to wait.

And wait. What were we thinking? David was right. Some things are forbidden. Gatekeepers are not permitted to enter anyone's Living Space. Unpaired men and women were not to meet in private.

But I didn't care.

Finally I heard the soft sound of his steps, saw his outline in the doorway.

"Come in," I whispered.

He stepped a few feet into my Living Space.

"Come in. Sit down."

"I better stay near the door. You know. Just in case."

I walked over to him.

"What was the day-shift Gatekeeper saying about me? I saw him pointing to my Living Space."

"Oh, him. He was just reminding me that an unpaired female was in the Compound. As if I didn't know."

"Are you paired?" I asked, and immediately regretted it. It wasn't any of my business.

"Night-shift workers cannot be paired because their partner would be alone every night. So, no, I'm alone."

I felt a silly sense of relief.

"They aren't going to let you remain unpaired for very long. You know that, right?" he asked.

"Not another Jeremy, I hope."

"I hope not. John says there aren't any available adult males ready to leave the Village. So I don't know. Just have to wait and see, I guess."

He stepped closer to the doorway and listened. All was quiet.

"You and John. You're friends, right?"

"He's my father."

My head was spinning. John used to be our neighbor so that meant David used to be my neighbor, too. "You knew my family? We were neighbors?"

Before he could answer, we heard the sound of someone crying out. A woman.

"That's Space Four. She has nightmares. I better go. Sometimes she wakes up and paces around."

With that he was gone, leaving me alone with even more questions than I'd had before.

CHAPTER TWENTY

The next morning I woke up and was met with a surprise. There on the counter was my nourishment cube, my water, and, beside them, a hard-boiled egg and a salt packet. And a sprig of flowers. Flowers! A long stem with little lavender buds, sweet-smelling and soft.

The egg was cold and smooth. It felt like a promise in my hand. The egg was too perfect, too special, to crack open just yet. I put it in my pocket. Before I hid the flowers between my mat and the wall, I touched the feathery softness of the petals with my fingers and then gently held them to my cheek, moving them across my face, letting them linger under my nose. The smell was beautiful enough to make me feel dizzy.

The Gatekeeper's footsteps were coming closer. He stopped by my doorway and stared in, his nose small and sharp, his lips thin. My skin prickled. He tapped the stick hanging from his belt and then walked on. I went over and closed the door.

I would have to tell David about this. It must be something to do with monitoring. Watching for infractions. I went to my board. I walked it step by step by step but my mind was full of thoughts. Voices and words tumbled together like a flock of birds, flitting from one thought to another, then flitting back.

Remember all Mother taught me. *Do what they can monitor.* Father's voice: *Do what they tell you. Promise me. Promise me.*

My feet slapped against the mat, pounding, marching.

Jeremy's high, whining voice. *I hate you. I hate you. So there.*

Then, comforting voices. *Little teapot. Little teapot. Little teapot. Family is important. Promised your Mother. Promised. Promised.*

The needle was moving slowly. I walked faster and faster, trying to keep up with the voices, with how the words made me feel.

Regret to inform you. Sorry for your loss.

I was sweating. My uniform top was damp and clinging to me. Rivulets of sweat ran between my breasts.

You can't see your baby. Ridiculous.

Mother reading from *The Little Prince: So I lived my life alone, lived my life alone, lived my life alone.*

El-sa. El-sa.

My face was wet. Was it sweat or tears?

The needle kept moving.

* * *

Just before dusk I heard John at my window slit.

"How do you get on the other side of the fence?" I asked him.

"Sorry, that's my secret."

"Tell me about the map. And Elsa."

"Best guess is that we're in Pennsylvania, or Ohio, or West Virginia. But it's just a guess. And I have something else to tell you. Listen carefully."

I glanced over my shoulder. I could see through the open door just enough to make sure the Gatekeeper was at his post. He was.

"Are you listening? Look at me!" John tapped his hand on the window slit.

Startled, I turned back to him.

"The Authority has been trying to solve the problem of what they should do about you. Young female, reproductive age, no available partner."

"What will happen?"

"It's a secret. You can't share it with anyone. Understand?"

"I understand."

"They're considering assigning you to the Children's Village."

I caught my breath. Elsa! I must have said her name out loud because John said, "Quiet. Keep your voice down."

"How do you know this?" I whispered. I put my hand on the edge of the window slit.

"I told Joan what you said. About her working there and you wanting to see Elsa and all of that. What you said made sense."

I held my breath, my chest tight, waiting to hear more, staring at him.

"She put in a request for more staff. The Village has some problems that she's worried about."

The trees behind him rustled in the breeze, green leaves fluttering.

"She hasn't heard anything definite yet. But I work Transport Team, remember? The Authority forgets that we are men. They act like we're horses. So they talk and I hear. As long as I am in my harness, staring straight ahead, I am merely part of their vehicle."

"When will they decide for sure?"

"I don't know. But they're discussing it." He laid his hand on mine and left it there. "But pay attention to what I am going to tell you. If they come to you with this plan, listen quietly. Keep your eyes averted. Say something like 'Thank you, sir, but I don't know if I am qualified.' "

"But I want to be assigned there."

"And they want to be in control. I guarantee you that if you say you don't think you're qualified, they'll say they are the ones in charge of deciding who is and who isn't qualified. If you act happy with the decision, they'll get suspicious. They don't trust happy people. We all have to be equally miserable."

I glanced out the door. The Gatekeeper was starting final rounds before the change of shift. "You've got to go. He's coming."

"Promise me. Eyes averted. Act humble."

"Can I tell David?"

"No! Not yet. Tell no one." Then he was gone, a shadow moving into the woods.

* * *

David slipped through my doorway after he made his night rounds. I had pulled the flowers out of their hiding place and was holding them when he came in.

"Do you like them?" he asked.

"Of course I do! But what if you get caught? What would happen?"

"Don't ask. Don't ask because I don't want to spoil our time together. For now just know that I'm very careful. Did you like the egg?"

The egg! It was still in my pocket. I pulled it out and began to shell it. The sharp little pieces of shell fell onto my lap. When I was done, I held it out to him. "Please share it with me."

He smiled and took the egg. I watched his mouth as he took a small bite. His lips were plump and soft-looking. He handed the egg back to me and I took a bite. He watched my mouth. I ran my tongue over my lips, savoring the morsels, savoring the moment.

An egg had never tasted so good.

CHAPTER TWENTY-ONE

The next morning I saw bits of eggshell on the floor. I smiled as I swept them up, smiled even wider when I found another egg beside my morning nourishment cube. I would save it for tonight, when David came back.

About mid-morning, when the sun was well above the tops of the trees, the clattering and groaning wheels of a bus-box stopped at the gate. I went to my doorway, wondering who might be coming to the Compound. It was the Central Authority vehicle. John was on the Transport Team. He stood tall and still, eyes straight ahead.

Two Authority Figures got off the bus and spoke briefly to the day-shift Gatekeeper, who kept his eyes averted, even when he made the circle sign. Odd. They started walking toward me. I had already put on my headscarf and checked again that the flowers were tucked behind my mat. All was in order by the time they reached the doorway.

The Gatekeeper lingered outside until one of the Authority Figures told him to return to his post. He made the circle sign again and walked away slowly, glancing back several times. Gossips, all of them.

When he was back at the gate, the Authority Figures came into my space and motioned that I could sit down.

My knees were shaking, and I was glad to be seated. They remained standing, looking down at me, deliberately not introducing themselves. Anonymous authority. I decided to think of them as Number One and Number Two. They both had mustaches, of course. And they were both tall. But Number One had a scar, a ragged red line across his left cheek.

Number One spoke first. "Praise be to the Republic."

I repeated it, eyes down. The tips of my shoes were dusty. I wanted to rub them on the back of my leg to remove the dust but I was afraid to move. My hands were folded on my lap.

"Citizen, as you know, unpaired reproductive females are to be paired as soon as possible. It is not acceptable that you are alone. That does not serve the Republic."

I nodded.

"However, if normal procedures are followed, there are no available reproductive males at this time. This, of course, is beyond the Republic's control."

How ridiculous he sounded. The Republic controls everything, but yet he says this is beyond its control. I kept my eyes lowered. I didn't need to know which one was talking. They both sounded the same, with their deep, echo-chamber voices.

"However, there are no cultural, economic, or social situations the Central Authority cannot address and solve."

"Praise be to the Republic."

"Praise be to the Republic."

The tips of their shoes were dusty, too.

"Central Authority has developed an innovative and appropriate solution."

My hands were sweating. I wanted to wipe them on my uniform but instead kept them in my lap.

"You have proven yourself capable of reproduction. Praise be to the Republic."

I repeated it yet again. My mouth was dry, and my voice was trembling.

"The Authority has identified a reproductive male, a nightshift Gatekeeper who is not yet paired."

My heart lurched.

"Normally, night-shift Gatekeepers aren't paired because their partner would be alone at night, which is not acceptable. To address this issue, the Central Authority's solution is this: you will be assigned as a worker in the Children's Village."

"But, sir," I said, "I don't know if I am qualified."

"The Authority decides who is qualified and who isn't." His voice was harsh. *Praise be to John.*

I wanted to look up. I wanted to watch his face. But I kept my eyes on my dusty shoes.

"Night-shift Gatekeepers are often males incapable of reproduction. But a reproductive Gatekeeper has been identified."

Looking up, I could see the hairs in his nose and a wart under his chin. I couldn't help staring as he talked.

"You'll be assigned to the night shift at the Children's Village. He'll continue as a night-shift Gatekeeper but will no longer reside in the night-shift barracks. That is until, and if, a day-shift position becomes available. If that occurs, your position at the Children's Village will be reevaluated. This solution demonstrates the wisdom of the Central Authority. Praise be to the Republic."

I was so stunned that I couldn't repeat the phrase.

He didn't seem to notice my silence. "You'll be taken to the Children's Village tomorrow morning for a general orientation. You'll be introduced to your partner in two days, and the Pairing Ceremony will be public at the Social Update Meeting. Because of the historic nature of this decision, it will be celebrated by all Citizens."

There was a brief silence. I could almost smell the flowers hidden near my sleeping mat. Flowers from David.

"You'll continue to live in this Compound with your partner. You will not be required to walk your energy board while working at the Children's Village, but you will be required to ride an energy bicycle there. One will be supplied for you. Do you have any questions?"

Yes, yes, but I shook my head no.

"Praise be to the Republic." Circle sign.

"Praise be to the Republic." Circle sign. With that, they left.

The bus-box lurched forward. John glanced over, and I think he smiled. The Gatekeeper looked over at me and then spit on the ground. Even for a Gatekeeper, he was a little man.

When the road was empty, it felt like the air had been sucked out of my Living Space. Like I was in a vacuum. I paced. Back and forth, around and around.

Praise be to the Republic.

I was to work in the Children's Village. In the Children's Village with Elsa! This was too good to be true. But they had said it. *I'm coming, Elsa, I'm coming.* And I'd be paired with a reproductive night-shift Gatekeeper. It had to be David. It must be David.

I wanted to run outside, feel the sun, look at the trees, touch the ground.

Calm down. Calm down. Finish the board.

Do what can be monitored.

* * *

Later, after his first rounds, David slipped into my Living Space.

"How are you?"

"Fine," I answered.

"I'm surprised you're still here. I thought by now—"

"I guess there are no available reproductive males."

I heard him take a sharp breath, like a wheeze.

So it isn't him, I thought. Or he doesn't know. And I couldn't say anything. I might be overheard, and I couldn't risk ruining this.

"I have the egg," I said. And I began to peel it. "Where do you live? What Compound?"

"They have a segregated place for night-shift Gatekeepers. Kind of a barracks near the Children's Village. We work twelve-hour shifts at night and we sleep during the day."

"What are the other night-shift Gatekeepers like?" I asked.

"Kind of scrawny. Products of the Children's Village, mostly. Younger than me, don't like to work, whine a lot. Why?"

"Just wondering." I finished peeling the egg. "Here," I said, settling the egg and the salt packet in the cradle of his palm. Our touch lingered. He raised the egg and took a small bite from its tip. The way he held my gaze as his lips closed over his teeth made my stomach feel floaty.

I knotted my hands together and stared fiercely at them. "Tell me more about the other Gatekeepers."

"Another time," he said.

Then he kissed me. A soft, hesitant gift that tasted of egg.

"I can't stay," he said. "But I want to."

"I know," I whispered, my head fit into the hollow of his shoulder, my arms around his back.

"The lady who has nightmares," he said. "I found her wandering around the Compound last night. Sleepwalking, I guess. I have to make sure she stays in her own space. I asked her last night what she was looking for and she said, 'My home.' I walked her back to her space and she kept saying, 'This isn't it. This isn't it.' Finally, her partner came to the door and took her in. He asked me not to report her."

"Will you?"

"Of course not. We're supposed to report the unusual. She's just a sad lady. Nothing unusual about someone being sad."

I thought of Mother. He was right.

He kissed me again and went back to his post.

David. A respecter of sadness.

* * *

The bus-box arrived the next morning just as I finished my morning cube. I was ready, headscarf in place. The day-shift Gatekeeper made a notation on his clipboard as I passed through the gate. I didn't look at him, but I could feel him staring. Even though the sun was barely out of the treetops, the day was warm. John was on the Transport Team and was already dripping with sweat. We passed the squirrel-feeding station, piled with grain. Birds twittered from the trees and flew about freely, sometimes darting down among the squirrels to pick at the plentiful food. The sun filtered through the leaves. Surrounded by the sound of birds chirping and tweeting, I closed my eyes and enjoyed the balmy air on my arms, breathed deeply of the fresh, green smell of grass.

And then we were there, at the Children's Village gate. The packed-earth play yard was empty of children again, its toy energy boards lined up. A woman in a white uniform waited by the main door. John's wife! She had been wearing pink when I saw her standing next to John at the Social Update Meeting. Now her uniform was white. I thought only chaperones wore white. She walked to the bus-box and motioned for me to step down.

"Hello," she said. "My name is Joan. I'm the supervisor of the Children's Village."

I held out my hand. "My name is Emmeline."

She shook my hand with both of hers, and then said to the Transport Team, "Please return in two hours. I've made the necessary requisition for it. Thank you."

She didn't look at John and he didn't look at her. That must be something that can be monitored.

I followed her into the building, down a long, dim hallway and into a room she called her office. She closed the door.

"Have a seat." She motioned to a chair. It looked flimsy and creaked when I sat down. Her desk was small and the surface scratched. The low morning sun shone through the window slits behind her so that I could hardly see her face. But her voice was kind and soft.

"You understand that you've been assigned by the Central Authority to work the night shift here at the Children's Village?"

I nodded.

She lowered her voice and leaned forward. "I changed the birth record of one of the babies before I requested additional help."

I put my hand over my mouth to stifle my gasp.

She leaned back in her chair and continued in a normal voice. "You understand the night shift is from dusk to dawn?"

I nodded again, but my mind was still reeling thinking of all the risks she had taken for me, for Elsa. "The night-shift staff works the pink rooms, the blue rooms, and the nursery."

My heart skipped at her last word. Elsa would be in the nursery. I would see her.

"Rounds are made on all areas so that the children's needs are always met. There have been concerns, lately." She paused.

"The concerns have to do, in general, with the children's apparent failure to thrive. I noticed it when I worked the pink room. Not all children fail to thrive, of course," she added quickly, "but many do."

"What does that mean, failure to thrive?"

"Oh, it means not gaining weight like they should. And not learning how to roll over, or sit up by themselves at an appropriate age. Things like that."

I almost asked about Elsa. But if she were failing to thrive, John would have told me. I pressed my thumbnail, willing myself to keep it away from my mouth and hide my nervousness.

"I mentioned my concerns at our last inspection," Joan said. "The

Village is inspected regularly and thoroughly. The future of the Republic rests with our children. Praise be to the Republic."

"Praise be to the Republic," I responded.

"As a result, I was appointed to be Supervisor. It's a new position. I'll have to wear white until they decide what color to assign to me. Prior to this, the Children's Village had no Supervisor. I don't know if I'm qualified to be Supervisor." She was twisting her hands together in tight little motions. "I'm afraid of what happens if I fail. If I'm not able to make things change, not qualified enough to make things better . . ." Her voice faded.

"The Authority decides who's qualified and who isn't," I said, trying to reassure her with her husband's own words.

"Yes, indeed. They do. And you learn quickly, don't you, Emmeline?"

I nodded. And smiled, but I kept my head down, eyes averted.

"Well, then. There is only one thing that I require of my staff: the children's needs will be met. It's the least we can do. Do you have any questions?"

"Your expectations seem clear," I said.

"Not to all, I'm afraid. Not to all. That's why you're here."

I looked at her. She looked sad.

"Why am I here?"

"Because I need you." She leaned forward, her mouth pressed right up against my ear, and whispered, "And because Elsa needs you."

CHAPTER TWENTY-TWO

Through the window slit I saw children walking behind adults who I assumed were their Caretakers. Little girls dressed in pink. Little boys in blue. They followed their Caretakers in straight, subdued lines to the energy boards. The Caretakers leaned against the fence. I could faintly hear the children chanting:

Every day I walk my board
Walk my board
Walk my board
Every day I walk my board
For my fair Republic.

Joan saw me looking out the window. "Those are our four- to six-year-olds. I wish there were more of them. The older groups are even smaller."

"Why is that?"

"It's part of what I'm worried about. The children"—she paused and shrugged—"they just seem to fade. Disconnect. They disconnect from each other. And from their Caretakers."

"Are the babies awake now?"

"Morning hygiene's been completed. So they're taking their morning nap. Toddlers are being taught the slogans of the Republic."

"May I see them? The babies, I mean." Please, please.

"Of course. But I've got a few things to go over with you, then we'll take a tour."

Patience, I told myself. *Have patience.*

"There are more Caretakers on the day shift than on the night shift because there's more activity during the day shift. Up until now, there was only one night-shift Caretaker. However, I feel the children would be better served if there were two."

"The other night-shift Caretaker is Lizzie. She's not paired. That's been the Central Authority's position on night-shift workers. Nonreproductive Citizens work night shifts. Up until now, that is." She smiled at me. "Lizzie sleeps in a separate area of the Village. She's asleep now, so you won't meet her until you come on duty for your first shift. I've never worked side by side with her so I don't really know her." She leaned forward, closer to me. "Not as well as I should."

John had told me: *Don't trust anyone you don't know.* Was his wife now trying to tell me something? I also leaned closer as though nearness to her would make her subtle message clearer.

"Your responsibilities will include hourly rounds on all the children. Between rounds you'll be stationed in the infants' area."

"With Elsa," I finished.

"You will meet the children's needs. For example, there are scheduled feedings for the infants. Nourishments and feeding schedules are found in the nourishment storage area. The babies are to be held when they are given their bottles."

She stood up and motioned for me to follow her into the corridor. It smelled of sanitizing solution. A warm breeze floated in from the door.

"You will not be restocking supplies. That would disrupt the children's sleep. Restocking is done on the day shift."

I nodded.

"If a child appears ill enough to need intervention, you'll hang the Children's Village flag and that child will be taken to Human Health Services. Illnesses requiring intervention include difficulty breathing, intractable vomiting, or prolonged crying with inability to comfort."

We walked slowly as she talked. I listened intently, determined to do just as she said.

"Fevers are treated with medication. Medication charts are available in the supply closet. Fevers that don't respond to medication within twelve hours are referred to Human Health Services. Do you have any questions?"

"Not at this time."

She stepped into a supply closet and closed the door after I followed her in. We were alone but still she whispered.

"Your first shift will be in two days. I understand you are to be paired tomorrow."

"Tomorrow? I didn't know that."

"Also," she leaned forward, "I want you to know that I had a daughter once. She died in the illness. Her name was Lois. She was about your age. And I have a son. His name is David. He was home-raised, as were you."

I studied her face, and found her smile written plainly there.

"He doesn't know yet," she said. "They'll tell him today."

I put my hands to my face. I couldn't speak. I was having trouble breathing. "Are you saying—"

"The Authority wanted to pair you with one of the older boys from the Village. It wanted to prove its success." She gave a little shrug of her shoulders. "Jeremy was a mistake. I tried to tell them. They didn't listen."

"After Jeremy, they came back, looking for another partner for you, a male from the Village. But none of the boys are mature enough. I suggested maybe one of the Gatekeepers. They had never even considered it! I may even have mentioned David's name." She smiled. "It worked!"

I leaned forward, listening to her every word.

"Home-raised children," she said, "are special. Trust me. I see them and I see the ones raised in the Children's Village. I see the difference." She set her hand on my shoulder. "Welcome to the family."

Family is important. That's what John had said. And I could feel the truth of it, flowing warmly from the firm pressure of Joan's hand.

"Well, then," she said, "are you ready for the rest of the tour?"

My heart was racing. I nodded.

As we stepped into the corridor, two Village workers walked past us leading a group of children in from the playground. The children were quiet and walked two by two in neat rows. Joan was silent until they passed. We continued down the hallway, which was lined with smaller rooms on each side. "The girls' classrooms are on the left, and the boys' on the right. The Central Authority mandates gender segregation after infancy, and you should abide by that rule as best you can in dealing with the children. The classrooms are labeled by age group."

The four- to six-year-olds' classrooms were empty. They were still outside learning their energy board duties. I remembered walking on my toy board next to Mother and how easy it had been, almost like a game.

"There's been some talk," Joan said, as if she could read my mind, "of putting a small amount of friction on the children's boards. Every ounce of energy counts, I guess. A decision hasn't been made yet."

I thought of the packed-earth common area, the play yard, and all the toy energy boards, lined up, neatly spaced. I thought of the children who had walked past us, quietly, two by two. Children who had never seen their mothers. If the toy boards were replaced with real friction boards, it would turn play into work. It would make quiet children even quieter. It would stifle laughter. All in the name of energy production. Sadness settled over me like a thick fog even though this should have been one of the happiest days of my life. I shook my shoulders as if to shake off the gloom.

"These are the seven- to nine-year-olds' classrooms," Joan said, and paused so I could see the children. Girls on the left, boys on the right. Both groups stood facing the flags of the Republic in their respective classrooms, the brightly colored blue-and-green Earth in the center. They were making the circle sign and repeating the Pledge of the Republic.

We pledge our allegiance
To the wisdom of the Central Authority.
We pledge our dedication
To the Earth and to its preservation.

The girls were reciting a little ahead of the boys, so the pledge had a discordant, disjointed sound. One of the boys, a smaller child with blond, spiky hair, was making the circle sign on his nose instead of his forehead. He was grinning, enjoying the farce. His Caretaker hit him sharply on the back of his head. He quickly put his hand to his forehead, and the look on his face made me think of a candle that had been snuffed out.

"The ten- to fourteen-year-olds make up the last group. Their classes focus mostly on the importance of the Republic and its regulations. All Republic, all the time," Joan said. "And now we're at the nursery."

My heart surged.

She pushed the door open and motioned me inside. I took a deep breath and stepped through the doorway. The room had a wet, milky smell. Small bassinets were lined up along opposing walls. On the left side, pink bassinets; on the right, blue. Most of them were empty. I walked down the center of the room, looking back and forth, left to right. Finally, two babies in pink bassinets, one in a blue one. I approached the pink ones. Joan made a motion as if to point out Elsa. I held my hand up and shook my head. I knew I'd know which of these two little girls was mine. They were both asleep. Both had their left arms extended and their heads turned in that direction. That one, that one. She has my nose. And George's forehead. Look at all that hair, a burnished pale yellow like mine in the picture in Mother's sleeping mat. Perfect fingers. Tiny, tiny fingernails of pale pink. Cheeks round and full as miniature apples. I pointed to her and turned to Joan.

She nodded.

I bent to pick her up but Joan held up her hand and shook her head no, warning me not to.

"It would be—*unseemly*, if the Caretaker saw you pick up a sleeping baby." She looked around. "I wonder where she is?"

"I'm here," a woman said, "in the storage room. I'll be right out." She came out, carrying an armload of diapers. She looked at me without smiling and began placing the diapers on the shelves under the bassinets. "Don't wake up a sleeping baby, you hear?" she said. Had she seen me bending over to pick up Elsa? Being watched, being overheard was like being monitored. Be careful what you say, what you do. I wondered why Joan didn't know that, and why she didn't address this woman's attitude. Was Joan afraid of this Caretaker?

Joan and I left the nursery and walked back to the main entrance. Already, I missed Elsa, missed seeing her, watching her sleep. The busbox hadn't arrived yet so we went back to her office to wait. She closed the door.

"Do others—I mean other mothers, come here? To try to see their babies?" I asked.

"No, not really."

"But why not?"

"First of all, the Social Reorientation has been very thorough and the Central Authority persuasive. People needed something to believe in, so they believed in the leaders. They repeatedly said that the children would do better if raised by the Authorities. That message was hammered into the people. They heard it over and over until it became truth to them. Besides, all their needs were being met. And not believing in the message, not following the rules, could be dangerous." She paused. "It worked on almost everybody."

"Did it work on you?"

She smiled. "Not really. There were a few of us who didn't accept their philosophies. Or their promises. Your mother and father didn't. There are others. But not many."

"How can you tell?"

"You watch. You listen. You wait. But you won't find them in the children. Over time, the system is all they know."

I saw the bus-box approaching. It was time for me to leave, but I didn't want to. I wanted to stay here in this building with Elsa. And with Joan.

"When will they tell David?"

"At dusk tonight, right before he goes on duty. Welcome to our family, Emmeline." Before she opened the office door, she hugged me and her arms were warm and strong on my back.

"Thank you," I said.

"Praise be to the Republic."

"Praise be to the Republic." And this time, I almost meant it.

CHAPTER TWENTY-THREE

The day-shift Gatekeeper made a note on his clipboard when I stepped off the bus-box at my gate.

"You still have to walk your board, you know," he said.

I nodded.

"Your *special* job hasn't started *yet,* you know."

I nodded again. He didn't have any facial hair. He talked like Jeremy, and he looked to be around Jeremy's age. He had to be a product of the Village. Joan was right. Watch. Listen.

"Did you know Jeremy?" I asked.

"What's it to you?"

I shrugged. "Just wondering."

"He was my friend. At the Village. I was moved out before him. He told me stuff after he came here."

"Stuff?"

"Yeah, stuff. Like who walked their energy board and who didn't. Like if one Citizen walked the board for another. Bet you didn't know he told me stuff. That's what friends do. That's what Citizens do."

I started to walk away. "And he didn't like you," he called out.

"You're one of those home-raised. Not like us. He told me about you. He told me about you waking up early. So there."

I couldn't change the past. I couldn't change what Jeremy said or did. I could only think about the future. I kept walking.

Later, as I walked my board, I heard a bus-box at the gate. The same two Central Authority men as before stopped to talk to the Gatekeeper. John slipped out of his harness and went to the back of the bus-box. He took an energy bicycle off the bus and pushed it toward my space. The day-shift Gatekeeper stared at John's back, but he couldn't see the big smile on John's face.

"Central Authority asked Transport to deliver this to you. I'm to show you how to hook it up to the energy download bar." He fiddled with a hose that was fastened to gears on the bicycle. "Don't smile so much," he whispered. "Look serious."

I turned so my back was to the Gatekeeper and the Authority Figures.

"I can't help it."

He plugged the hose into a valve on the download bar and turned a switch. The hiss of the download began immediately. When it was done he removed the hose from the valve.

"Okay, now, you do it."

I mimicked the demonstration and he nodded his approval.

"Praise be to the Republic," he said.

"Praise be to the Republic."

He went back to his harness and the Central Authority men approached.

I adjusted my headscarf to cover more of my forehead. I still had the white headscarf trimmed in black, a symbol of being partnered. After Jeremy was taken away, my headscarf hadn't been replaced. Maybe there was no color for an abandoned partner. No matter; I didn't really care.

"Praise be to the Republic," they said.

"Praise be to the Republic."

"Good afternoon," the first one said.

The other nodded.

I nodded back.

They walked past me into my Living Space. I followed.

We stood in the eating space, a triangle of three people, facing each other.

Oh, please, I hope you haven't changed your mind. Please. Say something.

"The Children's Village Supervisor reports that you did well during your interview."

"Praise be to the Republic," I murmured.

"Final arrangements are being made for your partnering ritual. Due to the extraordinary wisdom of the Central Authority, this will be a special ceremony."

"Please, sir, I don't know if I am worthy."

"That aside, the Authority knows best in all things. Do you understand?"

I nodded and kept my eyes averted. The second man was restless and paced around, touched my energy board, went into my sleeping space. I watched from the corner of my eye, willing him away from my sleeping mat.

"Tomorrow evening at the Social Update Meeting, you and your partner will be introduced. You will be escorted to the stage. That's where you will exchange your Partner Vows to the Republic."

The pacing man came back to the eating space. "It occurs to me," he said, "that we need to address the sleeping mat issue."

Oh, no, no, no. I felt a rough spot on my fingernail and pulled on it. The end of my fingernail ripped off, close to my skin, and a little drop of blood appeared. I wanted to put my finger in my mouth but I didn't.

"There is no sleeping mat issue," said his partner. "He can bring his from the barracks." He turned to me. "Would you like a new sleeping mat?" he asked me. His question surprised me because it sounded almost kind. I glanced up at him. His eyes were hard, turning me inside out, and he ran his tongue deliberately across his lower lip. His smile was wet and red.

"Oh, no, sir," I said. "The Republic has gone to so much effort for me already. I don't need a new mat."

"Very well, then. Arrive early at the Social Update Meeting. Stand near the stage so the Enforcers can find you easily and escort you. Do you have any questions?"

"Yes, sir. When will I work my first night shift at the Village?"

"Not the night of the Social Update Meeting. That would be—" He paused, then said, "That would be unseemly."

"And when will I get my Children's Village uniform?"

"It will be delivered with your evening cube on the day you are scheduled to begin work." He turned on his heel and started for the door.

"Please, sir, another question."

"Of course." He sounded like he was yawning.

"Should I walk my energy board on the day when I will be going to the Children's Village at dusk?"

"It's your duty to the Republic, isn't it?"

Do you walk a board? I wanted to ask, with sarcasm equal to his. Do you ride an energy bicycle? Instead, I kept my voice even and asked, "Can you tell me, sir, who will be my partner?"

"It's not relevant." He stared at me, eyes narrowed. "You have so many questions. Almost as if you expect the Authority to answer to you."

"I'm sorry, sir. Praise be to the Republic."

"Praise be to the Republic," he said, then slapped his glove against his hand while giving one long last glance at my sleeping mat. It was as though he was picturing me lying on it.

* * *

I didn't want to get back on my board, not just yet. I went outside to look at my new energy bicycle. How hard would it be to ride? I'd seen others ride their bicycles; I knew I could figure it out. How long would it take me to get to the Village? I disconnected it from the download bar and shut off the valve. Then I got on it. The seat was narrow and hard. The handlebars were high; I had to reach up, stretching my arms out. It felt good, stretching out like that.

And then I pushed off with one foot, got both feet on the pedals, and started riding. At first it was wobbly and it tipped low to the left. I put my foot out onto the dirt to stop the fall. Try again. Try again. Finally I felt the rhythm, the balance. I was riding.

I rode in a circle past all of the Living Spaces in our Compound. Twelve Living Spaces here at Re-Cy. Other Compounds were larger or smaller depending on the number of workers needed in those work-groups. Our individual worlds were small and fenced, under the dark umbrella of the all-controlling Republic. When I got near the gate, the Gatekeeper stepped in front of me and I had to stop. "What do you think you're doing?" he asked.

"Just practicing."

"Well, don't think you can leave the Compound. You can't, you know. Not unless you're assigned to leave by the Authority."

He remained standing in front of me, a barrier.

"I know the rules. I'm not leaving the Compound. I'm practicing."

He stepped aside but said, "I'm still going to keep an eye on you."

I made another circle around the Compound. The breeze shifted direction. I could smell the heavy rotten odor from the Re-Cy. It made me gag.

As I rode past Living Space 2, a woman with matted, tangled hair stood in her doorway, watching me. As I passed, she said: "I want to go home."

CHAPTER TWENTY-FOUR

Finally it was dusk. The sun drifted below the treetops and the common area was in shadow. Night owls began their haunting whoo-whoo-whoo. It was time for me to go to my sleeping mat. *Citizens will sleep from dusk to dawn to preserve energy. The Earth is robbed when artificial lighting is used. It is written.* But I couldn't sleep. So much had happened in one day. So much that my chest felt heavy, tight, hot, and my breathing was a shallow, rapid effort. I should be happy. After all, I'd seen Elsa. But I hadn't held her. Still, I should be happy. Joan had told me I'd be paired with David. But, then again, the Authority hadn't told me. So there was no guarantee, no certainty. Certainty came only from the Central Authority, and even then, it was only as certain as they wished it to be.

I put on my sleeping robe and took off my awful black-and-white headscarf and rolled it into a ball—a tight, angry little ball—and threw it onto the floor. Then I started pacing around and around my cement box. I wished I could remember more about the farmhouse in Kansas with the big windows and green grass. I wished I could remember the "good days" Mother used to tell me about. The vegetable soup and the cats in the barn—the "mousers," she called them. And the one house cat, a calico, she said, that always slept in the living room on the bay windowsill in the sunshine. I wished I could remember a living room. What must a Living Space be like if it has a room called a *living room?* A living room sounded like a peaceful place, somewhere your whole life could settle around you. I wished I could help the tangled-haired lady in Living Space 2 find her home, her living room, but that was beyond my power.

The only thing in my power was to do whatever could be monitored and care for Elsa while I was on duty at the Children's Village.

And to love David.

It was dark enough now for the Gatekeepers' change of shift. David should be coming on duty. I peered out through my partially opened door. I saw the two Gatekeepers, the day shift reporting off to David on the night shift. I saw my energy bicycle beside my door. The Gatekeepers' backs were toward me. I saw the day shift hand the clipboard to David. I saw the circle signs. I saw the day-shift Gatekeeper leave. I saw David turn toward the Living Spaces to begin rounds.

Except, it wasn't David. It was a tall, stoop-shouldered man, thin like a chicken bone standing on end. He began walking his rounds. He had a limp, a painful lurching gait as though one leg was shorter than the other. He went past Living Space 1 and stopped at 2. I heard him, faintly but clearly: "Get back into your space, you hag." David was a respecter of sadness. This Gatekeeper made a mockery of it. Is this the way others had seen Mother? As a hag? Mother, who had raised and protected me? I closed my door quickly.

I wondered where David was. I felt fear, like watching myself trip in slow motion over a rock and falling headfirst onto another rock, with no ability to stop. Knowing, knowing there would soon be pain. Or worse, having someone you love being taken away with ropes on their wrists. Or feeling the roughness of ropes on your own wrists. And not knowing what would happen next.

I stood, pressed up against the wall, the cement blocks cold against my back. The new Gatekeeper stopped outside my door. I stood as still as I could, frozen in place. Even though my door was closed, I could hear his breath wheezing in and out. He had no reason to be standing there. He stood outside my door for a long minute, then said, "I wonder where David is. Yes, indeed, I wonder where David is." Then, he moved on.

I shivered and slid down to the floor, feeling the rough wall on my back, the frigid floor through my clothes. I don't know how long I sat there, worrying about David.

Finally, too weak to stand, I crawled to Mother's mat. Her smell had completely faded, leaving only the dank odor of the room. *The Little Prince* dug into my cheek. Something was terribly wrong. I was so close, so close to holding my daughter, but I hadn't. I was so close, so close to telling David we might be paired. But I hadn't.

I turned over on the mat and the covers twisted around my legs, trapping me.

I had failed myself, failed those I loved. Why didn't I object when they took Mother? Why hadn't I blocked the doorway, daring them to push me aside? Instead I just stood by, childlike. And why hadn't I opened my door tonight and demanded that the sickly, harmless Gatekeeper tell me where David was?

I was no longer a child. But I still felt powerless. I still did what was expected of me, whatever could be monitored. But I didn't do what was important to *me*. I let the Authority have power over me. Power they didn't deserve.

Finally I began to drift off to sleep, the covers twisted around my legs and the gold thing clenched in my hand, and I wondered when exactly I had exchanged my conscience for fearful obedience.

CHAPTER TWENTY-FIVE

I slept well past dawn and woke with a dull, throbbing headache. I rubbed my forehead, trying to think. I wanted to find John and ask him where David was. I reached deep into Mother's sleeping mat, wanting to touch the things she had touched. I needed to feel something that wasn't being controlled by the Republic. I reached past the pictures, past the recipes, past *The Little Prince*, and felt something else. Something small, smooth, cold, round. I pulled it out slowly. A golden color. An image of an Indian on one side. I slipped it back inside the mat.

I didn't bother to get my nourishment cube from the box, though it was required. *Citizens are required to eat their nourishment cubes upon awakening, before beginning their assigned duties, to maintain productivity.* Forget the rule, I thought. For once, forget the rule. Thanks to the headache, my stomach felt queasy. Reluctantly, I put on my Re-Cy Compound uniform and started walking my board. Walk. Walk. Walk. Tonight was the Social Update Meeting. Tonight I would be paired. And tomorrow night I would work at the Children's Village.

I walked until noon, facing the bare cement walls, keeping a steady pace, making the board move beneath my feet. Birds called in the trees on the other side of the fence, and when the cool autumn breeze shifted, I smelled the putrid Re-Cy odor. Luckily, the breeze from the Re-Cy plant was infrequent and brief. Eventually my headache faded, and I felt hungry. I regretted the recklessness of not following the rule.

I went outside to my storage box, but it was empty. There was no cube. The Gatekeeper sat in his booth with his back to me, oblivious. Just yesterday I promised myself to do everything I could to protect my family. Do everything that could be monitored. And now, this— something that I could easily be reported for.

The old lady from Living Space 2 stood outside her door, looking in my direction. She was saying something I couldn't hear. The Gate-keeper was still watching the birds beyond the fence, so I walked over to her.

She grinned at me, showing several gaps in her teeth. Then she held up a nourishment cube.

"I took it," she said. "I took your cube."

"Why?"

"I need it."

"Why?"

"I'm saving it. For my children. For when they take me home."

I didn't know what to say. Obviously, no children lived in her space, nor had any lived there recently. She looked a little younger than Mother, but she was so unkempt, so untidy, that her sadness seemed to have aged her by the decade.

"Who is going to take you home?" I asked her.

"My children. Elizabeth and Andy, of course. They're coming for me. I hear their voices. Listen. You'll hear them, too." She cocked her head to one side and closed her eyes. Her eyelids were crusted with dry skin and the corners of her mouth were red and cracked. "Do you hear them?"

I didn't answer. She didn't notice.

She reminded me of someone from long ago, from a different Compound, when I was still too young to walk a real energy board. A lady who used to stand in our doorway and wave to me.

"Go away," Mother would tell her, waving her hands toward the woman. "Stop staring at us." And then Mother would complain to Father about her. "Something about that lady isn't quite right. Not since they took her children away."

"Now, Elsa, what harm is there in letting her visit our Emmie?"

But Mother was adamant. "Remember the illnesses?" she asked Father. "Remember that? Remember when the Authorities ran out of routine vaccinations? Oh, the perfect, perfect Authorities who regulate medications but can't provide enough of them! Shortages of this and shortages of that and children got whooping cough and polio and measles and who knows what else. Emmie didn't. I kept her safe, away from everyone."

The discussion stopped at that fact, always. And after a while, the lady stopped coming to our door to wave at me.

This woman with the toothless mouth might have been the same woman.

The Gatekeeper stood up and began walking toward us.

"Please give me my cube," I said to her quietly. "I won't tell." It is forbidden for one Citizen to take from another. Everyone is given equal amounts. No one can have more than anyone else. Only the Authority can give, and only the Authority can take away.

"Is there a problem here?" he asked, first of me and then of her.

I shook my head no and turned to leave. But the old lady shook my cube in his face and said, "This is mine, and she can't have it."

He frowned and opened her storage box. Inside was a single cube. "Then whose is this one? And why is it still in the storage box?"

"My husband," she said. "He didn't eat his. That one is his—this one is mine." She put both hands on the cube and clutched it to her chest so tightly that her knuckles turned white.

"I saw your husband leave for Re-Cy this morning. He was eating his cube. The one in your box is yours. Give the one you're holding back to her." He motioned to me.

She shook her head no; her hair fell across her face.

"Citizen! Now!" He was visibly angry.

Reluctantly, she held the cube out to me.

"Have you walked your board today?" he asked her.

She didn't answer him. Instead, she closed her eyes and cocked her head to the side as though she was listening to something.

"I'll file a report on this event," he said to me. I breathed a small sigh of relief. Obviously, he didn't realize I hadn't checked my box first thing in the morning. I was safe. But she was not. What kind of a person had I become, glad that an old woman would be reported instead of me?

I went back to my space and he went back to his post. As far as I know, the old lady remained standing there with her eyes closed, listening. I couldn't eat the cube. It felt dirty. And I wasn't hungry anymore.

* * *

Later that afternoon, I heard the bus-box at the gate and watched as the Enforcers took the old lady away. She was smiling as they walked her to the bus-box, wrists tied together with dirty ropes. She said to one of them, "You must be Andy. My, how tall you've grown."

I couldn't hear his answer but I saw him shake his head no.

"You look like my Andy."

He shook his head again. The Enforcers, one on each side, held her by the elbows, practically lifting her feet off the ground.

She turned to the other one. "Are you taking me to my Elizabeth, my little Lizzie?" She sounded so hopeful.

A few minutes later, a metal screeching sound drew me back to the door; the Gatekeeper was raising the flag at the gate, the signal that a Social Update Meeting would be held this evening. Then a dark thought, a dreadful thought, came to me: What if they decided to pair me with that old lady's partner? Was he still able to reproduce? Oh, what a terrible thought. What a terrible, awful thought.

I picked up my headscarf and went to the washing-up area. It was time to get ready. The special Pairing Ceremony would make this one of the strangest Social Update Meetings ever. The meetings were always about the total community—how much the farm co-ops produced. How many healthy births there were. Updates on the size of our army and speculation about the size of the armies of other republics. Rumors of war. Citizens were not recognized as individuals there. Ever. Unless, of course, they had broken some law, violated some pledge. Those individuals were publicly pointed out, humiliated. Some were never seen again. But that, we were told, was for the good of the community.

But what happened to the ones who were never seen again? Who decided their punishment? Citizens who didn't do what was required, didn't produce enough energy, were they treated the same as, say, someone who hurt an animal or picked a flower? I finished my washing up and tucked my hair into my headscarf, resolving to find answers any way I could.

The only variation in Social Update Meetings occurred once a year, when the army—or whatever part of it we were privy to seeing—marched in a parade past the Central Stage. Young men passed in lockstep, heads turned toward the Authority Figures, their boots creating little puffs of dust in unison. They carried black guns that rested against their right shoulders. The first time I saw a gun, Father had to explain to me what it was. That was the only time any of the army was actually visible to the Citizens.

* * *

The Gatekeeper rang the bell. It was meeting time. As I started out of my space, I saw the man from Living Space 2 sitting on the ground in front of his door. He wasn't really all that old, just worn-out. The Gatekeeper checked my name off his list. I walked slowly, glancing over my shoulder every few minutes. After everyone from the Compound was checked off, the Gatekeeper went back to the man sitting in the dirt. The man said something, then the Gatekeeper said something. But the man didn't get up. The Gatekeeper hit the man across the face and, even at a distance, I could hear the dull thud of his nightstick against skin. Everyone else was walking forward; no one seemed to notice or care about the man from Living Space 2. He was lying down on the dirt, curled up on his side, his hands in front of his face. The Gatekeeper took ropes out of his pockets and tied them to the man's wrists. I stopped looking back. I had to hurry. They had told me to stand near the front. But there were so many people in front of me, too many for me to move forward.

As I walked, I had the cold realization that something in me was hoping they would take the old man away so he could never be a potential partner. I knew decisions made by the Authority could be changed at the last minute, and they might pair me with him since his wife was gone. They might keep David in the barracks.

Thinking like that made me no better than them, and I flushed with shame.

We converged into a mass as the Authority Figures mounted their elevated platform.

How many of these meetings had I attended over the years? Fifty? Hundreds? As a child with my parents, not understanding the speeches but learning the pledges. *Praise be to the Republic.* Mother never said the words out loud. She just made her lips move. Then I came as a young adult with George. Dear George, who never knew Elsa. I came to only one meeting with Jeremy. Childlike, poisonous Jeremy. If he had reported Mother for not walking her board, then he was the reason they took her away.

And now, for the first time, I was alone in the middle of this mass of Citizens. People were still gathering, rushing past one another. No one wanted to be the first one or the last one in. No one wanted to be noticed. Someone brushed against me and whispered: "There's been a change of plans." John's voice. I turned, but he had already melted into the group.

A change of plans?

Not enough oxygen. Not enough air. Breathing too fast, hands sweating, faces swirling around me, a ringing in my ears, folding upon myself, falling. People backed away from me. Faint murmurs. And then nothing.

CHAPTER TWENTY-SIX

At first the voices were far away and blurred, then closer and clearer. The Authority Figures, speaking in their great big outdoor voices. I opened my eyes and realized I was lying on the ground. I could feel dirt on my face and grit on my lips. Slowly, I pushed myself up to a sitting position. No one came to help me. No one would even look at me. They had shifted and moved away, so as not to be noticed. I was far enough away from the platform that the Authority Figures probably couldn't see me. I sat for a minute until the spinning in my head stopped, then stood and faced the platform.

I hadn't eaten today. Maybe that's why I fainted. Maybe John had not said "a change of plans" after all.

Corn production exceeds last year's crop by ten percent. Praise be to the Republic.

I looked at the Transport Team area, but couldn't see John.

We have not met our quota of healthy births this month. Reproductive-ability testing is ongoing. Babies born today will be our workers in fourteen years. Babies born today will be producers of our energy in fourteen years. Healthy babies born today will be protectors of this Republic and of the Earth. Praise be to the Republic.

There was a woman in white in the transport area. That had to be Joan, but I couldn't see her face. I was desperate to see someone I knew, someone I trusted. I stood on my tiptoes, trying to see over the heads of people in front of me, but I couldn't. All the people around me were Compound 18 people and yet there were no friendly smiles, no friendly glances or nods hello. We were all strangers, isolated in the same Compound.

There is news of conflict south of the Republic. Our army is on full alert. The conflict to the north has subsided for the time being.

"Wars and rumors of wars," Mother used to mutter when they announced the news regarding conflicts. She would mumble and end it with a little *humph* sound. Father would nudge her when she did that. And so I, standing alone, muttered, "Wars and rumors of wars."

The sky was growing darker and the wind began blowing through the trees on the other side of the fence. They bent and fluttered, first this way, then that. Birds stopped flitting from branch to branch and instead huddled on the biggest branches. As the wind grew louder, the Authorities spoke louder, trying to sound more powerful than the wind.

Energy production remains consistent with the needs of the Republic. There will be no increase in requirements of energy production this month. Praise be to the Republic.

Praise be the Republic came the reply from the Citizens. This time, they sounded like they meant it.

Rain began, slowly, hitting against the leaves, hitting the dirt, leaving little dents in the packed surface, hitting my headscarf, flecking my arms. Harder and faster, and rain ran down my face and down the faces of those around me. We weren't permitted to leave the Social Update Meeting just because of rain.

Praise be to the Earth. Praise be to the rain. Praise be to the Republic.

Circle sign with wet fingers.

A tarp covering was pulled over the elevated platform. The Authority Figures and Enforcers would stay dry.

Thunder began to roll in from a distance, coming closer and louder. One sharp crack of lightning, bright and shining and flashing like white fire from the skies. The Authority Figures said once more, *Praise be to the Republic,* and we responded once more in unison. The Authority Figures climbed into their special bus-box, and that's how we knew we were dismissed.

Everyone turned and headed back to their Compounds. All but me. I stood there in the rain, in the thunder, in the lightning, looking for someone, anyone, I could trust.

At last, I turned and started walking alone back to Re-Cy. Back to my space.

The day-shift Gatekeeper checked my name off his list as I passed through the gate.

"Rather late, aren't we?" he asked, pointing his pencil at me.

I just kept walking. Let him write down that I was late. I didn't care.

Alone, I removed my wet headscarf and hung it on the bar of the energy bicycle to dry. Then I went to the washing-up area to dry my face and arms. Bits of dried flowers were still in my hair, little flecks here and there. I shook my head and some of the bits drifted down like snowflakes. I started to take off my Re-Cy uniform when I heard a familiar voice at the back window slit. John.

I rushed to him, almost tripping over the corner of my sleeping mat.

"John, John," I whispered, my voice shaking. "What's going on? Where's David?" I put my hand through the window slit and he held it, his fingers wet and cold with rain. He was holding the map and it was getting soaked. He passed it through the slit to me and I wiped it on my clothes to dry it off.

"It's okay, little one," he said. "David's okay. Don't worry."

Another jagged white finger of lightning, followed by a roaring rumble of thunder came. In the distance, we both heard what sounded like a tree falling.

"I can only stay a minute." He still held my hand. "I ran here after the Update Meeting because I knew you'd be worried. The Authority Figure who told you there would be a special ceremony at the Social Update Meeting overreached his power. He was a low-level Authority and didn't have the power to make that decision. He'll never make that mistake again."

More thunder. More lightning. "David will explain everything when you see him tomorrow." With that John was gone, into the trees, but I felt like he was still holding my hand. He had said *when you see him tomorrow.* But where was David tonight?

CHAPTER TWENTY-SEVEN

Morning. Bright sunlight. A new day. A new beginning. John had said everything was going to be all right. Funny how I believed those simple words from a friend more than news and rumors of war spoken by Authority Figures.

The storm had stopped and the raindrops on the leaves beyond the fence sparkled like crystals in the early morning light.

"Everything's going to be all right," I said out loud to myself as I got my nourishment cube out of my storage box. "Everything's going to be all right." I changed into my Re-Cy uniform.

The map had dried overnight but now was crinkly harder to fold. I did the best I could and then pushed it back deep into the mat. There, in the mat's far corner, a place where you'd never lay your head, I felt a smooth, firm lump. Mother had placed something deep in the mat between the layers of padding. I pulled and ripped until I felt an object. Looking around, making sure no one could see me, I pulled it out.

A strange little book. Red leather, cracked with age, its cover lettered in faded gold. *The New Testament.* The pages were thin, the print tiny, the wording different from anything I had seen before. Inside the front cover Mother had written a note in her beautiful, flowery writing, full of loops and curlicues: *For Emmeline, my beloved daughter. May she read and understand.* The *m*'s in *Emmeline* and *May* swirled like the petals of a wildflower. I kissed her handwriting, then wondered where she was. Was she somewhere thinking of me just as I was thinking of her? Was she lonely? I swallowed hard, feeling the pressure of tears building in my eyes. I let a few minutes pass, then began to glance through the book. It seemed to be made up of different stories told by different people: Matthew, Mark, Luke, John. No last names? Some pictures. A man on some kind of wooden thing. Nailed to it. How strange. Mother taught me how to read. I'd do my best to understand.

I slipped the book back into the mat, far into the corner, and felt something else. Hard and cold. This, too, had been buried between layers of padding. I pulled it out. It was a strange object, oblong in shape, only about three inches long, and made of metal.

I pushed a small button on one side and a blade snapped out.

I dropped the knife on the mat and stepped back. Like a snake, it seemed to threaten me from the floor. A knife! Citizens were not permitted to have knives! The only Citizens allowed to handle blades were those who worked in the uniform Compound. And Father told me a long time ago that they were counted at the end of each shift and locked up. What was Mother thinking? And why had I never felt something so hard and firm in my sleeping mat before? I pulled the cover off that far corner of the mat. She had actually cut away some of the padding on the bottom and moved it to the top, over the knife. She put it in a place where, even if the mat were rolled up, it would not be discovered.

I tried to figure out why she saved what she did. The things I had found earlier. The photograph of her and me as a child. A favorite book of my childhood. A map of the United States of America. Recipes. Then the round gold thing. Now this book. And this little magic knife with its snap-out blade. Nothing seemed connected. Nothing.

I picked up the knife and tested the tip of it against my finger. A bubble of blood appeared, slick, wet, red. I put my finger in my mouth. If Mother were here I would wrap my arms around her and cry against her shoulder. I'd whisper against her ear that I would protect her forever. And she'd smile and say, "Get your fingers out of your mouth." If Mother were here, I could have asked her why she wanted me to have these things. I wished I had asked her more questions when I was growing up. I wished she hadn't recoiled and withdrawn from questions. I tried to fold the knife blade back into the holder but it wouldn't move. I glanced out the door, wondering if the Gatekeeper was making rounds.

Sweating, I took the knife into the washing-up area and tried again to close it. It remained rigid and lethal. Finally I tried pushing the button and the blade at the same time. It snapped shut like the jaws of a wild animal. Quickly I returned it to the far corner of the mat under some padding. I felt strangely proud that I had figured out how something worked, something new to me, something from Mother. As I pulled my hand out, I felt something else. Something small, square, smooth. Retrieving it, I saw it was a cardboard box with a little slide-out drawer. Inside, small, smooth wooden sticks with red tips. The label said: SAFETY MATCHES. Back into the mat it went, over on the side by the wall, right below the knife. My buried treasure.

Time now to walk my board. Time now to do what could be monitored. Hands on the metal sidebars, feet slapping against the rotating black mat. Everything's going to be all right. Everything's going to be all right. Think, make a poem. Everything's going to be all right. I'll be with David tonight. Walk, think, hope. El-sa. El-sa.

When my needle hit the halfway mark, I stopped for a break and stepped outside. The air was warm and soft, and the breeze was blowing toward Re-Cy, so it had a sweet smell. I took a deep breath and turned my face to the sun. As I was standing there, I heard a bus-box at the gate. A young man, thin, with dark hair flopping over his forehead, got off the bus and held his hand out to help an even younger woman off the bus. She was obviously pregnant, her belly pushing against what looked like a brand new Re-Cy uniform. Her black-trimmed headscarf covered her hair and most of her forehead. She looked pale, tired, and swollen. They both carried rolled-up sleeping mats. The Gatekeeper walked them to Living Space 2, made some notations on his clipboard, and walked away.

I felt an impulse to greet them, even though socializing is forbidden by the Central Authority. I walked quickly to their Living Space and stopped at their doorway. They were standing there silently, holding their mats as though they didn't know what to do next.

"Hello," I said.

Startled, they edged back a step.

"Hello and welcome. My name is Emmeline."

The man nodded without expression and said, "We don't want trouble."

"I'm not here to make trouble. Just saying hello, that's all. How are you feeling?" I asked her. "When are you due?"

She didn't answer but just rested her hands on her belly and looked down at the floor.

"Where were you before? I mean, before you were relocated here?"

"Farm co-op," he said. He spoke so quietly that I could hardly hear him. "They put us there. They didn't think we were reproductive." He smiled. His teeth were small, too small for his face, like baby teeth in a grown-up. "But they were wrong. Praise be to the Republic," he said. They both made the circle sign.

Automatically, I raised my fingers to my forehead. Their discomfort was like a wall between us. I felt stupid and awkward and realized that the Authority no longer needed to frown upon socializing—their Citizens made it almost impossible. Getting too friendly, too close with anybody, and they might turn out to be the kind of Citizen who might report you to the Authority. Trust is risky business.

"Well, good-bye then. I have to finish my board." I left them standing there, still holding their sleeping mats, and walked away with the secret knowledge that I, not they, would hold their baby and comfort it in the Children's Village.

I walked my board until the needle hit the peg and I had done what could be monitored. Then thoughts, like buzzing flies, swarmed into my head. Why did I have to walk the board? Why did anyone have to walk a board? Just because the Authority said so? And where did the energy go? Who used it? Certainly not me. For my effort, I got a nourishment cube and a cement cell to live in. That didn't seem like a fair or equal trade. The breeze had shifted direction and the putrid smell of Re-Cy drifted through my window slits.

I heard the Gatekeeper making his rounds to distribute the evening cubes. Lids opened with a little, tinny screech and then plopped closed. I waited until he moved on before I went to my box. Inside were two nourishment cubes. The Gatekeeper must have made a mistake. Back when Father told me about the scissors being counted and locked up, he told me that the nourishment cubes were also counted. "Rationed" is what he had called it. At the end of the day, the Gatekeepers had to turn in a tally. "And the count had to be right," he added, shaking his head. "Sad state of affairs."

Mother had almost hissed the word back at him. "Sad? Sad? Despicable and controlling," she had said. "Control the food and you control the people. Control the food *and* the energy and you control everything."

I started to call out to the Gatekeeper, to ask him to take away the extra cube, but before I could get his attention, a bus-box pulled up and David got off with two Authority Figures. They were walking toward me.

CHAPTER TWENTY-EIGHT

David stood before me, a thin line of sweat shining above his lip. Two Authority Figures, looking stiff as the nightsticks the Gatekeepers carried, stood on either side of him. He had a clean spare uniform and his mat rolled under his arm. I lowered my eyes and waited for the Authority Figures to speak.

There in the dirt by my shoe was a ladybug, lying motionless on her back. I focused on her, afraid to look up. If I looked up, I might smile. I might look happy. I might ruin everything. The ladybug didn't move. I didn't move. It hurt my chest to breathe.

The Authority Figures droned out the Pledges of Pairing. I saw their boots, shiny and black with heavy metal eyelets and thick laces. David's shoes were not as sturdy, not as shiny. The hems of their uniforms, the heavy black fabric folded up into crisp cuffs, carried bits of dirt along the bottoms.

And still they droned on.

"Praise be to the Republic."

I almost dropped one of the nourishment cubes while making the circle sign.

"Praise be to the Republic."

With that the Authority Figures turned as one and stepped in stiff unison back to the bus-box. The Transport Team jerked away from the gate, and the Gatekeeper made a notation on his clipboard. The wooden side rails of the bus-box rattled and clattered and then faded out of earshot.

David and I went into the space that was now ours. We stood there in the eating area. He was still holding his extra uniform. We stood there not knowing what to do next. Finally I held out one of the nourishment cubes.

"Later," he said. "Later." His voice was thick and deep. He dropped his extra uniform, put both of the cubes on the eating counter, and held his hands out to me.

"First this," he said, as he pulled me closer to him. I felt the heat of his hands, of his arms around me, of his face next to mine. He kissed me and I felt the softness of his lips.

"And now this," he said, picking up his sleeping mat and unrolling it next to mine. I watched him undress, watched him toss his clothes onto my energy board. I undressed slowly, methodically, folding my clothes, my hands shaking.

"You are such a beautiful woman. I had no idea how beautiful. Yes, praise be. But not to the Republic."

We spent the evening on his new sleeping mat, twined around each other like vines on trees.

Later, much later, we ate our nourishment cubes.

CHAPTER TWENTY-NINE

I woke up first, just as the sun rose enough to let pale light through the window slits. I had never slept naked before. My skin felt smooth and vulnerable. I pushed the sheet away and looked at my body. David had said I was a beautiful woman. No one had ever called me beautiful. I ran my hands down my sides, feeling the inward dip of my waist and the gentle flare of my hips.

I watched him as he slept, curled on his side. The firm muscles of his arms. The way his hair curled just a little against his neck. How long his legs were. Long and straight and strong. I leaned near him and took a deep breath. The smell of his skin was warm and earthy.

He turned toward me and opened his eyes.

"Hello there, my beautiful wife." *Wife.* What an amazing word. The way your lips have to move when you say it. Wife. I smiled at him.

I sat up and pulled the sheet around me.

He pushed the sheet off my shoulders. "Don't cover yourself. Not just yet." He smiled and touched the hollow of my throat.

I heard the tinny clinking of the nourishment box lid. The Gatekeeper was making rounds, delivering morning cubes. I pulled the sheet back up and across my chest.

"We better get dressed," I whispered. He nodded and reached for his rumpled pile of clothes. He dressed quickly, putting on his dull gray Gatekeeper uniform, then handed me my clothes from the energy board.

The scuffling sound of the Gatekeeper's footsteps faded, and David retrieved our nourishment cubes.

"Not many people say wife. Or husband. They mostly just say paired or partnered."

"I guess you could call them before-time words, words we used, back then."

I dressed quickly. "Mother used to talk about *back then*. But then she would get really quiet and wouldn't talk anymore."

He gave a little sigh and put his cube down.

"Here's another before-time word. House. Nobody says house. They say Living Space."

"Mother told me about our house. Our back-then house. That always made her sad."

"I used to hear Mom and Dad talking about your mother. They said they saw changes in her. They said that long before the relocation. They saw it when she was still teaching. I was too young to notice. She was a teacher, you know."

"I knew that."

"Well, then. What else do you know?"

I thought back to the day Father and I walked around the Compound. "She was George's teacher. Father told me that. And some things I didn't understand. Things about laws changing."

The sun was higher now. I could see dust motes floating and twirling in the light streaming through the window slits. I should be on my energy board by now.

"What else?"

"Laws about animals. Laws about who owned the farms. Laws about energy."

I felt a dull headache, a heavy pressure in my forehead that increased as I tried to remember what Father had told me. I went to my energy board. I had to get my board, get my meter all the way to finish.

"What are you doing?" David put his hand on its metal sidebar.

"I have to walk my meter."

"Why? Aren't you working tonight at the Children's Village? Why do you have to walk your board today?"

"The Authority Figures said I had to. Today is my last day on the board. At least I think it is."

"No," he said firmly. "No. Yesterday was your last day on the board. I'll walk it for you today."

"Why would you do that? You have duty tonight, too, don't you?"

He tugged on my arm and held my hand as I stepped off the board. "Why? Because you're my wife, that's why."

There was that word again. *Wife.* That lovely before-time word.

CHAPTER THIRTY

I sat cross-legged on the sleeping mat and watched as David walked the board. How much faster he was than me. And so much faster than Mother had ever been. He made the black mat rotate so quickly that it seemed to blur. I admired how tall and strong he was, admired the dark hair that dipped across his forehead. Dark eyebrows curved just so above his eyes. Lips full, soft; chin firm, square.

And valuable to me. I thought of the gifts of flowers, the eggs, and felt a melting sensation in my chest as though the sun were shining inside me, somewhere under my skin.

I wanted to learn everything about him and everything he could teach me.

"Was my mother ever your teacher like she was George's?" I asked him.

"No, she taught high school history. I was in elementary school before the relocation."

"Yes, history. George told me that." The memory of George had blurred around the edges. Not much was left of him except Elsa. Elsa and some special moments. How he called me teapot. Little teapot. Never wife. And then I remembered Father telling Mother that George's *wife* had been taken away and the Authority was pairing him with me. That word, *wife,* had slipped past without my even thinking about it. So much had slipped past me without my notice. Now I notice everything; now I hear words and learn what they mean.

"But she was my Sunday school teacher," he said, as if I knew what that meant. "She brought us cookies every week. And then things changed. She changed."

"Sunday school?"

"Another before-time word." He smiled at me. I only nodded. He frowned and slowed down his pace on the board. His knuckles were white from gripping the sidebars. "Time for a break," he said, and went into the washing-up area. He must have splashed sanitizing solution on his face because, when he came out, his dark hair was damp against his forehead. He sat down facing me on the sleeping mat.

"Sunday school. Hmm. Well, then, let me try to explain. Remember, I was just a kid. I don't have all the answers."

"Just try. Just tell me what you remember." I pushed his hair back from his forehead. He took my hand and pressed my fingers to his lips for a brief, warm second.

"There used to be churches."

"I know. Father told me."

"Well, Sunday school was where kids went to learn about God. But the new Central Authority didn't approve of churches or of Sunday school." He was quiet for a moment. Outside, beyond the Compound fence, I heard birds twittering. I went to the window slit and watched them flying freely from one tree to another. The smell from Re-Cy was faint today. David asked, "Did you know your father sang in the church choir?"

I stared at him. "Father? I never once heard him sing."

"That's too bad. He had a big, deep voice that could fill a room. He played the guitar, too. Sometimes he and your mother would have picnics at the farm, and all the neighbors would come. The grown-ups sat around eating and singing. Us kids ran around playing and stuff."

"I don't remember any of that."

"Of course you don't," he said, smiling at me. "You were only a baby. I was about ten when you were born. And I thought you were a nuisance, the way everybody fussed over you. Like you were something special." He leaned toward me and kissed my forehead. "Turns out they were right."

He went back to the board. I walked over and looked at the meter. It was far past halfway and the sun wasn't even overhead yet.

"Do you want me to walk for a while?" I asked. "Will they know it's not me walking?"

He shook his head. "No. Only the meter matters. You need to rest today. You'll be up all night at the Children's Village."

"What's it like, being up all night?"

"You get used to it. You learn to sleep through the daylight and work in the dark. An upside-down kind of world."

Outside, I heard the wooden clatter of the bus-box near our gate. The Gatekeeper was walking our new neighbor, the pregnant one, toward it. She was clutching her belly and I heard a low moan. Her partner was probably working. She would be as alone as I was when Elsa was born.

David came and stood beside me in our doorway. He put his arm behind my back, resting his hand on my hip.

"Maybe you'll have a newborn to take care of tonight."

John was on the Transport Team. He didn't look over as they pulled away, but I saw him give us a little wave by pretending to swat a fly in front of his face.

"He works so hard," David said.

"So did Father," I answered.

"So do all of us," David said. "And I'd better get back to the board."

"Let me walk for a while. You're going to be up all night, too. You should rest."

He shook his head. "I'm used to being up all night; you're not. Let me do this for you."

I sat back down on the mat and watched as he walked, the board turning, the energy hissing through the hose. "Where were you the night before last?" I asked him.

"What?"

"Night before last. I was worried. Some other night-shift Gate-keeper was mumbling outside. Saying 'I wonder where David is.' That scared me."

"Sorry. I had no way to get a message to you. The Authority wanted me to, you know, rest. They wanted me to rest before we were paired."

I squirmed a little. I didn't want to think about the Authority planning our pairing, imagining us pairing.

"So they assigned Randall. He usually works the Children's Village."

"Why did he say, 'I wonder where David is'? It really did scare me."

"That's Randall. He's odd. I don't like him. Steer clear of him at the Village. But," he added, with a crooked little grin, "he's probably just jealous. And I can understand why." He smiled at me and got off the board. "All done. Now we can rest."

We curled together like puppies on his sleeping mat. It seemed strange lying down to sleep while there was still daylight. But we didn't go to sleep right away. We slowly rocked together in rhythm until our bodies melted into one.

Later, just as I was falling asleep, I heard John's voice at the window slit.

"Emmeline," John whispered, "see Joan tomorrow morning before you leave. Let her know how your first shift goes." With that, he was gone.

Before I drifted off, I asked David what his father might have meant about any problems I might have on my shift. And I wanted to ask him why my mother had changed so much.

But he was already asleep.

* * *

David kissed my shoulder to wake me up when the sun was still above the treetops.

"Look what I found in our nourishment box." He was holding my new uniform, a pink top and matching pants. The seam stitches were of typically poor quality. "The Gatekeeper left it with our cubes."

I clutched the uniform to my shoulders, measuring it against my body. The material was smooth and cool and had no odor of a previous worker. I went into the washing-up area to sanitize myself before I put it on. No more green Re-Cy uniforms for me. No more board walking. I felt like I was sanitizing my world, not just my body.

"Well, just look at you," David said, with his eyebrows raised and a happy look on his face. "That's a good color for you." He had already put on his Gatekeeper uniform and it looked good with his dark hair and eyes. He handed me my cube.

"Eat something. It's almost time for you to leave. You have to be there by dusk for the change of shift."

"I've never gone there on my own. I went in the bus-box for my interview. Maybe I'll get lost or be late." My stomach churned. What if I threw up when I got there? I clenched my hands so that I didn't chew on my nails. Even so, I caught myself a moment later twirling a lock of hair around and around my finger until it tugged my scalp.

David took my hand, gently freed it from my hair, and cradled it to his chest. "You can't get lost."

"But I've only ever been in the Transport and Re-Cy Compounds. And I've always been with someone else."

He squeezed my shoulder. "You can't get lost. Let me show you." He wet his finger and drew a damp circle on the eating counter. "All the Compounds are arranged to make a big circle. See?"

I nodded.

"Each Compound backs up against the fence. Just like we do." He motioned to the back window slit and the trees beyond.

He wet his finger again. Inside the big circle, he drew a smaller circle. "That's the circular road. It goes past each Compound. No matter which way you go on the circular road, you eventually end up going past every Compound. See?"

I nodded again.

He made some marks between the big circle and the road circle. "Say this is our Compound, Re-Cy." He pointed to one of the marks. "And this is the Children's Village." He pointed to the opposite side of the circles. Then he made wet straight lines from each Compound to the center of the circles. "All these lines are the paths to the middle. You know, where they hold the Social Update Meetings. But you can't go straight through the center to get to another Compound. You have to go on the circular road. The only time Citizens can be in the middle is when the Authority holds Social Update Meetings."

He wet his finger again and drew some squares behind the Children's Village and in some of the Compounds. "These are the work centers. Re-Cy, Nourishment, Clothing, Sanitation, Gatekeepers' barracks, the Authority's supply storage, all kinds of places outside the living spaces but still inside the compounds. They're all surrounded by fences."

He made it look so simple. I felt a little better about finding my way. We ate our cubes quickly. I felt like I had to hurry. I wanted to hold Elsa.

"So I won't get lost?"

"No, you'll be fine. You can go left or right out of our Compound, it doesn't matter. The Children's Village is about halfway around, either way you go. Oh, but one other thing: the Gatekeeper at each Compound you pass will make a notation of you."

"Why?" I finished my cube and wiped the crumbs from the corners of my mouth.

"Because. It's just the rules. The Authority wants to track all Citizens at all times and have records of their activities. So, if you are passing a Compound and the Gatekeeper holds up his hand, that means he wants you to stop. So, just stop." He rubbed his hand on the counter, blurring the wet lines and circles he had drawn. "He may ask you to identify yourself and your destination."

"What should I say?"

"Just answer the questions. Don't say any more than you have to. Some of the Gatekeepers will just wave you on without stopping you. Trust me, they all know who you are and where you are going. Remember, all the Gatekeepers live in the barracks behind the Children's Village. Just like I did until we were paired. And Gatekeepers who live together talk."

"And the ones who don't wave me on will try to stop me? Oh, David, I hate this."

He touched my cheek with his finger and gave me a crooked smile. "Some like the power. The power of the clipboard. The power of being able to stop people. Some think they are part of the Authority."

"Are they? Are they part of the Authority? Would they have any reason to report me?"

He pinched my cheek. "One question at a time!"

"Sorry." I smiled, too. There was so much I wanted to know.

"Okay," he said, "the only true power is held by the Authority Figures. And the ultimate power is in the Central Authority. The clipboards are just an illusion of power. I guess you could call them a symbol, just like the nightsticks, the flags, the fences." He helped me tie my headscarf, adjusting it so my hair was hidden, then he kissed the side of my neck above the curve of my shoulder.

"Thank you," I said.

He put his hands on my shoulders; his face was just inches from mine. How clear and smooth his skin was, how dark his eyelashes and eyebrows. He put his mouth near my ear and whispered, "There's just one more thing I need to tell you." His voice was low. "It's been a wonderful first day with you."

"The first of many," I whispered back.

The Gatekeeper rang the bell. The half-hour-till-dusk warning bell. David helped me disconnect my energy bicycle from the download bar. The bicycle was wobbly at first, but soon I was on my way, passing through the gate, under the flag, past the Gatekeeper, who made a notation on his clipboard.

* * *

I wish I could say that everything went well once David and I were paired. I wish I could say that spring slid into summer on a soft breeze, and our world was just the two of us and Elsa when I was able to cuddle her. I wish I could say that and make it the truth.

But I can't. Time and events pushed us forward in ways I never could have imagined.

CHAPTER THIRTY-ONE

I decided to turn right. David had said it didn't matter. The sun had slipped a little below the treetops, but there was still plenty of light beaming through the humid air. I pedaled as fast as I could, but the circular road was rough, with ruts carved into it from the bus-box wheels. I seemed to be the only person alive. Soon the Re-Cy Compound was behind me and ahead I could see another Compound, another flag. I was sweating, my headscarf moist against my forehead and my hands damp on the handlebars. There was a squirrel-feeding station on the other side of the fence. Squirrels and birds squawked at each other, a flurry of fur, feathers, and noise. Below the feeding station were small flowers, pale pastels on short stems. Mostly pink, some yellow. Probably sprouted from seeds dropping off the feeding station. Bees dipped into one flower, then another. I could hear their buzzing, like a fly near your ear. The flowers were so close to the other side of the fence that I could almost reach them. Almost. How had David gotten flowers for me? How did he have the courage to break the laws protecting the Earth? I smiled. He did it for me.

Enough of that. Tonight I would focus on learning my job at the

Children's Village. And I would focus on Elsa—holding her, smelling her hair, learning her features, counting her fingernails and eyelashes and toes, teaching her the feel of my skin on hers. My Elsa. My child.

I passed the gate of the next Compound. The Gatekeeper didn't stop me but did make a notation on his clipboard. A record was being kept of me. An account. The Compounds looked deserted, but there had to be people inside because they each had a Gatekeeper. Wherever there were Citizens, there was a Gatekeeper. Knowing that made me feel lonely; I didn't know why.

I bicycled past more Compounds. Past the flags—Nourishment, Transport, Clothing. They all looked the same except for the flags. Square, squat Living Spaces backed up against the fence. Packed-dirt common grounds. Some of the Gatekeepers were making rounds, but even they took note of my passing, marking their clipboards. Sometimes one of my feet would slip off a pedal and the hard metal would hit my heel. I had to stop once because it hurt so badly.

There was a spot of blood on my stocking. I rested a minute, one foot on the ground, the other still on a pedal. The other pedal spun needlessly. There was no breeze and the leaves hung limp in the heat. Birds were beginning to roost after a day of carefree flight and song. Dusk was approaching. I started to bicycle again.

Walking this road would be easier than cycling. Cycling used different muscles because you had to keep your balance. I should have practiced more. I was used to walking. I did it every day on my board. But walking wouldn't make enough energy for the Republic.

I understood the layout of the compounds better since David had explained it to me; I just didn't understand the rules any better. Who made them? How did they get so much power? And what did they do with all the energy the Citizens created? I would have to remember to ask David.

I pedaled faster, trying to ignore the sweat on my face, the pain in my heel. The stocking glued to me with dried blood. And then, there it was: the gate to the Children's Village. The blue and pink flags. And the Gatekeeper, walking with a lurch.

Randall.

He held his hand up as I approached.

I put my feet on the ground, straddling my energy bicycle.

"Your name?" he asked. A voice deep and harsh.

"Emmeline," I answered. My throat felt tight as though a hand were squeezing around it.

"Your purpose?"

"Dusk-to-dawn shift at the Children's Village." I nodded my head toward the building and my headscarf slipped back, off my head, exposing my hair. I quickly pulled it back but it felt uneven, askew. I tried to straighten it with one hand, holding my bicycle up with the other. I felt clumsy, as though I might fall onto the dirt. My heel throbbed.

As he leaned against the gate, I realized he was trying to stand straight, trying to hide the fact that his left leg was shorter than his right. And when he talked, the left side of his mouth didn't move the same as the right side. And his left eyelid drooped a little. He was not a perfect Citizen.

I straightened my shoulders and repeated, a little louder, "Dusk-to-dawn shift here at the Children's Village."

"I heard you the first time." He made a notation on his clipboard. "Park your bicycle over there." He nodded to a metal bar beside the entrance. "Secure it. Secure it well."

I got off my bicycle and started to push it through the gate.

"Stop!" he said. "Aren't you forgetting something?"

I didn't know what to say. I stood, looking down at the dirt, afraid to meet his eyes.

"Citizen," he said. "Praise be to the Republic."

I looked up. He was making the circle sign.

"Praise be to the Republic," I replied, making the circle sign.

He nodded without a smile, without any sign of approval, and motioned me through the gate. He didn't stand aside, not even a little, so I had to brush against him. He smelled wet and musty, like dead leaves rotting around the bottoms of trees.

I secured my bicycle to the bar between two others. The metal securing chains were rough and rusty. I wouldn't download my energy until I got back to my own space and I didn't want anyone to download my energy into their cycle or storage bar. Energy was too valuable.

Little flakes of red metal fell from the chain and clung to my fingers. I brushed them off as best I could, one hand against another, then finger by finger. I wanted my hands to be as clean as possible when I held Elsa. Maybe there was sanitizing solution inside the Village.

I pushed open the door and immediately heard the sounds of sleeping. The soft in-and-out breaths, the tiny puffs of moving air. The hallway was dim. Off to the left was Joan's office, empty now, but I remembered the first time I met with her when the sun came in the slit and made a sort of halo around her, making it hard for me to see her face. John had said I should check in with her in the morning, at the end of my shift.

I walked down the hallway, classrooms on the left and right, empty now. No little voices reciting praises to the Republic. Past the sleeping rooms of the older children. Deeper into the building and toward the nursery. My shoes made no noise. I could hear voices. Two women, from the sounds of it. There were two dancing lights in the dimness, lights that moved as the voices rose and fell.

"So she's here tonight?" one said. She talked through her nose in a high, whiny voice.

"Sure enough," said another, and the light bounced up and down.

"And you met her?"

"Didn't exactly meet her. Joan had her come in. For an interview." She said *interview* like it was something to make fun of. "Good old Joan. And we're all supposed to be equals. Equal Citizens." Whoever was talking coughed a wet, rattling cough and then made a throat-clearing noise. "Caught her getting ready to pick up a sleeping baby. Can you imagine?"

I held stone-still, waiting.

"Which baby?"

"Don't know for sure. One of the girl babies. And Joan just standing there. Far as I can tell, Joan thinks this one is something special. Something more than equal."

"Well, we'll see to that, won't we?"

And they laughed, together, the strange lights bouncing up and down. Another cough.

"So, anyway. Anything to report?"

"Not much. One was born today. That's what I heard from Human Health Services."

"And? Was it viable?"

They must be talking about that childlike woman from my Compound. The one who, holding her swollen belly, left on the bus-box.

"No. Crooked foot. Turned way in at the ankle. Too bad. A boy. Took him straight to Re-Cy."

"The regulations have gotten tighter lately, haven't they?"

It was getting darker in the hallway. My shift was about to start, and I couldn't risk being late.

"Hello," I called out. "I'm here."

The lights were turned toward me, shining in my face. I held my hand up to my forehead, shielding my eyes.

I couldn't see them. But they could see me.

CHAPTER THIRTY-TWO

"Almost late, aren't you?"

Both lights were shining in my face. The one on the left was talking. She sounded like the same one I met the day I came for my interview with Joan. The one who told me not to wake a sleeping baby.

"Almost, I guess," I said. "But I'm here now."

"Did you bring your torch?"

I didn't know how to answer. "My torch?"

They shuffled closer together. One of them reached up and turned off the light she was wearing. It was attached to a band that went around her head.

"Well, did you or didn't you? Did you or didn't you bring your torch?"

I shook my head. "I don't have one."

"How do you expect to work night shift without a torch?" The other one turned off her light, too, and the room was murky, the only light a faint haze coming through the window slits. "Look how dark it's getting. My, my. Glad I have my torch. Wouldn't want to be without it." They both turned their lights back on.

One of them was wearing pink. The other, blue. Neither was very tall nor very heavy—both were altogether unremarkable.

"I'd best be leaving. My shift is done." The one who was working the day of my interview turned her back to me, her pink uniform wrinkled and sagging around her hips. I didn't know her name. "Have a good shift, Citizen."

"Praise be to the Republic," they said in unison and made the circle sign.

My arms hung down uselessly. Should I be making the circle sign? Should I ask their names, give them my name? Should I have known about the torch? I felt ignored and ill-prepared.

The one in pink started down the hallway to leave but called back to her friend. "I'll say hi to Randall for you."

"Don't you be bothering Randall, you hear?"

And they both laughed.

The one in blue turned to me. "Well, then. No torch, huh? Guess you'll have to stick close to me all night. Can't have you bumping into things in the dark, can we?" I followed her down the hall and we turned into what looked like a large supply cupboard. Her torch shone up and down the shelves as she took stock of their contents.

A shelf of white cloths. A shelf of small bottles with nipples. A shelf of sanitizing solution and basins. More shelves. More supplies. The clean, sharp, almost acid smell of cleaning solutions. Propped in the corner was a worn, frayed broom next to a cracked dustpan. In another corner, a small red stepstool for reaching things on the higher shelves. Off to the side was a rocking chair. Hanging from a nail in the wall was a clipboard with a list of words, maybe names.

"What's that?" I asked, pointing to the clipboard. I wanted her to turn her light onto the list.

She acted like she hadn't heard me. She was taking stacks of the white cloths from the shelf, cradling them in her arms.

"What are those?" I asked, pointing to the cloths.

"What's that, what's this?" she said sharply. "Just full of questions, aren't you? Just follow me and try to figure it out as we go. Understand?"

I nodded.

"All right then. Follow me."

She shut the door and headed for the nursery. Finally I would see Elsa. I had to walk closely behind the woman in blue because the light from her torch was dim and cut only a narrow path through the darkness. I could smell her hair, oily like the fish-flavored nourishment cubes. She stopped abruptly, and I bumped into her back. She turned, her torch shining directly in my eyes.

"Be careful."

The sharp tone of her voice made me feel cold and afraid.

"I'm sorry," I said. "I didn't know you were going to stop. I was just trying to keep up."

"There is no keeping up here. There is just doing. I have things to do. I stopped because I wanted to. I stopped just to see what you would do. Understand?"

I nodded, even though I didn't.

"Here's the deal. I've had this night shift since I graduated from the Children's Village. It's been mine. All mine. I do it my way. No matter what you've been told. Understand?"

I heard a small cry from a child somewhere down the dark hall. Elsa? No. It sounded like an older boy, not a baby. A child dreaming, maybe, of something dark and scary.

She didn't seem to hear it, or she had no interest in checking on the child. My legs, my arms, my head wanted to find that child, smooth his covers, stroke his forehead. More than that, I wanted to see Elsa and hold her.

"First thing we do is restock. Get it?"

"Restock?"

"Yes. Restock. Put fresh diapers under the cribs. We do it for the day-shift workers."

I remembered Joan saying restocking was not done on the night shift. But I didn't say anything. Somehow, here in the dark, it didn't seem safe to disagree.

"After we restock, well, we do what we have to." She turned and went into the nursery.

We moved from crib to crib, with only her light to guide us. There were few babies in the nursery. Which one was Elsa? The woman didn't shine her light on the children, only on the shelves under their cribs, and only long enough to take diapers from the cradle of her arm and move them onto the shelves. I had to move closely with her because the cone of light didn't allow me to see anything except what she chose to show me.

"My name is Emmeline," I whispered, finally.

"I know that," she said. "Everyone knows that. No one cares." She didn't tell me her name but, from what Joan had told me, I knew she must be Lizzie.

She turned and went back to the supply cupboard. I followed, but not too closely.

This time she took some of the bottles with nipples off the shelves. For each bottle, she took a diaper and handed it to me. The bottles rattled against each other when she turned and left the supply cupboard.

The diapers felt rough against my skin. I had expected them to be soft.

I followed her back to the nursery. She stopped by the first crib and told me to hand her a diaper. She rolled it into a kind of round tube or pillow, using just one hand. Then she laid the rolled diaper next to the child in the crib. Finally, her light shone on the child. It wasn't Elsa. It was a little boy, sleeping with his arms flung out beside him. She had to move one of his arms to get the diaper next to his face. She tugged on the back of his little shirt so he was turned slightly onto his side. Next she took one of the bottles and propped it onto the diaper so the nipple touched his lips. Tiny pink lips like the petals of a flower. He opened his mouth and she pushed the nipple into his mouth. He began to suck on it, his round, smooth cheeks moving, but he didn't wake up. She had done this whole procedure without actually touching the child. She had only touched his clothing.

She started toward the next crib.

"Don't you hold them to feed them?" I whispered to her.

She turned to face me. "I told you already. I do things here my way. Just follow me. No more questions."

We went from crib to crib. Roll the diaper, put the diaper in the crib, turn the child slightly, put the bottle on the diaper, the nipple by the mouth, in the mouth, move on. As her light bounced back and forth, I looked at each child as carefully as I could. Two boys and three girls so far. No Elsa. As we walked to the last crib, my hands began to sweat. What if this last child was not her? What if she was gone?

CHAPTER THIRTY-THREE

Walking to the last crib seemed to take forever, as though each step had slowed, and then become deliberate and motionless—like a mere mockery of walking. I could hear my own breath. It seemed loud enough for Randall to hear outside. Loud enough to wake the children.

When we finally reached that crib, the last one on the left-hand side of the nursery, Lizzie held out her hand for the last diaper. I stared into the crib, waiting for the light from her torch to fall on the face of this child. She rolled the diaper, placed it as she had done the others, and shifted the child slightly. Still no light. Finally, she placed the bottle and I could see clearly. I could see my Elsa.

I put my hands to my cheeks. Oh, how beautiful she looked, how peaceful. Her hands were curled into little fists, round and smooth. So tiny.

The bottle was against her lips but she turned her head away.

"This one gives me fits," said Lizzie. "Stubborn from the first day she came in. Four months now she's been here and stubborn every day." She pushed the nipple against Elsa's lips, but Elsa turned away each time. "She got started on regular baby food last week. About time,

I say. Enough of this bottle stuff." She moved the bottle again, rubbing it across Elsa's lips. "Come on, come on. I don't have time for this."

"Maybe she's not hungry right now," I whispered. "Maybe if I held her?"

The light from her torch was turned onto me.

"It's eating time. She'll eat now or she'll get no food."

The light was still shining onto my face, into my eyes.

"And why would you want to hold *her*? What's so special about Baby Six?" The way she said *her* sounded like her lip was curled up over the word, as though she was sneering, but with the light in my eyes, I couldn't see her face to tell. I wanted to scream out that her name was Elsa. Not "Baby Six," Elsa!

I blinked and tried to turn away from the light.

"I just thought—" I started to say, but she interrupted me.

"Oh, you just *thought*. Oh, yes, Emmeline just *thought*. My, my, my. Isn't that interesting." She pushed the nipple one more time against Elsa's lips. This time Elsa accepted the nipple and began to suck.

"I already told you. Twice now I've told you. We do it my way."

She turned and started to walk out of the nursery. Quickly, briefly, I touched Elsa on the top of her head, feeling her soft, feathery hair.

"Are you coming?" Lizzie asked, talking to me over her shoulder.

I had no choice but to follow. If she left the nursery, there would be no light. I needed her light, dim and distant as it was.

We returned to the supply closet. Outside the building, the metallic rattle of a nourishment box lid caught my attention. Lizzie's, too.

"Good," she said. "Break time. Before we have to gather up the empty bottles and diapers. Wait here." She went into the corridor, leaving me in the total darkness of the supply closet. I heard her footsteps against the concrete floor, a scuffling sound that faded away briefly and then returned as she walked back to the closet, the narrow beam of light preceding her, bouncing from side to side like a firefly.

When she came back in, I saw she was carrying a hard-boiled egg.

Just one. She sat down in the rocking chair and began to peel off the shell, putting the small fragile pieces in a Re-Cy container beside the chair.

"Guess Randall forgot to requisition an egg for you. Funny, he did take the time to write my name on this egg. Look here. It says Lizzie. So it's mine. Better luck tomorrow night." I heard the tiny bits of shell pinging into the metal container. "In fact, I'll remind Randall that you need an egg. That's only the right thing to do, don't you think? And Randall pretty much does anything I ask. Know what I mean?"

She took a bite of the egg and smiled at me, bits of yellow yolk stuck on her teeth.

"You know, working the night shift has its benefits. Like this egg." She held the last bit of the egg up, like a trophy. "The Authority makes sure we get a middle-of-the-night nourishment. Praise be to the Republic." She ate the last of the egg and leaned back in the rocker. "And now we rest."

With that she turned off her torch. The darkness was immediate. I couldn't see a thing, but I could hear the collective breathing of the children. The older ones turning in their beds. One of the babies was crying but Lizzie didn't seem to hear that.

"Lizzie," I whispered, "one of the babies is crying. Shouldn't we check?"

The rocker creaked as she shifted her weight.

"So? Babies cry. That's what they do. I bet I cried when I was a baby. And I bet nobody ever held me." I thought her voice sounded sad. Or maybe mad. A strange mixture of the two.

"We should check, just to be sure."

"Just to be sure of what?" The rocker creaked again.

"Maybe the baby needs something. I don't know. Maybe a clean diaper. Or some more bottle. Joan said—"

She snapped on her light, aimed it directly into my eyes, and leaned forward.

"I've been in the Village longer than Joan. She came from what, the farm co-op? Please, you think she knows anything? We diaper them all at the end of our shift. They eat what we give them. When we give it. End of story. No child, no baby, gets more than any of the others. That's the rule." Snap. The torch was turned off again. "That was the rule when I was raised here. No one ever held me." I didn't like hearing those words in the dark. This time I didn't hear sadness or anger. Just a voice as flat and cold as ice on stone. "Besides," she added, "it's good for them. Good for them to learn straight away how things are."

"Do you really believe that? That it's good for them?"

"Of course I believe it. I was raised that way and I turned out okay."

"But—"

"But nothing. It's how it is, and it's what's right."

I leaned against the wall, feeling the cold concrete through my uniform. The baby was still crying. Nothing seemed right. Joan said not to restock on night shift. Yet we restocked. Joan said I would be stationed in the nursery. But here I was in the supply closet. Joan had said nothing about a torch.

Soon I could hear Lizzie's deep breathing, a snoring sound with a bit of a whistle at the end of each breath. Regular, in and out, the sound of deep sleep. I couldn't believe she would actually fall asleep while on duty. I tried to remember if Joan had said anything about sleeping. Even if she hadn't, sleeping on duty made no sense. Didn't seem right. A baby was still crying. If I had to, I would report Lizzie for sleeping. Whatever it took, I would do it.

I felt along the wall, moving slowly, until I came to the open door. The air in the corridor was cooler than in the supply closet. Quietly, keeping my hand on the wall, I walked toward the nursery, toward the crying baby.

I passed the twin hallways that led to the older children, boys on one side, girls on the other. Moving forward, slowly, ever so slowly, with my arm out, wanting to feel the touch of the wall when it resumed. Picking my feet up tentatively, trying to remember if there was anything in the corridor that I might bump into, anything that would make a sound and wake Lizzie.

The baby was still crying. The closer I got, the louder it got. A long wail followed by little sobs, little short-of-breath sobs, then another wail. Long, short, short. Long, short, short. A rhythm of need.

Finally, the nursery. I felt my way along the line of cribs, evenly spaced cribs, evenly spaced babies, and moved closer to the crying. It was the first baby on the boys' side. The nipple had fallen from his mouth. I repositioned it close to his lips and patted his back. Soon he was quiet and eating.

I moved farther into the nursery, toward Elsa, moving from crib to crib, feeling the wooden edges until I came to the last one. In the darkness, I leaned over Elsa, felt the warmth of her on my hands. I picked her up and held her against me. How light she was, how easy to pick up. She curled against me, her head on my shoulder, her cheek next to mine. Skin to skin. I breathed in the smell of her, milky and warm, wanting to pull it into me and never let it go, never forget it. I patted her back and swayed back and forth, holding her. She nestled even closer, and we fit together perfectly. My baby, my Elsa. Warm tears slid down my cheeks—warm, happy tears.

I forgot about the Gatekeepers and their clipboards. I forgot about the Authorities and the Enforcers. I forgot about Randall and Lizzie. There was only Elsa in my arms and I wanted it to go on forever.

A torch snapped on. Light in my eyes. Lizzie stood in front of me, hands on her hips, shining the light without mercy on my face.

"Citizen," she said in a low, menacing whisper, "you have broken the rules."

CHAPTER THIRTY-FOUR

I tightened my arms around Elsa and took a small step backward. Lizzie took a step closer to me, her hands on her hips.

"The rules?" I asked.

"Yes, the rules. Like I told you."

Elsa moved her head against the side of my neck. Her hair was soft and warm, but I felt cold and afraid. Through the window slit I saw the dim light of the moon and heard the clumping steps of the Gate-keeper.

"I know you told me," I whispered because I didn't want to wake Elsa. She moved her head again, and squirmed in my arms, her legs pushing against my chest. I had to think of something, anything, that would explain my actions without making it worse. "I was doing what Joan had told me we were to do. Comfort the babies. She's my boss, and she's your boss, too. Besides, I was afraid the crying baby would wake you up."

She took another step, her face pushing closer to me. I took another step back, against the wall.

"Are you crazy?" she asked. "I wasn't sleeping. Hear me? I wasn't sleeping." I could smell her breath. I turned my head away but I could still smell the hot, musty egg yolk.

"As far as Joan goes, I got friends that will say I comfort babies. I got friends that will say you're lying. Joan doesn't have friends here. You don't have friends here. I do. I'm not farm co-op. I'm not home-raised. So put that baby down. Now." She stepped back and I could see the shadow of her arm pointing to the crib. "Or you will be sorry."

"Everything all right in there?" Randall must have been outside by the window slit. He must have been listening, hearing everything. "You need my help in there, Lizzie?"

"Not right now. Least I don't think so," she answered, still pointing at the crib. "But I caught this new worker sleeping. Can you believe it? Sleeping. First night on duty."

"Well, then," he said through the slit, "that needs to be reported, don't you think? I mean, after all, you know—"

"I'll think about it. Don't you go telling anybody till I decide. I might let it go if she promises never to sleep on duty again."

At first I was stunned. But then I knew with clear, cold certainty exactly who Lizzie really was: a snake. An evil, slimy snake who, just like the real snakes, was being protected.

Randall said, "I've got to finish rounds. Got to make sure the Authority's special supply building is locked. But I'll check back. Put out a flag if you need me." I heard him clumping away on his uneven footsteps.

Lizzie turned back to me. "Put the baby down. Now. We've got some talking to do."

I moved to the crib, felt the hard wood of the side against my thighs, and bent forward to lay Elsa gently on the mattress. I took my time doing it, savoring every second, making Lizzie wait. Lizzie turned her light on the crib and watched me. Elsa curled on her side, still asleep, her pink fist by her mouth. Her nourishment bottle was still half full.

"Follow me," Lizzie said.

We went back to the supply cupboard. Lizzie sat in the rocking chair and motioned for me to sit on the stepstool. Lizzie rocked and her torch bounced up and down. Shining off the walls, off the bottles of nourishment, sweeping past the clipboard with its list of names, up to the ceiling, across my face, down to the floor. The stepstool was low and my knees were up around my chin. My back was cold against the wall. Somewhere down the dark hall a child was coughing.

We sat that way, in silence, for what seemed a long time.

Finally Lizzie spoke, her voice gruff. "Well, what do you have to say for yourself?" She kept rocking.

My mouth felt dry, as though my tongue were made of shoe leather. "Nothing," I said. The words seemed to quiver and hang in the air in front of me as Lizzie stopped rocking and the torch settled on my face.

"You bet you got nothing to say." She rocked awhile, the chair creaking with movement. "And I know why you don't understand. You were *home-raised*. Aren't many of your kind left, thank goodness. Bet your mama never taught you anything, now did she?"

"She told me about the before-time."

"Before-time! It's over. Forever. So why even tell you about it? I heard she was a little bit crazy. Word gets around."

Through the window slit, I could see dirty gray clouds slide over a sliver of the moon.

"Heard she didn't like the idea of change. None of them liked the idea of change. They were stuck in the muck of the status quo. That's what I heard."

I could hear Randall walking past the building, making rounds, his footsteps shuffling.

"If you had been Village-raised you'd know the real history. Like I do. Had to memorize it. Got good grades, too. That's how I got this job.

"Real history had its beginning with the Republic. So let me tell you about it. Then maybe you'll understand."

She sounded proud and sure of herself. She paused, as if deciding where to start, and then went on. "Did she tell you how hard people had to work before the change?"

I thought of the photograph of Mother holding me, the way she was smiling, how green the grass was, the big house behind us.

"She never said anything about working hard, nothing like that—"

Lizzie interrupted me. "That just proves she was crazy. See, before the Republic, people had to work hard. Either grow their own food, or work and get money to buy food. Had to pay for their houses, too. And clothes. All that stuff. Big, big companies made the rules because they owned the energy and drilled the Earth for it. Regular people didn't have a chance. The Earth didn't have a chance."

From the nursery, I heard a baby cry. I wanted to go there. I didn't want it to be Elsa.

"Sit still," Lizzie said, as though she could read my mind. "It's all part of their learning. Sleep when it's time to sleep, eat when it's time to eat. I was raised here. I learned it. They will, too. That's how it works."

"But they're just babies," I said.

"They're Citizens," she answered. "We all live by the same rules."

The crying slowed, harder to hear. A brief quiet. Then it started again.

"Back to your history lesson," Lizzie said. "Stuff your crazy mama never told you. Bet your daddy didn't tell you much, either."

"He taught me a lot." *Do whatever they ask.*

"You don't act like he taught you a lot. Guess he had his hands full keeping your mama under control." She shifted in the chair, crossing one leg over the other. Her pant leg pulled up and I could make out the bony knobs of her ankle.

I stood up and stared down at her. "Don't talk about my parents like that. You have no right! They loved me and took care of me."

"And where are they now?" she asked in a cold, flat voice. "Are they here now?" She stared back, blinding me with her torch. "Sit down. We're not done."

I remained standing, ignoring her command. She either didn't notice, or didn't care.

"Things got worse," she continued. "Some kind of new crisis every day. Food prices skyrocketing, energy shortages, riots in the streets. People grew restless, scared. That's when the Republic was born. One wise and powerful man became the Ultimate Authority. His name was Fabian. He chose other wise and powerful men to join his Authority and the people became Citizens. Proud Citizens. *Praise be to the Republic.*"

Her voice had slipped into a monotone, almost trancelike.

Another baby was crying. Then another. The babies needed me. I needed to go to them. I started to walk out of the room.

"Sit," Lizzie said. "I'm still teaching. Remember, I can report you for sleeping, for breaking the rules. And Randall will, too. And then what will happen to you?"

She rocked. Babies cried. I felt tears behind my eyes, a burning pressure.

"But it wasn't easy," she went on. "There were some who didn't believe in the Central Authority." She said *didn't believe* in a way that I could imagine her lip curling up over the words. She rocked harder, the light from the torch bounced faster, like lightning in all directions.

"Your mama didn't believe. And her mother and sister didn't believe." Her mother? Her sister? That would be my grandmother and my aunt, but I never knew a grandmother or an aunt so how did Lizzie?

"How stupid. How very stupid they were. The Central Authority was promising to take care of them, give them food and clothes and housing. Meet all their needs. And at the same time, protect the Earth." She had slipped back into the monotone, the rocking slowed, and she fell silent for a long moment. Then she started again. "Those stupid people tried to organize against the Central Authority. Can you imagine that? Organize against the Central Authority?" She made a snorting sound, like a hiccup and a laugh mixed together. "And when the relocation of Citizens began, they held protests. Right there at the train stations. Protests. Big protests by small people. Status quo people."

"Why don't you just stop talking?" I asked.

She ignored me. "What do you think happened next?"

"I have no idea."

"They were shot. Right then and there. In front of everyone."

"Shot?" I tried to imagine that scene. I couldn't. I couldn't imagine it. I'd seen guns on the army members when they marched on display at the Social Update Meetings. But they never seemed real.

"Yep. Shot. Killed. I heard that your grandmother and aunt were shot. Right in front of your mama. Others were, too. Guess there was a whole pile of bodies. Different people told me that. Randall saw it for himself, before he got on the train."

The room was silent, except for the rocking. Except for the noise in my head, in my ears.

"From what I'm told, that's when your mama started acting crazy. Some of the others did, too. Your daddy worked hard to keep your mama from acting out. Had to remind her, from what I hear. Had to remind her not to say anything."

Again, silence. In that silence, in that darkness, I felt like I couldn't breathe. Did David know all of this? Did Joan and John? Surely they did. But no one ever told me. Father never told me. Piles of bodies, and nobody told me? Mother digging at her skin with her fingernails, and turning away from me when I asked questions. The questions, the memories tumbled in my head, pushing against each other, throbbing and pounding, making me dizzy, making me feel like I was going crazy.

"Only reason they didn't shoot your mama was that she had to raise you. They didn't have a Children's Village yet. See, they were busy making sure everyone had food and shelter. And they had so much to do to start healing the Earth. The most necessary things first. So they needed her to raise you. From what I've seen so far, you'd have been better off

if they'd shot her. Right then and there. You'd understand the rules better. Raised by a crazy mama, that's what you get."

"She wasn't crazy! She was my mother. How dare you talk about
her like that!" My voice was shrill and loud. I wanted to slap her oily,
dull face.

She rocked again, the creaking of the chair loud and regular.

"I talk. You listen. That's how it works here at the Village. Understand now?" she asked.

Oh, I understood all right. I understood hatred. I understood fear
of the Authority. I understood, perhaps for the first time in my life,
what it felt like to be trapped.

CHAPTER THIRTY-FIVE

The darkness through the window slit began to turn lighter shades of gray. Lizzie stood up and stretched. "Time to get the children ready for the day," she said. I followed her out of the supply cupboard and into the corridor. As much as I despised her, I had to work beside her so I could see Elsa, make sure Elsa was cared for. *Whatever you do, Emmeline, don't fight them.*

We went into the boys' dormitory first. Their room had a mousy smell of bedding that needed to be sanitized. Their sleeping mats were lined up along the walls. In the gray light I could see small wooden chairs between each mat, and a pile of folded clothing on each seat. The mats were a dark color and the small faces of the sleeping boys were pale against their dark pillows. Lizzie went from mat to mat touching each boy on the shoulder. One by one they stirred, sat up on their mats, rubbed their eyes, and yawned. I followed, unsure of what she wanted me to do. My legs felt weak and my feet heavy. The boys looked puzzled. Perhaps it was because there were two workers instead of just one. They remained silent but glanced at each other as we passed. I counted twenty in all.

The older boys were closest to the door. When Lizzie had finished waking all of them she paused at the doorway. The boys stood and went to the end of their mats, facing her.

She raised her hand to her forehead and made the circle sign. "Praise be to the Republic," she said.

Small hands rose to small foreheads.

"Praise be to the Republic," they said in such unison that I caught my breath. I saw the little boy who had made the circle sign on his nose when Joan had walked me through the Village. This time, he made it on his forehead and there was no trace of a smile on his face.

"Next time," Lizzie hissed at me, "do the pledge with me. It's a requirement."

Lizzie made a motion with her hand, and the boys walked out into the corridor, tallest first, smallest last. They lined up against the wall and waited for her. She opened a door I hadn't noticed before and I immediately smelled a recycling toilet.

"Morning ritual, boys," she said. "Washing-up time. Then get dressed."

She left the boys there, standing in line, waiting their turn for the washing-up area. I paused to look back at the boys before following her. Some of them were pushing each other. It looked like they were having fun, but they stopped when they saw me looking.

I caught up with Lizzie.

"I wake the boys first. They don't take as long washing up as the girls do. But they take longer getting dressed. So it works out that both the girls and boys finish their morning ritual at the same time." She smiled proudly. "I figured that out all by myself." Her voice was different from the voice that talked in the dark about shootings and piles of bodies. "Now we wake the girls."

The routine in the girls' room was the same. Their smell was less pungent, though, and sweeter. The smallest girl was curled on her side and tried to shake Lizzie's hand off her shoulder. She rolled to her other side, and pulled her cover up over her head. Lizzie shook her shoulder harder. The child sat up reluctantly and looked down at the floor. She had a curly frame of light hair around her face, like flower petals aglow in the pale light.

"Morning ritual," Lizzie said and walked to the doorway. All of the girls, except the last one, went to stand at the end of their mats.

"Morning ritual," she repeated.

The small child remained on her mat. One of the older girls, almost as tall as Lizzie, walked back to that child. She bent and whispered something to her and took her hand. Maybe she was saying, "Do whatever they ask. No matter what, do what they ask." Yes, I thought, do whatever they ask.

Finally, Lizzie raised her hand to her forehead. I did the same.

"Praise be to the Republic," we said, together, in perfect unison.

"Praise be to the Republic," the girls responded, eighteen girls, eighteen circle signs.

The boys were shuffling back to their room to dress. The girls lined up in the corridor for their turn. I had never been around children before. I was surprised at how fragile they looked. Frail and vulnerable. Knobby little ankles, thin elbows. Outlines of shoulder blades under the thin fabric of night clothes. Necks that looked too thin to support heads of sleep-matted hair.

"And now the babies," Lizzie said. She went back to the supply cupboard and gathered nourishment bottles, cradling them between her arm and chest. "Get the propping diapers. And diapers for changing." I did as I was told. My hands were sweating and I rubbed them against my uniform.

I heard Randall outside, making his final rounds.

"Come on, we're running late. All this stuff needs to be done before the dawn workers arrive."

I heard the half-hour-till-dawn warning bell. Half an hour before I had to leave Elsa. Half an hour before I had to meet with Joan.

Lizzie went quickly from crib to crib. Took off wet diapers, dirty diapers, and dropped them into the recycle bins. Wiped little bottoms with sanitizing cloths, and dropped those cloths into the bins. With no wasted motion, she put out her hand for a clean diaper, and, like a machine, I handed her one. Then another diaper for propping the morning bottle. The babies, smelling fresher than they had, curled hands around the bottles, small cheeks pumping and sucking, making little wet noises.

Finally we were at Elsa's crib. She was awake, looking up at the ceiling with eyes as blue as the best sky I had ever seen.

"Go ahead, change her. I want to see if you know how," Lizzie said.

My hands were shaking. Lizzie had to notice how nervous I was.

"Go ahead. Show me you can do it," she said.

I bent over the crib and Elsa turned her head toward me. I felt an odd throbbing in my breasts. It was like water moving under my skin.

Biting my lip, I removed her wet diaper. Her bottom looked red and splotched. The sanitizing cloth was cold in my hand but I had no way to warm it. I rubbed it against her and she pulled her legs up toward her tummy and squirmed. But she didn't cry. For some reason, that made me proud. Quickly, I diapered her, wishing the cloth were softer against her skin.

As I worked, Lizzie cleared her throat as if she was nervous. "You and Joan. You got a special deal from Joan? Being paired with David and all that?"

I shrugged. Let her think I got a special deal. Let her squirm.

" 'Cause if word got around that you got a special deal, well, you know. And since you can't be here all the time and Joan can't be here all the time, well . . ." She stopped talking for a long, silent minute. I fastened the diaper and smoothed Elsa's sleeping clothes over her legs. The material was the same pink material of my uniform. Her feet were bare and pink and her ten little toes were curled. Curled and smooth, not yet calloused from walking a board, nor dirtied by walking the Earth.

"Thing is, if some of the workers thought you got a special deal, if maybe they took something I said to mean you got a special deal, well, maybe, I don't know for sure . . ." She was talking fast, her words bumping into each other. "Maybe this little one might miss a daytime feeding or something. Besides, I heard Joan isn't doing such a great job here. Heard the Authority is watching her closely."

I stared at her, realizing the cold power of her threat. "I have no special deal," I said finally.

Lizzie handed me the last bottle. "Want to hold her?" she asked. It felt like a trick. Was Lizzie trying to tease me or make me break the rules she so often reminded me of? "Go ahead, pick her up."

I didn't care what her reason was. I slid my hand under Elsa's head and back. How warm she was! How soft! I stood there, cradling her in my left arm. My baby. It felt so perfect, the way she fit against me.

"Want to feed her?"

My head felt wobbly on my neck as I nodded.

"Well, then. Was I sleeping on duty?"

I didn't know what to say.

"Remember, I got Randall. Randall will say whatever I tell him to say. Know what I mean? You say I was sleeping, well, me and Randall say you were sleeping. Two Citizens against one. Understand?"

She was offering me something. Some kind of deal. All I had to do was lie. So easy. She stood staring at me, blinking and chewing on a thumbnail.

"I never saw you sleeping," I said.

To feed Elsa, I would lie. To hold Elsa, I would lie. I would do whatever I had to. Whatever it took.

I stared at Lizzie as she handed me the bottle.

I stared, but I did not blink.

CHAPTER THIRTY-SIX

Elsa took the nipple eagerly, her round cheeks pulling so hard that one small dimple emerged. Her eyelashes were so long that they fanned against her eyelids. Then her eyes focused on my face, and I felt like we were locked together in some magical way. A tear slid down my cheek before I even realized I was crying. Then another, and another after that. She would never know her grandmother, but I would make sure she knew her mother.

Lizzie broke the magic.

"The dawn shift's coming," she said. "Put that baby down."

I heard the metal clang of an energy bicycle being fastened to the bar. Faintly, Randall's voice spoke to someone who was coughing. The sounds seemed so far away, muffled and distant. Not part of the world Elsa and I shared.

"Come on—put her down." Lizzie sounded nervous, rushed.

Reluctantly, I bent over the crib and laid Elsa down. She curled on her side, and Lizzie took the bottle from me and propped it on the rolled diaper. My arms still felt warm and strong from holding her. I didn't want to walk away. I didn't know if I *could* walk away.

"Come on. And wipe your face."

Lizzie started to walk out of the nursery. I bent over Elsa's crib and whispered, "I'll be back. I promise." I wiped my face with the back of my hand and caught up with Lizzie.

"I'll give change of shift report to Barb. She's the day shift. You don't have to hang around."

"Shouldn't I be there? Isn't that part of the job?" I asked.

"Not necessary. Not today. Go back to your Living Space."

Lizzie stopped at the supply cupboard where Barb was waiting. From the closed, tight looks on their faces, I knew it would be a mistake to stay.

"Well, then, good night," I said and kept walking. Outside, Randall was still talking to the day-shift Gatekeeper and handing off his clipboard. They both looked up and stared at me as I walked down the corridor. I could feel Lizzie and Barb staring at me from behind.

I never felt so alone.

Joan had asked me to stop in at the end of my first shift. Her office was ahead, on the right. I couldn't stop in. I couldn't risk it. Lizzie would take that to mean I had a special deal or whatever she called it. And she would be sure the word got around. I had no doubt of that. She said if word got around, Elsa might not . . . I couldn't bring myself to finish the thought.

It felt like Lizzie had more power than Joan, especially if it was true that the Authority wasn't pleased with Joan's performance. Joan wanted to help me. But Lizzie could hurt me. And hurt Elsa. The ability to hurt had more power than the desire to help. I couldn't talk to Joan. Not today.

I walked as quickly as I could past her office and kept my head turned away. If she was in there, she must not have seen me. She didn't call out, and I kept walking as quickly and as quietly as I could out of the Village.

I fumbled with the lock on my energy bicycle. The Village flags fluttered above the gate, making little rippling sounds. Through the fence, the trees cast shadows on each other, making different shades of green that moved like bird wings in the early morning light. Finally, the lock released, spraying rust flakes onto the packed dirt. I pushed the bicycle through the gate, past the Gatekeepers. The day-shift Gatekeeper was older than Randall, heavier, and taller. He made a notation on the clipboard as I passed by. I think he nodded at me, but I was so set on leaving that I wasn't sure.

I bicycled on the rut-filled path away from the Village, leaving Elsa behind. What kind of person was Barb? Would she diaper Elsa gently? The tears started again, this time faster and faster. I began to sob, great huge sobs that pulled my shoulders forward and up. Uncontrollable. I had to quit cycling. Alone on this path, I gasped for breath, my head against the cold metal handlebar of my bicycle until I couldn't cry any- more and had no choice but to keep pedaling.

I passed Compound after Compound, Gatekeeper after Gatekeeper. Some were making rounds, putting nourishment cubes in boxes. Some were leaning against their gates, holding their clipboards. The rotten, spoiled smells from Re-Cy were beginning to rise into the air, and a wave of nausea passed over me, up into my throat and mouth, making me gag.

Everybody must have known about the shootings, the cruelty. Ev- erybody must have known, but nobody told me. Not Mother or Father, and I trusted them the most. Not George or Joan, either. Not John, who somehow knew how to get outside the fence. Not even mean little Jeremy. David must have known, too. They all must have known, and yet no one spoke of it. Why? I felt a hot anger building in me, and I pedaled harder, trying to get away from the rage and the smells and the injustice.

Finally I arrived at my Compound. David was standing in our doorway, waiting for me. He was actually smiling. I let my bicycle fall instead of hooking it to the download bar and pushed past him into the dim interior. How dare anybody in this world smile, I thought. What is there to be happy about?

He stepped outside and I heard him fasten my bicycle to download. Then he came in with a puzzled, cautious look and a frown line between his eyebrows. Our nourishment cubes were on the counter. I gagged again, just looking at them.

"Did you get to hold Elsa?" he asked, holding his arms out to me.

I started crying again and turned away from him.

"Emmeline, what is it? What's wrong?" He stepped closer, touching my shoulder so that I would face him. "Is Elsa okay?"

Rage rushed through me, fast as lightning, scorching as fire. My hands curled into fists. I ran to my energy board and began hitting the side rails as hard as I could until my hands hurt too much to continue.

David wrapped his arms around me, holding me tightly. His arms were strong and hard, and I felt his thighs against mine.

I brushed my face against his shirt and saw the wetness of my tears on it.

"Did you know?" I asked him, tilting my head back to watch his face. "Did you know about the shootings?" The word *shootings* came out of my mouth as sharp as nails.

"There were shootings? Today? Where? I didn't hear anything." Two worry lines formed between his eyebrows, straight up and down.

"Not today. No, not today. Shootings at the beginning. People. Lots of people. My own family! Shot. When the relocation started. Did you know?"

"You didn't?" His lips looked dry and white as chalk.

I shook my head no.

He held me even closer.

"Could it happen again?" I whispered against his chest, against the gray Gatekeeper uniform. "Could it happen again?"

He hung his head and didn't answer. He didn't have to. His face told me everything.

And so it began. Knowledge.

CHAPTER THIRTY-SEVEN

David continued to hold me.

"I'm sorry. I'm so sorry, Emmeline. I don't know what say." He ran one hand up and down my back. "I thought you knew. I thought everybody knew."

"Obviously not."

We stood together. A bus-box rumbled by, wooden sides rattling. David leaned down and kissed the side of my neck. I pulled away; the anger was still there, inside me, twisting, pulling.

"What did they think, what did anybody think? I mean, what good was it not telling me anything? What good did that do?" I was breathing fast and talking fast. My hands twisted around each other.

He didn't answer.

The rumble of the bus-box was fading. I wondered if John was on the Transport Team but I didn't have the energy to look outside. I glanced around. The grayness of the walls and floor struck me as the most helpless and hopeless color I had ever seen. My nourishment cube on the counter. Dry, tasteless thing. I grabbed it, ran outside, and threw it as hard as I could over the fence. It bounced against a tree and fell among the greenness on the forest floor. I heard a rustle in the grass. A small brown animal, no bigger than my hand, was sniffing at the cube.

David grabbed my arm, but I pulled away and went back inside. He followed me and stood in the doorway, his shoulders slumped.

"What you just did was very dangerous, Emmeline." His voice was a low whisper. "What if the Gatekeeper saw you throwing away your ration?"

"I don't care. What are they going to do? Shoot me? Let them!"

"You don't mean that. I know you don't mean that. Think of Elsa." He came in and closed the door behind him. "Think of Elsa. Think of me."

He stepped closer and I could smell the sanitizing solution on his skin, on the strong muscles of his arms. The same smell as Elsa's cleansing wipe. The same smell that was still on my hands. And somehow it connected us. David, Elsa, me. The smell wrapped itself around me as heavy as a blanket, and I had to sit down on my sleeping mat. David sat next to me, cross-legged with an arm around my shoulders. I leaned against him, letting my weakness rest against his strength. I started to put my fingers in my mouth but stopped. They gave no comfort anymore.

David took my hand and pressed my fingers against his lips. We sat that way in silence while outside the Gatekeeper made rounds and the smell from Re-Cy wafted through the trees and into our window slits.

Fatigue washed over me. "I'm tired, David. So tired."

He got my water ration from the counter and handed it to me. "Please drink some."

The first sip tasted good. I took another. The outside of the bottle was sweating. Today was going to be hot and sticky again. I held the bottle next to my cheek, feeling the coolness.

David watched as I drank, his face sad. "Who told you? Who told you about the shootings?"

I handed the water bottle back to him and he sat it on the counter.

"Lizzie. The night-shift Caretaker."

"I'm sorry you had to hear it from her. And I don't know why your parents didn't tell you. Maybe it was just to . . ." He paused. "To keep things secret. Their way of protecting you."

David put his hand under my chin and tipped my face up. With his other hand, he stroked my cheek. Maybe he was right. I had already lied to protect Elsa.

"I promise to tell you everything I know," he said. "No secrets. But right now, you need to sleep."

I lay down on my mat, still in my Caretaker uniform. Not enough energy to change my clothes. Not enough energy for anything.

As I lay there, I felt the hardness of some of the things Mother had left for me. I could picture them all, buried within the mat. The smooth edge of the book by my cheek. Along the side, by my fingers, the small hardness of the knife that opened like a snake. I hadn't told David about these things.

We all had our secrets.

CHAPTER THIRTY-EIGHT

I tossed and turned, somewhere between rest and restlessness. Images, unconnected and fragmented, floated past each other, twisting and turning. Mother on her board, face turned to the wall. Mother at the end, curled on her mat, face still to the wall. Elsa in my arms. Father in his sweat-stained shirt. Joan smiling at me, the sun behind her, a halo around her. Lizzie biting her fingernail. The two girls in the bus-box with me on reproductive-testing day. They faded away, gray ghosts. Me, alone in the bus-box, being pulled along by a Transport Team past squirrels swirling like fog. In my sleep, I reached out to touch them, but they were too far away. David taking the first bite of an egg. His hand, holding the egg out to me. His fingernails, smooth and pink, against the whiteness of the egg.

And then I fell into a deep sleep, with David still beside me and my hand resting on the far edge of the mat, near Mother's treasures.

When I woke up, David was seated beside me, vigilant and watchful. He stroked my cheek with one finger. A soft, smooth touch that made me smile even though my eyelids felt hot and swollen, and my lips rough. He went to the counter and came back with some water for me in his right hand, his left hand behind his back. After I drank some of the water, he took the ration cup then held out his left hand.

Flowers.

A fragile cluster of short-stemmed beauties. Small pink buds, unopened, tucked in between bigger flowers with white petals, yellow centers. Some purply sprigs that I could smell already, like the breeze across the trees and grass after a rain. A fern, lacy and soft, that swayed up and down even as he held the bouquet. There was even a soft blue bird feather among the stems.

I reached for them. They felt as fragile as Elsa, beautiful but dependent. "I held her," I whispered, my nose buried in the flowers, the feather brushing against my cheek. He looked so happy when I said that, smiling so hard his eyes almost crinkled shut.

"What does she look like? How long did you hold her? All night, I hope."

"Not exactly," I answered. "Tell me. Do I have a dimple?"

"What? Do you have a what?"

"A dimple. A little dent in my cheek that gets bigger when I smile?" I tried to smile so I could show him, but my lips were dry and my face felt stiff.

He touched my right cheek. "Yes, right here, you have a beautiful, perfect dimple." He leaned forward and kissed me on the cheek. "I love your dimple."

"Mother had one, too. On her right cheek. But it seemed to get lost on her. Elsa has one. Her skin is so smooth, so perfect. I wish you could see her."

"You can tell me about her. Every morning when you end your shift. You can tell me everything."

I clenched and unclenched my fists, pushed my hair behind my ears, and took a deep breath. Surely, he didn't believe just hearing about Elsa secondhand and never holding her would be enough!

"David, someday I will have your baby."

He smiled, a shy little smile. "Oh, Emmeline, that would be so, I don't know, so wonderful. A baby. Maybe a boy." He paused. "Or a girl. Either way."

"And, if I did have your baby—a girl or a boy, either way—you would never be able to hold that baby. Never. It would be a Children's Village baby. Raised by the Republic." I paused, studied his face, and then continued. "Perhaps," I took a deep breath, "perhaps we shouldn't have a child. Because it would never really be our child."

He turned away from me. The air felt heavy with quiet sadness. "I don't know what to say, Emmeline." He turned back to me, his shoulders slumped. "It's beyond our power. All of it."

"Beyond our power," I thought. That ugly word. *It*. Mother used to say that. *It is what it is.* I didn't think that was good enough anymore. Not since I held Elsa. *It* was ugly and *it* hurt and *it* wasn't good enough. But the whole idea of *it* was too big for right now, too big for the two of us in this Living Space. A Children's Village worker and a Gatekeeper. We were nothing against *it*. I took a deep breath and tried to slow my breathing. Tried to push away ugly thoughts, tried to think of something good, if just for a little while.

"How did you get these?" I asked, pointing to the flowers.

"I didn't," he admitted shyly. "They were on the window slit when I woke up. Father must have left them."

"But how? How does he do these things?"

"The first question is 'why?' I bet it was my mother's idea." He took the flowers and put them in the little bit of water left in the ration cup and then handed it back to me. "Back before the relocation, in the before-times, she had flower beds everywhere. Your mom was leading protests. My mom was pruning roses. Your dad and my dad and I were baling hay. Look where all of that got us." He looked around our dismal area with a grimace.

I set the bottle and the flowers on the floor by my feet. I looked at my toes. So much bigger than Elsa's. No longer pink and smooth.

No longer soft, uncalloused, or unsoiled. Strong toes. Strong feet. Strong legs from walking the board. Flowers were good and sweet, but strength was better.

"How? How does he get them here? To our window slit. How, with Gatekeepers and fences around all of us? How?"

David went to the eating counter and came back with the one morning cube that was left. He broke it in half and handed me a portion. "You have to eat, Emmeline. Please. Share with me."

I took his offering. He was right. I had to eat to be strong. We shared the cube, the dry sustenance from the Authority. It had no taste today, but it did have nourishment. From nourishment comes strength, in spite of the source.

"You didn't answer me," I said. "How does he get outside the fence? Can anybody get out there?" Outside the fence sounded like freedom.

"It's Dad's secret," he said. "I can't tell you."

"No, David, no. Never again. No secrets. You promised me." I knew if there were secrets between us, there could never be hope. Not for David, not for me, not for Elsa. "Did you hear me? No secrets. Not ever." I put my hand under his chin and turned his face toward me. "Look at me."

He looked at me with clear gray eyes, unblinking.

"I need to know everything. Everything you know. Everything that happened. The before-time. The relocation." I paused. "How? Why? Tell me all of the terrible things that happened."

"I don't know if I can answer all of that. The how and the why—like I told you, I was just a kid." He paused. "I wish there was a way we could spend time with Mom and Dad. They know more than I do. I'd rather they told you about it."

I thought about what he was saying. Maybe he was right. Or maybe he was afraid of upsetting me. Maybe his memories were all buried. Deep, dark, ugly things. But I still wanted to know about these things the same way I want water when I am thirsty. Even a tiny sip is better than none at all.

"Then start with something small. Something you do know. How does your dad get outside the fence? Can you at least answer that?"

He nodded and walked to the doorway and looked out. I saw him look in both directions.

"Not now, Emmeline. Not now." He put his finger to his lips, motioning me to be quiet. So many times I had seen Mother do that. I never knew why. Not until now.

The Gatekeeper was making rounds. I could hear his boots walking on the ground, in a circle from the first Living Space and on and on, past ours, his shadow past our doorway and then on, fading away to the last space. Finally, he must have returned to his post, making his notations on his clipboard. What kind of people are these Gatekeepers? I thought, before remembering that David was one of them. There must be degrees of Gatekeepers, degrees of Transport Team members, degrees of Village workers, degrees of all classes. The secret was figuring out what degree someone was. Not all Citizens were the same. Regardless of what the Authority said or wanted. Not all Citizens were the same.

"Right. No secrets. Not ever. Not between us." He sat next to me on the sleeping mat and talked quietly. "I heard him tell my mother that there is an old bus-box with a broken wheel parked beside the Children's Village. All the bus-boxes are parked to the right of the building at night. They line them up for morning transport."

He paused and went to the doorway again. The sunlight cast his shadow into our space but he soon came back and sat next to me.

"That one bus-box with the broken wheel has been there for a while, parked right alongside the fence. The Central Authority is inefficient when it comes to fixing things." He laughed when he said that. "They are so busy making sure the Citizens do everything right, but they aren't real good about doing their own work right."

The flowers sat in the ration cup at our feet. I held his hand and it felt strong and sure. His long fingers curled around mine—they made me feel safe.

"Anyway, behind that bus-box, there's a small break in the fence wire, right above the cement base. Every evening when dad parked his bus-box, he would go to that break and pull on it and make it a little bigger. The fence wire is thick so it took a lot of effort, a lot of time." He smiled, and I knew he was proud of his father. I could just see it in the way his lips curled up at the corners and his eyes crinkled around the edges.

"After a while, the break in the fence became big enough for a person to slip through. No Gatekeeper can see the hole because it is hidden behind the bus-box. Dad would slip through it just to be where things are green and growing. Mom was upset when he told her about it. Said it was dangerous to go outside the fence."

"Well, your mom is right."

"Maybe she is. But," he said smiling at me, "being out there is important to my dad. Just look at those flowers."

He was right. Those flowers, those beautiful flowers, symbolized so much more than just love. They symbolized freedom. A life outside the fences. A life without Central Authority and Gatekeepers and nourishment cubes. A life with Elsa and David.

I liked the sound of that.

CHAPTER THIRTY-NINE

David said it would take a while for me to get used to sleeping during the day and working the night shift, so we tried to nap again. He rubbed my back, trying to get me to relax, but soon he was kissing the side of my neck, right above my shoulder. Then he took my fingers, one by one to his lips, loving each. As he moved from finger to finger, it felt like my body was melting against the sleeping mat. He began to fumble with his clothes but stopped when we heard the shrill three-blast whistle warning of a Social Update Meeting.

He groaned and sat up, holding his head in his hands.

"I forgot. Social Update tonight." He smacked his hand against the sleeping mat. "I'm sorry, Emmeline."

I sat up next to him and put my head on his shoulder. "I'm sorry, too. Maybe later?"

He smiled. "Promise?"

"Promise," I said, and my voice felt like it came from deep in my throat. I went into the washing-up area to get ready for the Social Update Meeting. David got our evening cubes from the box and we took turns eating them, taking bites from each other's cubes, sharing in a way that seemed so natural, like it had always been this way and nothing would ever change. The terrible things Lizzie had told me last night seemed, briefly, far away and unreal.

The Gatekeeper was raising the Social Update flag by the gate. It made a screeching metal-on-metal sound. Time to go. Reluctantly we left our space and went together into the common ground of our Compound.

The couple from Living Space 2 came out at the same time. They were so much younger than the old man and woman who used to live there, but I could see the beginning of the same vacant expressions on their faces. They didn't walk close together, instead leaving a big space between them, making them look unconnected to each other, or to anything else, for that matter. I reached for David's hand and looked away from the young couple. They were too much of a reminder of how easily things could go wrong. Her poor baby, born not viable. That void in her life was the space between them as they walked; a space too big to be filled by any amount of tears. A space that destroys all hope.

And then I thought of the old lady being taken away from that same Living Space, away from her husband. Her matted and tangled hair, her scuffed shoes. She never looked back toward him, never called out to him. I remembered her voice, frail and quivery. "Are you my son, my Andy? Are you taking me to my Lizzie?"

We kept walking, merging with the people from all of the Compounds, moving like tall grass in the wind. David and I went into the Re-Cy section and stood ramrod straight, facing the elevated stage, waiting for the words from the podium. We stood with our shoulders touching. Paired. Over to the left, in the Transport Compound, I saw John in his orange uniform, and beside him, Joan. They were in the back row of their section and craned their heads, scanning the crowd. Finally John spotted us and nudged Joan. She touched her hand to her heart, so briefly that no one would really notice it. But that small gesture meant so much to me. I touched my heart in response.

This Social Update Meeting would be the same as all the others. Pledges, circle signs, information, announcements. But I felt different this time. More awake, maybe. Listening harder, watching, waiting for clues, information, anything. I looked at the faces of the Citizens, trying to tell what they were thinking or feeling. If they were afraid. If they really believed the pledges.

The Authority Figure, in his gold-trimmed black uniform with shiny black boots almost to his knees, came onto the podium. He was followed by two Enforcers, their boots just above their ankles. Citizens were never issued boots; we only got shoes. I looked at mine and those of the people around me. Flimsy shoes with thin soles, worn to nothing from so much walking on energy boards.

The uniforms of the Enforcers could not hide their bulk, their broad shoulders and large arms. Their thighs were as thick as tree trunks. They stood on either side of the Authority, but slightly behind him. They scanned the crowd mechanically, their eyes sweeping from Compound to Compound even though their heads barely moved. Polished nightsticks hung from their belts. But something was different this time. They all had rifles slung across their backs.

I glanced at David. His lips were as pale as his skin. He had noticed the guns, too.

The pledges started and we responded in unison, circle sign to forehead, pledge to protect the Earth, pledge to protect the animals and the plants, pledge to produce energy, pledge to remain loyal to the Authority, pledge to be thankful for the generosity of the Authority, for our shelter and our food and our health care. Circle sign, circle sign, circle sign until my fingers cramped.

Finally, the announcements. People began shuffling their feet, moving them a little on the dirt, and the shuffling almost sounded like sick, tired people being forced to march. Except no one was moving.

"Citizens," said the Authority Figure, "I have news. News that is not good."

The shuffling grew a little louder. Someone coughed. A collective *sshh* went through the crowd like a breeze.

"Groups outside of our Republic have been disrupting our food supply. They have vandalized the train tracks that bring our food from the farm commune. They may soon attack our farmworkers."

All around us, Citizens raised their hands to their mouths and a communal whisper of "No" spread around the stage.

This would have been Mother's cue to say, "Wars and rumors of wars." And Father would tell her to be quiet.

The Authority Figure went on. "The damage to the tracks has been significant. Until that can be repaired, your cubes will, of necessity, be smaller."

This time the communal "No" was a little louder. The Enforcers stepped forward to the edge of the platform, and the voices fell silent.

"The army has been dispatched to guard and repair the tracks. And to protect the farmworkers, if necessary."

He was silent for a moment and looked at some papers he held in his hand. "The groups outside of our Republic are envious of us. Of how much energy we produce. Of how we work together. Jealous of how we worship the Earth and all that is good on the Earth. We are stronger than them. We will destroy them. Praise be to the Republic."

"Praise be to the Republic," we said, following his lead.

"They are not like us!" he thundered, holding his clenched fists above his head. "They do not believe what we believe!" He lowered his voice, but it still sounded like thunder. "We believe that all Citizens are equal. Equally responsible for working, equally responsible for producing energy, and equally deserving to share the rewards."

I looked at his brightly painted bus-box with its high sides. Better than any bus-box used for Citizens. Their shiny boots. Did he think we were fools? Yet, around me, most Citizens were listening with rapt attention, even adoration. Yes, perhaps some of us were fools. At my side, David was staring at the ground.

The Authority Figure looked at his script again. "While the military is deployed, I call on all of you to be vigilant. Use your eyes, your ears, report anything that could be harmful to our Republic. Praise be to the Republic."

"Praise be to the Republic."

"One last announcement." He took a cloth from his pocket and wiped his forehead. "Birthrates have fallen. Again. Fewer viable new Citizens were born last quarter. We need new Citizens to grow our army and increase production of energy." He paused, scanning back and forth over the crowd, looking dark and powerful. "Reproductive pairs who do not meet expectations will have their pairings dissolved and new pairings assigned. No exceptions."

The Enforcers escorted him to his large bus-box.

The crowd of Citizens silently turned and shuffled toward their Compounds.

I stayed as long as I could, staring at the empty stage. His last words still hung heavy in the air.

No exceptions.

CHAPTER FORTY

We had no sooner entered our Living Space than the half-hour-till-dusk warning bell sounded. Time for David to strap his energy cell on his thigh; time for me to unplug my bicycle from the download bar; time to do our duties as Citizens, but no time for the promise I had made earlier to David.

I took my headscarf off and ran my fingers through my hair, putting pressure on my scalp with my fingertips. "Who are the other groups outside the Republic?" I asked. "The ones the Authority says are disrupting the food supply."

"From what Mom and Dad told me, it sounds like there were three different kinds of people when the Republic was being formed." He took off his Gatekeeper shirt and pulled a clean one on while he talked. "First, the believers, the ones who wanted everything Fabian and the Authority promised." His voice was muffled through the fabric.

He pulled this shirt down; his hair flopped across his forehead. "Second, the protesters, who didn't believe the promises and held rallies, spoke out. They were at great risk." He bent down and adjusted his shoelaces. I watched his fingers, his strong hands. "They were dealt with by force."

I thought of my aunt and my grandmother and wondered how many others had died alongside them—how many at the train depot that day, and how many across the country.

"The last group was quiet, watchful. Kept their eyes and ears open, but stayed back, sort of in the shadows, you could say. Some of them slipped away. Left their homes and disappeared before the actual relocation. They're out there, somewhere. The Authority calls them 'traitors' but we call them the 'shadow people.' " He motioned with his hand, pointing at the window slit and beyond. "Those are the ones he was talking about. I don't think they are an actual army. The Authority is always looking for them."

"Are they a threat? The ones who slipped away? Should we be afraid?"

He looked thoughtful for a minute, then answered, "I can't say for sure, but I don't think they would hurt Citizens. Their battle is with the Authority. And, I would guess, they are busy trying to survive."

"So, you really don't think they're dangerous? Those others out there? Disrupting the food supplies—"

"Emmeline, the Authority wants us to be afraid. Fear makes us more dependent on them. I worry much more about the Authority's power than I do about the shadow people."

I brushed nourishment cube crumbs off the counter into my hand and tossed them through the window slit for the birds.

"Well, what about your parents?" I asked. "I don't see them as anything like what you described."

He nodded. "You're right. I guess there was a fourth group. Like my parents. And yours. I don't know exactly how to describe that group. They really didn't believe all the grand promises but, at the same time, they didn't realize exactly what was happening. They were sort of passive nonbelievers. And then it was too late."

I wondered, if I had been an adult when this was happening, what group I would have belonged to. And, for that matter, what group did I belong to now?

David tucked his shirt into his uniform pants. "I do worry about something else that was said at the meeting."

I already knew what he was going to say. Knew that, no matter what we did, some sadness would follow. I was no longer a contained child in a contained space. Life had pushed me forward and now life was mine to deal with, any way I could.

"If we have a baby, that baby will never be ours. It will belong to the Republic, not to us. Just as you said." He shook his head and his dark hair fell across his forehead again. I brushed it back with my fingers. I liked the feel of his hair and the little wave across his forehead. "But if we don't reproduce," he went on, "then our pairing is dissolved. We'll be reassigned. No exceptions. That's what *he* said." He put his hands to his face, covering his eyes as though shutting out the thought of reassignment.

I took his hands and held them tightly in mine. "We can't let that happen," I said.

He stared at me, not blinking, not smiling, and asked again, "What choice do we have?"

What choice, indeed. It was either have a baby and give it up to the Republic, or have our pairing dissolved. Two terrible, evil options. Surely there must be a third. I would think of it. I just needed time.

"I don't know, David. I don't know what I'm saying." And, in truth, I didn't know. Who was I to say we could prevent something from happening? Who was I, a mere Citizen, to say we could change anything?

"It's too big right now to think about." I went to him and he wrapped his arms around me. They were strong across my back, his chest wide and firm against mine. My David, my fortress. "We can talk more later."

He nodded and pressed his lips to my forehead, then pulled the energy cell strap through its loop, tightening it on his upper thigh. The conversation was pushed deep into the corners of our Living Space, where it would linger in the shadows—a lurking darkness, ever present.

"I think I know something about Lizzie," I added quietly, putting on my own thigh cell.

"What?"

"A while ago, before we were paired, I saw a woman who might have been Lizzie's mother being taken away."

"What makes you think she was Lizzie's mother?"

David picked up my headscarf from the counter and helped me tie it firmly under my chin.

"She took my nourishment cube. Said it was for her children. Elizabeth and Andy. That's what she said to me. Then, when she was getting on the bus-box, she asked the one Enforcer if he was Andy and if he was taking her to Lizzie."

"At least for one brief moment she thought she had something to look forward to. How sad."

"Later I saw them beat the old lady's husband, but I don't know what happened to him after that. I never saw him again."

David pushed a stray bit of hair into place under my scarf.

"I hate hiding your hair. It's so beautiful." He opened the door but we lingered inside, still talking, reluctant to leave each other. "Are you going to tell Lizzie? About her mother, I mean."

"Should I?"

"I don't know. I can't tell you what to do. But it's interesting, isn't it, that you know something she doesn't."

The tight, tense feeling in my chest eased when he said that.

I started to remove my bicycle from the bar. David reached down and did it for me. He made it look so easy.

"Randall's still the Village Gatekeeper?"

I nodded. "Lizzie and he . . . I don't know . . . they act like they're somehow connected. Like they're a team or something." I straddled my bicycle.

"I knew him from the Gatekeeper's barracks. He was always on edge about one thing or another. That limp of his. If he were born now, since the Perfection Standards were imposed . . ."

I grabbed the handlebars. Dusk was fast approaching.

David leaned closer and whispered, his breath warm against my cheek. "I don't trust Randall. Be careful."

I dreaded leaving David. I dreaded spending the shift with Lizzie and her horrible histories. But I would see Elsa. Maybe even hold her, feed her. I could deal with Lizzie if it meant I could hold Elsa. I could deal with *anything* if I could be with Elsa.

I pushed my bicycle past the gate, past the flag, and then started to pedal toward the Village.

I pedaled in rhythm to my thoughts. El-sa, El-sa. Da-vid, Da-vid. Care-ful, care-ful.

CHAPTER FORTY-ONE

The day-shift Gatekeeper was alone when I got to the Village. He smiled at me, made a note on his clipboard, and took the handlebars of my bicycle.

"You must be Emmeline," he said. "Let me help you with this." He walked the bicycle to the security bar and fastened it. "I'm Paul." He nodded and went back to the gate. He was tall and thin, and his face had a golden tan from so much time in the sun. I wondered what group he would have belonged to in the before-time.

Lizzie and Randall came around from the corner of the building, heads tilted toward each other, talking in whispers. They looked so serious, worry creasing their foreheads. I couldn't tell if they were arguing, and I didn't want to stare. But they saw me standing by my bicycle, straightened up, and fell silent. Randall went to the gate. Lizzie went into the building and I followed her.

The corridor was shadowy and cool, filled with the smells of childhood: sweaty boys, milky babies, chalky classrooms, sanitizing solution. I could hear their sounds, too, the stirring and rustling of blankets as they struggled to fall asleep. A cough, a giggle, a whisper.

Barb gave the change-of-shift report in the dim light of the corridor. She had a toothy face, with large, uneven teeth.

"Nothing to report, really," she said. "Classroom teachers report no problems. Babies have been diapered. Some took their bottles. Some didn't. The older children did their sanitizing washings."

I wanted to ask about Baby Six—Elsa—but I couldn't let this woman know I cared. I didn't know what group she would have belonged to.

"Supplies arrived," Barb continued. "Transport team delivered them on schedule. No additional torch was received . . ."

That would be my torch. I would still be working in the dark, dependent on Lizzie.

" . . . and that is it. Nothing to report, really."

How can that be, I wondered. A whole village full of children and there was nothing to report? Some babies eat; some don't? And this is the future of the Republic?

Lizzie yawned.

"All right, then. I'm out of here," said Barb. She started to leave, then turned back. "By the way, Joan wants to see you in the morning."

"Did she say why?" I was afraid to look at Lizzie.

"No. But she sounded serious. Maybe even angry. So I don't know." She shrugged. "Hard to say. But you better follow directions." And with that, she was gone.

Lizzie was rigid, tense, and silent. She started pulling diapers off the shelf. She handed some to me and I followed her down the hall to the nursery. It was a repeat of the night before: the restocking of diapers and then back for the nourishment bottles, the silent propping of bottles without touching the babies or making soothing sounds. In the darkness, the babies were merely little mounds covered with blankets, small and curled.

We moved like two pale shadows through the nursery—me trailing behind her like an afterthought, her cutting our path with the torch. Lizzie, her thick body blocking my view, propped Elsa's bottle last.

We went back to the supply closet and Lizzie sat down heavily in the rocking chair. She may have been silent, but her body language was speaking loudly. My job was to figure out what it was saying, and how it could help me.

I sat on the stool again, with my knees against my chin and my back against the wall. Such a cold, hard wall, it sucked the warmth out of a person. Lizzie switched off her torch. She and I alone in the dark, with only the sounds of our breathing and the creak of the rocker in that tiny room. The longer we sat, the louder the sounds seemed. Sounds trying to fill a vacuum. Louder and louder. All the while, I only wanted to hold Elsa. It was up to me to break this vacuum.

"When do you think my torch will arrive?" I asked her.

"Beats me," she said. "That's up to Joan. Used to be my job to order supplies. I was good at it, too. Now it's her job. Seems to me, seeing as how she's David's mother and you and David are paired, well, I'd have thought she'd take better care of you."

I listened for the message beneath the words. What was important to her? Being good at something? Yes, that was it. Last night she told me she made good grades. And she was proud of her system for waking up the older children. Tonight she told me she was good at ordering supplies.

"Oh, Lizzie," I said quickly, "I thought you knew. She told me in my interview that her job, under the rules of the Authority, was to treat all the workers equally. Said she had to follow the rules."

The rocking slowed and I heard Lizzie shifting in her chair.

"She said that?"

"Yes. She also said you were a very good Caretaker, and said that I would learn a lot from you."

The rocking stopped.

"She did?"

"Of course. And she was right. Just look at what you taught me last night. I mean, about the history of the Republic. Things no one ever taught me before."

"I was lucky to be raised in the Village, where I could learn stuff. Lucky that I wasn't quite four when they made the announcement. You weren't so lucky. And I got really good grades in history."

There it was again.

As timidly as I could, I asked, "If I don't know about something, well, I can ask you, can't I?"

"Depends."

"Depends on what?" I asked.

"Depends on what you ask me."

We were both quiet for a few minutes. I stood up just to get away from the cold wall. I would have to figure out what I was allowed to ask.

"Where are you going?" she asked.

"Nowhere. Just standing up."

"You could go hold Baby Six."

I took a sharp, startled breath.

"You can go hold Baby Six," she repeated, "while I go outside to talk to Randall."

She turned on her torch and handed it to me.

"You can use this while I'm gone."

My hands were shaking as I slipped the band over my headscarf. Was this a trick?

"One more thing," she said. "You can ask questions. But don't ask about Randall."

She left the supply cupboard and I heard her footsteps fading down the corridor.

I had a torch and it seemed as though Lizzie and I had a deal.

She went to Randall. I went to Elsa.

CHAPTER FORTY-TWO

Elsa was asleep on her belly, her knees pulled under her, covers off, her little bottom a raised round mound. Her nourishment bottle was almost empty, and had become wedged between the rail and the mat so that the nipple stuck up like a pink thumb. She was making sucking motions, her round cheek and rosebud lips moving in rhythm. Standing there watching her in the light of my torch, I was filled with warmth, but at the same time, an overwhelming sense of responsibility. She was mine, not the Republic's.

As gently as I could, sliding my hands under her face and belly, I lifted her. She was light and warm, like sunshine in my arms, and I cradled her in my left arm. With my right hand, I stroked her cheek. She stirred and opened her eyes for a second, a bubble of nourishment on her lip, then she curled against me.

How much time did I have before Lizzie returned? I listened but heard no footsteps. Somewhere a child whimpered. Carrying Elsa, I went to the corridor and listened. There it was again, a whimper. I followed the sound into the boys' sleeping room, my torch moving across the beds, one by one, until it lit on one boy, sitting on the edge of his sleeping mat. He was bent over with his hands on his belly and he looked frightened.

I walked to his side and slid my torch away from the center of my forehead so the light wouldn't shine in his eyes. "Are you okay? What do you need?" I whispered to him.

He looked down at the floor as though he was ashamed. "I need to go to the washing-up area."

"All right, then, I'll walk you over. I have my light to show the way."

He shook his head.

"Why not? It's okay. Come on." Our whispers hadn't wakened Elsa. All around us were little snoring noises, like punctuation marks in the dark.

"I can't," he said. "It's not washing-up time. I'll get in trouble."

Washing-up time? At first, I didn't understand. And then, in an instant, I remembered.

The rules. Always, the rules.

"Well, I give you permission to use the washing-up area now. I'll walk over with you."

"You can do that?" He looked at me, his eyes wide and unblinking. "You can break a rule?"

I smiled and looked down at Elsa. "Yes," I said. "Sometimes."

When he was finished, I walked with him back to his bed. I smoothed the blanket over him, rough fabric on young skin. Before he turned on his side, he motioned for me to bend closer. I leaned over and Elsa squirmed in my arms.

"Will you be here tomorrow night?" he asked.

"I hope so," I said.

"So do I," he said, and he curled up on his side, making his body as small as he could against whatever dark things might be lurking about in the Children's Village. I waited till he was asleep, then walked through the girls' sleeping area.

This is where Elsa would sleep in about three and a half years. Here, one among many. She would be no better than anyone else. No extra hugs, no extra anything. And if she woke in the middle of the night, needing to use the washing-up area, would the Caretaker on duty be willing to break a rule? I walked past one row of beds, then back past another, my torch sliding across the children. Each was lit up for a second before I passed on to the next child. All the girls appeared to be asleep. Still holding Elsa in my left arm, I used my right hand to pull the blankets up around those who had kicked theirs off. Tucked them around shoulders, frail and thin. The air from the window slit had grown cool and damp with the green-brown smell of wet grass and leaves.

I wondered why Lizzie had gone outside to talk to Randall. Had they been arguing? It certainly had looked that way. Questions, answers—eventually, piece by piece, I would learn whatever I needed to keep Elsa safe. Information was my currency.

I carried her, still asleep, into the supply cupboard, and sat in the rocking chair. We rocked with a slow, even rhythm, and I murmured against her soft, silky hair: *"Ladybug, ladybug, fly away home. Your house is on fire and your children will burn."* I felt strands of her hair, fine as cobwebs, lift against my lips. I could feel her, smell her, hear her, and, in the bouncing light of the torch, see her.

Lizzie came into the supply cupboard, startling me.

"My chair," she said. "My torch." Her voice had a rasp to it, harsh, demanding.

I stood and slipped the torch off my head. My headscarf tangled in the strap. Lizzie reached out and grabbed it roughly. The torch fell against Elsa's forehead with a smacking sound. Elsa startled, stiffened, her back arched against my arm, and she cried, a shrill, sharp sound that pierced the shadows of the supply cupboard and echoed down the corridor. I propped her against my shoulder and patted her back with a sense of urgency, a rapid pat, pat, pat as though that would somehow take away the surprise and the pain of the injury. "It's okay," I murmured. "It's okay. I'm here." But even as I tried to soothe her, I felt a fierce rage.

"What's wrong with you?" I asked. Lizzie didn't seem to hear Elsa crying. She just sat, still as a stone, holding the tangled torch and headscarf on her lap.

She glanced up at me, then looked away. "Nothing," she muttered. "Nothing you need to know about." She fumbled with the headscarf, pulling it free from the torch, and handed it to me. Elsa's crying was easing into little hiccups. I moved her to my other shoulder, felt the roundness of her head against the curve of my neck.

"Try me. I'm a good listener." I heard Randall's uneven footsteps outside as he made rounds. Lizzie cocked her head toward the sound, then sighed.

"It's time to diaper and feed." She led the way for me to take Elsa back to her crib, I put my headscarf back on, then together we went through the robotic routine of diapering babies and propping bottles. Finally, we finished and went back to the supply cupboard. She sat quietly, frowning as if thinking hard thoughts. Without looking at me, she started to talk.

"So, you're a good listener?"

"Yes."

"Sometimes a person just needs to talk," she said. "Know what I mean?"

"Yes."

She rocked, her hands gripping the arms of the chair so tightly her knuckles were turning white.

"It's Randall. I'm worried about him."

I waited.

"You can't say a word about this. Hear me?"

I nodded.

"Say it. Say you won't tell anyone."

"I won't tell anyone."

"Not Joan. Not anyone."

"Not Joan. Not anyone." This was eerily like repeating the pledges to the Authority.

"He heard something about the Perfection Standards."

I'd heard that phrase before but wanted to know what Lizzie knew. I gave her my best blank stare.

"You don't know Perfection Standards? Typical home-raised—otherwise you'd know. Makes me tired having to explain everything."

"I'm sorry. But no one else explains as well as you do." Her face softened into a shy smile.

"Okay, then. Here's the history; you'll understand. The Authority, right from the start, knew that resources could not be wasted. The old government wasted everything. Under them, the Earth got sick and the people suffered."

The light in the corridor was changing from night darkness to a lighter shade of gray. She wouldn't have much more time to talk.

"Then what?"

"Well, with the Authority in charge, things got better. You know. Like if someone is sick, really sick, and needs a lot of care, well, that turns out to be a waste of resources. They call it futility."

The word illuminated a memory—George's first wife. Mother had told me about her. Renal failure, a case of futility. And they took her away.

"And then when someone isn't productive enough, doesn't produce enough energy or isn't able to do their assigned job then, well, that's just not fair to everyone else. I mean, we all have to give and receive equally."

My poor mother, curled on her mat, not walking her board. And they took her away.

"Babies can't give equally," Lizzie said. "Everybody knows that. But they're kind of like investments. When they grow up, they can start producing energy. But . . ." She paused, as though trying to think of the best way to explain something. "The Authority soon realized that some babies would never be productive enough to warrant that investment. So they announced the Perfection Standards."

Another memory illuminated: that young couple in Living Space 2, and the absence of their baby creating a void between them.

"Randall's worried. He heard some rumors. I tell him rumors are like poison. Once they get into your head you can't get them out. He shouldn't listen. But he does. He thinks the Authority might expand the Standards. And he's got that limp." Her voice was low as if she was talking to herself, worrying out loud. "It's getting worse. He thinks he needs a special shoe."

"You really care about Randall, don't you?"

"Of course I do. He's my brother."

"I thought your brother's name was Andy," I blurted out.

She stood up, pushing the rocking chair back. It hit a shelf and some nourishment bottles crashed to the floor.

"How do you know that? Are you some kind of a spy? I should have known better than to talk to you. I should have listened to Randall."

I took a step back from her, and held one hand up in front of me. "I'm not a spy. I promise. I heard your mother say that. I heard your mother tell someone . . ." I paused, took a breath, and went on. "I heard her say her children were named Elizabeth and Andy."

"When? When did you hear my mother talk?" She was leaning forward, her face red with anger, her neck muscles tight like thick ropes.

I took another step back. "It was just a coincidence," I said, and told her what I remembered from that day. The nourishment cube, the Gatekeeper, the Enforcers. Her mother saying she needed the food for her children, her Lizzie and her Andy.

"Andy," she said, relaxing a little, not leaning forward as much. "Randall was ten years older than me. Everyone called him Randy but I couldn't pronounce it right. It always sounded like I was saying Andy.

It turned into his nickname." She stared at me for a minute, shaking her head. "You're saying my mother was stealing? Stealing food for me and Randall?"

I nodded.

"Then what happened?"

"They took her away."

CHAPTER FORTY-THREE

Dawn broke. I left Lizzie looking pale as a moth's wing as I walked down the long dim corridor to Joan's office. Her door was open and light from her window slit cast a narrow beam on the corridor floor. I could hear Lizzie saying a toneless good-bye to the day shift. Through the window slit I saw Randall by the gate, scuffing the dirt with the shoe of his crippled foot, sending up little puffs of dust. The day-shift Gatekeeper stood tall and smiling next to Randall, who looked sullen, like a cloud ready to rain down great drops of bad news. Above him, the flags hung limp. As I watched, Randall's dark mood seemed to transfer onto the day-shift Gatekeeper—his head started to hang low and his shoulders slumped.

Joan was at her desk. She looked up at me and smiled. I couldn't help but feel love for her. How much David looked like her, with the same full lips and smooth, dark eyebrows. She gazed past me into the hallway, and a spark of fear flashed in her eyes.

"I expected you to report in yesterday morning," she said in a loud, firm voice. "You were instructed to do so, and you disobeyed that directive." She put her finger to her lips, pointed toward her door.

I didn't know what to say. I glanced in the direction she was point-ing and there, in that narrow beam of light, I saw the shadow of a per-son standing outside the door, blocking the light of the main entrance. The shadow didn't move. Lurking.

"Well, answer me," Joan said, glancing toward the shadow, then looked at me with a stern expression. "You disobeyed. That's against the rules."

I flailed around in my mind, searching for the right answer. Should I be giving an answer to Joan or to the shadow? I said the only thing I could think of.

"I don't know what to say." The words came out in a jumble, hardly a space between any of them.

"Speak up. I can't hear you."

"I don't know what to say."

Joan shifted in her chair and turned slightly toward the doorway.

"Well, let me ask you this. Maybe you can handle a simple yes-or-no question."

The shadow didn't move at all. I could make out the shape of a headscarf at its top.

"Did you follow Lizzie's instructions? Did she teach you?"

The shadow seemed to lean forward a bit, as if to hear my answer. Joan nodded her head up and down, giving me a silent instruction.

"Oh, yes. She taught me so much both nights." I paused and could hear the footsteps of children far away at the other end of the corridor. Maybe they were going for breakfast cubes. Or maybe to class to learn to recite Praise Be's. "She's a very good teacher. She knows so much about how to care for the children."

The shadow seemed to straighten up and puff out wider.

"I know how good Lizzie is," Joan said, but she had a tightness around her mouth, the opposite of a smile. "That's why I assigned you to work with her. It's important that you learn as much as you can from her."

The shadow got shorter and slipped away. And then, a few seconds later, through Joan's window slit, I saw Lizzie and Randall walking along the fence toward their barracks. They looked like they were having the same serious conversation they had been having at the beginning of our shift. Randall walked as though his foot hurt, lifting it and putting it back down slowly, gingerly. Joan saw me looking through the slit and turned toward it.

"Quite a pair, aren't they?" She looked at me, eyebrows raised.

I nodded. I didn't know if there might be other shadows lurking about. Lizzie had said trust was important. And she was right, at least on that point.

"Lizzie only knows what she learned at the Village. That's it. Randall had a fairly normal childhood but then was ripped away from his family and had to grow up in the barracks. He has no understanding of the history of the Republic, no understanding at all. And he trusts no one." She stood up and went to the window slit, watching Lizzie and Randall disappear around the corner of the fence. "And he's different. He has that limp. In the Republic, it's not good to be different."

She came back to her desk. "Why didn't you stop in yesterday morning, Emmeline?" she said. "I was worried."

I didn't want to tell her the real reason so I changed the subject. "Lizzie told me about . . ." I twisted my hands in my lap. "She told me about people being shot. Back then. My aunt. My grandmother. That was the first time"—I felt my throat tighten, my voice tremble—"the very first time anyone told me."

She started to say she was sorry, but I couldn't hear her anymore. There was a roaring in my head, like bees swarming, drowning out her words. In a heartbeat, in the space of a breath, I had erupted into hot rage. Out-of-control rage. I thought I could hear the gunshots, the people screaming, dying. I thought I could see people herded into trains.

"What did you do, Joan? What did John do? You let it happen. If there had been more who protested, more who tried . . ." My voice rose, then I couldn't go on. My throat was as tight as if a headscarf had been tied around it. No air could get in; no air could get out.

Joan came around her desk toward me. I held out my hands in a feeble attempt to keep her away. If she touched me, I would fracture into a million little pebbles. But she kept coming, and soon I was sobbing in her arms and she was patting my back with one hand and smoothing my hair away from my forehead with the other. My headscarf had slipped down and was hanging around my throat.

Joan adjusted it, pulling it into position and retying it. Her hands were cool and smooth on my skin.

"I'm sorry, Emmeline," she whispered into my ear. I felt a cool wetness on my cheek. Tears. Joan was crying, too, and her tears were mixed with mine.

"I'm so sorry," she said again. "We were wrong."

I pulled away from her and looked at her face. Strands of her hair had slipped out of her headscarf and were curled wetly against her cheeks. How gray her hair was. Her eyelids were heavy and swollen. For the first time I saw her as more than just kind. She was defeated, too.

"We were wrong. We didn't see what the others saw. We trusted too much."

There was that word again.

Trust.

"Who did you trust? What did you trust?"

She went back to her desk and sat with her head in her hands, her long fingers that were so much like David's making tight little circles around her temples. It was quiet in the corridor. The children must all be in their assigned spaces. I wondered about the little boy, the one who wanted to use the washing-up area in the middle of the night. How was he now? How awful it must have been for him, awake in the dark, needing something personal, private, that was not allowed by the rules. And the sad tone of his voice when he said he wanted me to come back tonight.

Finally, Joan looked at me and started to talk.

"We trusted—John and me, and a lot of others—the way things were. We couldn't imagine anyone being able to change that."

"And what does that mean? The way things were?"

"Our life. Our family. Working. We had our farm. If we worked hard, we would succeed. Same as your parents. A work ethic. Individuals could work and be rewarded for their effort. Not just farmers. Teachers. Factory workers. Anybody. Some were more successful than others, of course."

She tapped her fingertips on her desktop.

"We didn't mind the work. Really. Maybe others did, I guess. When the Authority came in to power they said we didn't have to work so hard. Said everyone could share everything. We would all be equal. They called it the Fare Well plan. They spoke so eloquently. And they made the changes so quickly! Seemed like almost overnight."

She fiddled with a clipboard on her desk, looked at some of the numbers written down. "The babies aren't thriving," she said. "My job is to find out why—or, to find some reason other than the obvious." Her shoulders were pulled up tense and tight, almost touching her ears under her headscarf.

She was changing the subject, but I needed to know more, to understand. And I couldn't stay too long here in her office. Others would notice. I had to get her back on the before-time, how it had all happened.

"And this work ethic. How did it change? Under the Authority, I mean."

"Think about it," she said. "Your energy board, for example. Say you are young, full of energy, strong. You want to walk your board past the peg. Gain credits. Maybe get an extra cube. What happens? What happens when you walk your board?"

I had never thought about it like that. When my energy board meter pegged, that was it. I didn't have to give any more. I would get my cube once it pegged. When it pegged, I stopped.

As though she could read my mind, she said, "When it pegs, you stop. Right?"

I nodded.

"So nobody can be better than anyone else. No one can be stronger or smarter. No one can be outstanding. All Citizens are equal. All get the same rewards. There are three ways a Citizen can be different," she said, leaning forward and staring at me so hard I felt hypnotized. "One way a Citizen can be different is by not meeting the Standards set by the Authority. Another way they can be different is by needing more than other Citizens. Giving less or needing more. Both of those ways are punishable."

"And the third?"

She glanced through the doorway to the corridor before she spoke.

"The third way is for one Citizen to report another to the Authority. Report them for acting or talking against the Authority. The reporting Citizen is rewarded."

"And the other Citizen? The one who is reported?"

"No one ever sees them again." She said this in a flat voice, as though the words were heavy and hard coming out of her mouth.

She picked up the clipboard again. "The babies aren't thriving," she said. "They're not gaining weight. I'm frightened about this. I was assigned here to fix this problem."

"They're not being loved," I said.

"What?"

"They're not being loved."

I leaned forward, waiting for her to respond.

She raised her eyebrows, adjusted her headscarf. "Some things I can't mandate. Like love."

Maybe not, I thought. Not when you look and sound so hopeless.

"You can mandate rules. Make the workers follow the rules. You're in charge."

"I've tried. Believe me, I've tried." She shifted in her chair. "Truth is, Emmeline, there are more of them than there are of me. The workers are *organized* against me."

"What happens next? If you can't fix this? If the babies don't thrive?"

"I'm afraid, Emmeline, the Authority will close this Children's Village and relocate it to another Planned Community."

Relocate Elsa? I could feel the little hairs on my arms stand up and something like a round stone rolling and shivering down my spine.

"They would do that?"

"My dear Emmeline," she said with a shallow sigh, her face in her hands, "you know so little. So very little. And we are running out of time."

CHAPTER FORTY-FOUR

The day-shift Gatekeeper didn't help me with my energy bicycle as he had the day before. Something had changed.

"Long meeting?" he asked. "Not much fun, those meetings."

I shrugged. "Just some extra training."

I fumbled with the rusty chain locks on the bicycle bar; he didn't offer to help. His eyes never met mine, but twitched back and forth as though looking for someone or something.

"Did you miss your egg last night?"

The question jarred me, but he was right: Randall had not brought any eggs, not even one for Lizzie.

"I forgot all about it until just now. I guess Randall forgot."

He lowered his voice to a whisper. "No one forgot. There aren't going to be any more eggs for the night shift." He cocked his head to one side, birdlike, and his eyes searched the shadows again. "It's the new rule."

I adjusted my headscarf and set off. I wondered what else the Gate-keeper had learned that made him act so differently today. And was it only yesterday that I had learned so much? Had I changed just as he had? Of course I had. Knowledge changed us all.

The ride home was easier. My leg muscles had already adjusted from walking on the energy board to pedaling an energy bicycle over a rutted path. David stood in the doorway of our space, looking worried. Probably remembering how upset and angry I had been the morning before. To me, it seemed as if a whole year had passed between the two mornings, and far longer than that since David and I had paired.

Seeing him standing in the doorway, the sun on his face and the concern in his eyes, made me want him again—just the tangled two of us. My mind, my body, my spirit needed him. I *needed* David. I had to somehow make compartments in my head, to lock away all the evil and hateful things I had learned, just for a while. Long enough to catch my breath and gain my balance.

"How was your shift?" he asked. I didn't answer. Instead I put my fingers on his lips to silence him. He pushed my headscarf back and ran his fingers through my hair, then closed his eyes and leaned against me, passive and still. We went to his sleeping mat, and lay with each other, taking comfort in our nearness. Later we slept deeply, drained of all emotion and energy.

When I opened my eyes, David was sitting cross-legged on the mat, holding our cubes, frowning.

"It's started already," he said.

"What? What's started?"

"The cubes. Look how much smaller they are."

I took mine from his hand. They had always been exactly three inches on all sides, the width of four of my fingers pressed together. Now they were maybe a half-inch smaller in all directions. They didn't feel as dense, either—they were already crumbling inside the wrapper.

"They stopped the eggs, too," he said. "At first I thought it was just a mistake that I didn't get one. Then I realized they don't make mistakes."

"That's what the day-shift Gatekeeper at the Village said. And he seemed all fidgety."

David nibbled on his cube and grimaced. "Doesn't have any flavor at all. They left something out."

He walked across our space and put his cube on the counter. "We need to talk," he said. His voice held the dark timbre of faraway thunder. He came and sat next to me on the mat, his arms dangled across his knees and his back curved. I ran my hand down his back and felt the knobby little bumps of his spine.

"I'm listening," I said, and he glanced sideways at me but didn't smile. His face looked like stone.

"Something's going on," he said, "and I'm not sure exactly what it is. The day-shift Gatekeeper said all the guys in the barracks are wired up. Tense. Nobody's sharing much information."

"Tense?"

"You know. Ready to pick a fight. No one knows who's telling the truth. No one knows who to trust."

Trust, again.

"Telling the truth about what?"

"That's just it. Nobody's talking except a little comment here or there. Nothing makes sense. None of us know anything. And that makes everybody nervous. The cubes are smaller. There are no more eggs for the night shift. There's less for everybody. Those are facts. There's not a good explanation for the shortages, just rumors. Facts beat rumors every time."

"Well at the Social Update Meeting the Authority said—"

"The Authority *said*. They *said* what? Armies? Armies tearing up the railroad tracks? Armies interrupting the food supply? I don't believe them. I don't believe there are foreign armies out there. Only the Authority has an army. Not a very good one, either. Fewer and fewer strong men."

"If you don't believe it's an army out there, then who are they?"

He looked away and was quiet for what seemed like an eternity. Finally, he answered. "They're the ones who slipped away."

"The shadow people?"

"Yes. The ones who slipped away before the relocations. They knew they'd die if they fought. So they slipped away. And they're out there now, trying to survive. Maybe somehow they're interrupting the food supply."

The shadow people. Out there, free, on the other side of the fence.

"Keep talking," I said.

"All I know for sure is that there are no more eggs and smaller cubes. But I just have a feeling. I don't know how to explain it, but it's not good. Everyone just seems nervous. Change of shift last night, the day-shift Gatekeeper asked me what I knew." I'd never seen him look so worried. "I told him I didn't know what he was talking about and he just clammed up."

David went into the washing-up area and I could hear him splashing sanitizing solution on his face. I could smell the sweet-sour lemony tang of it. I wondered what a real lemon looked like. I knew what apples looked like. *Apple, Apple, A-A-A.* Mother would sing to me, pointing to the picture of the apple. There were no pictures of lemons.

He came back to the mat and sat the same way, hunched with his arms dangling over his bent knees.

"Then this morning when he came to relieve me, he asked me if I had heard anything about the Perfection Standards."

"Oh, wait," I said, pulling the sheet up over my shoulders and across my chest. The fabric was coarse and rough but had the warm smell of David on it. "Lizzie said Randall was worried about an increase in the Perfection Standards. He needs a special shoe—"

David interrupted me. "Special shoe! When has anybody gotten anything different or better than anyone else?"

"Well, I got you."

That made him smile, a real smile, and he touched the tip of my nose with his finger. But he quickly became serious again, the smile gone and the two little ridges between his eyebrows back.

"So, your turn," he said. "How was your shift? What about Randall and his special shoe? Did you talk to my mother?"

"Well, to use your words, everyone was wired up. Tense. Randall looked like his foot hurt when he walked. He talked for a long time to the day-shift Gatekeeper. Whatever he was saying, I don't know, but the day-shift guy was in a bad mood after that. Lizzie and Randall were, I think, arguing but I couldn't hear them. They spent a long time outside."

"And my mother?"

"She seemed, oh, I don't know. Distracted. The babies aren't thriving. That bothers her." I didn't have the courage to tell him what else she'd said.

"Did you get to hold Elsa?"

"Yes, I did." My arms came together like a cradle and rocked back and forth. "She liked it. And she took her whole nourishment bottle."

"So, what aren't you telling me?" he asked, staring straight at me, not blinking. Somehow he knew it would be something bad. "What aren't you telling me about my mother?"

And then I realized that I was doing the very thing that had been done to me: withholding information to protect someone. But that only makes them more vulnerable. No matter how terrible the information, I had to share it with David.

"Your mother said . . ." I swallowed hard, then plunged forward. "She said the babies aren't thriving and the Authority might relocate the Children's Village to another Community." I put my hands over my face, pushing away the image of an empty crib and an empty Village.

"Oh, sweet Jesus," David said.

Sweet Jesus? Mother used to say that. *Oh, sweet Jesus.*

But Father made her stop.

Oh, sweet Jesus.

CHAPTER FORTY-FIVE

The Gatekeeper was making rounds. His nightstick rattled as it bumped against the cell strap on his thigh. I knew all the sounds of our community. The irregular flapping of the Compound flag when the wind blew. The rattle of the wooden sides of the bus-box combined with the undercurrent of grunting from the Transport Team as they passed by. The screech of the nourishment box lid when it was opened and the pinging rat-a-tat when rain hit the lid. Bees on the flowers on the other side of the fence. But the best sound, the very best sound, was the twittering of birds.

David moved from his mat to mine when he heard the Gatekeeper coming closer. His eyes grew large when he sat down, and he gave me a puzzled look as he ran his hand along the far corner of the mat. He must have felt one of Mother's treasures, but now was not a good time to explain. I was trying to keep the sheet over my shoulders and chest, clutching it with my fist, and I put my finger to my lips.

The Gatekeeper tapped at our door. A tentative sound.

I slipped into the washing-up area quickly before David opened the door. I had to get dressed. I wouldn't be issued a clean uniform for two more days now, since the change. This one was wrinkled but it was full of Elsa's smell, her white milkiness. I turned my head to my shoulder, closed my eyes, and breathed deeply. Birdsong and baby smells.

The Gatekeeper didn't seem to notice me when I came out of the washing-up area but just nodded his head sideways at David, a tilt of the head that seemed to be asking David to come outside.

They didn't talk long, and I couldn't hear anything but the soft murmurs of their voices. Soon David came back into our space.

"What is it?" I asked. "What's going on?"

He leaned against the counter with his arms crossed over his chest. "He heard that another rail line was ripped up. Might just be a rumor. He didn't know where."

"By the shadow people?"

He nodded.

"How many other communities like ours are out there?"

"Nobody knows for sure. There's no way to communicate from one community to another. I kind of think they're all along the coast, from what Dad said."

I thought for a minute, sorting out what I knew, putting pieces together as best as I could.

"Okay, then. Let me show you something. Something that I have."

I flipped Mother's old sleeping mat over, exposing the rip and reaching inside, feeling with my fingers until I found the map. I pulled it out and carefully unfolded it. It had torn a little along the fold lines but, other than that, it was usable. David stood statue-still, staring at the map as though it were a poisonous spider.

"Mother kept this. There are other things in there, too, but first I want to study this. Your dad said our before-time farms were here." I pointed to Kansas.

"My dad knows about this map?"

"Yes. I showed it to him. Before we were paired. He studied it, then brought it back."

"You never told me about it." I could hear the hurt in his voice and I could see it on his face. "You said no secrets, but you kept this a secret."

"David, we've been paired just three days. I wasn't hiding this from you." I touched the side of his face. "There's been a lot of stuff going on. You know that." *Stuff.* There had to be a better word than *stuff* to describe everything I had heard and felt in the last three days, but I just couldn't think of the right one. "I'm showing you now and there are other things in the mat I'll show you later. But, right now, let's look at this." I ran my finger along the East Coast, with its deep blue border of ocean. "If the Planned Communities are along the coast, and the farm co-op is somewhere over here"—I pointed to a place farther west, right at the edge of a mountain—"well, how do the railroad lines get from there to here?"

He looked closer at the map, studying it. "I know there's a depot some distance out from our Community. Far enough that we never hear the train. Dad told me that's where they offload the supplies onto bus-boxes. The Transport Team never actually sees the train. The supplies are just there, waiting. They haul them back to the storage area next to the Gatekeepers' barracks and unload them. Then it's up to the Gatekeepers of each Compound to pass them out."

"So you don't know if there is a separate track to each community, like this?" I used my finger to indicate straight lines from the middle of the map to different spots along the coast. "Or if somehow there are other tracks that connect one track to another?" I traced more lines, like arcs, that crossed over the straight-line tracks. How much I wanted a crayon and piece of paper like I had as a child. Imaginary lines weren't enough.

David looked puzzled. I wasn't explaining this very well.

"Come over here," I said, and went to the counter. I wet my finger as he had done when he showed me how the Compounds lined up along the fence. I made a wavy line, like the coast. "Here's the coast."

Then some wet dots, up and down the coast. "Planned Communities."

Another dot, bigger, farther away, and to the left. "Farm commune."

Wetting my finger again, I drew straight track lines spoking out from the farm commune to the communities. "Train tracks."

Next, some curved lines across all of the straight lines. "Connecting tracks." I turned to him. "What do you think?"

"I don't know," he said, still looking puzzled. "Could be either way. What does it matter?"

"It matters," I said, "because if there are only straight-line tracks to each community, then, well, any community that had its track ripped up would be without food."

I thought for a minute, picturing what it must look like out there. Out there with the tracks and the shadow people. And I thought of our smaller cubes. The pieces came together in my head.

"We're missing something here," I said. "Forget all of this about the tracks."

"You're confusing me," David said.

"If the tracks were destroyed, we'd get *no* food. Instead, we're getting *less* food. Smaller cubes. No eggs. But *why* are we getting less?"

And then, I knew. The answer was so logical.

I ran my hand over the counter, blurring the dots and lines.

David was frowning, concentrating.

"We are getting less food," I told him, "because there *is* less food. Something's happening to the food or someone is taking the food. The farm co-op is failing. Just like the Children's Village is failing. Just like the broken wheel on the bus-box that never gets fixed. The Authorities are lying about the tracks."

He looked at me in a new way, proud but very serious. "Perfect sense. It's not the tracks. It's not the tracks at all."

CHAPTER FORTY-SIX

I folded the map more easily this time and slipped it back into Mother's mat.

"What else is in there?" David asked.

I pulled the mat as far into the corner as I could, where it would be hard to see from the window slit or the doorway if somebody was standing at either of those places. David knelt down beside me as I retrieved Mother's treasures, one by one.

First the recipe cards. He glanced through them, flipping them from one hand to another, reading them, his lips moving as his eyes scanned the cards.

"I remember some of these foods. Look, this one is in my mother's handwriting. The bread pudding. With raisins. They must have exchanged recipes. And this one. Pumpkin pie. We always had that at Thanksgiving."

"Thanksgiving?"

"You don't remember?"

I shook my head no.

"Thanksgiving. It had a certain smell about it. Mom would start cooking early in the morning. I would wake up and hear her in the kitchen and smell the onions and celery and melted butter for the stuffing. It was incredible." He had a look of sadness about him. His mind was in a place I had never been.

He looked through the recipe cards one more time, then held his hand out for another item. I gave him the gold thing.

"It's an old gold coin. I thought the Authority had confiscated all of these." He rubbed his thumb over it, then handed it back, and I put it deep into the mat.

Next: *The Little Prince*. He opened it and the picture I had drawn fell onto his lap. He picked it up and smiled.

"You drew this?"

I nodded.

"I'm glad she saved it." He touched the drawing to his lips.

Then the New Testament. He held it gently and was quiet for a long minute.

"You Mother took a great risk, saving this." He handed it back to me. "We have to do everything we can to protect this."

I slid it back into the far corner of the mat.

Then the picture of Mother and me. He stared at it for the longest time, then looked at me. "I remember that day. At your house. I remember it so well." Tears welled in his eyes and rolled down his cheeks.

I moved closer to him, my shoulder against his. "Why are you crying?"

He brushed his cheeks with his forearm and looked at me.

"Look at you. Look at you in this picture. So happy. And now you don't even remember Thanksgiving."

He didn't have to explain.

"Someday you can tell me more about Thanksgiving." I took the picture from him and put it back in the mat.

The box of safety matches was next, and then the knife. He paled when he saw it and a little ridge of sweat formed above his lip.

"What was she thinking?" he said, more to himself than me. He opened and closed it easily, as though he had done so many times before. Quickly he shoved it back into the mat, into the deepest corner, glancing at the window slit and doorway as he did.

Then I flipped the mat, torn side down, slid it back where it belonged, and pulled the fabric tight and smooth. No bulges—good enough.

"So," I said, "why do you think she saved what she did?"

"I guess you save what you think you're going to lose. I saved salt."

"You did?" I remembered the little salt packets he used to give me with the eggs.

"I once heard a rumor they were going to outlaw salt. You know how those rumors are. Nine times out of ten, before you know it, it's a fact. Things can happen so fast. So I saw this little box of salt packets in the storage area. You know, where the Gatekeepers pick up the cubes for their Compounds. I grabbed a handful. Guess where I hid them? In my sleeping mat." He smiled at me. "You liked it on your eggs, didn't you?"

I nodded. But I was still thinking about what he said.

You save what you think you're going to lose.

CHAPTER FORTY-SEVEN

I was running late for work. The sun had slipped down far enough that dusk would soon become dark. I bicycled as fast as I could, my heart racing and my headscarf fluttering around my face, sliding across my eyes. If I was late, I could be reported. I didn't want to even think about that. The Children's Village was directly across from my Compound, separated by the great area of land the Authority used for Social Update Meetings. I could get to the Village in no time if I were allowed to cross that area. But all Citizens had to stay on the path. All activities, all movement, had to be tracked.

Finally, out of breath and sweating, I was at the Village.

Oddly, there was no one at the gate. I had never seen a gate or a Compound without a Gatekeeper. It was quiet, too, as though the dusk muzzled the birds and breezes.

I kept looking over my shoulder as I fastened my energy bicycle to the download bar. Still no Gatekeeper. I was completely alone in the yard, though somebody surely had to be watching me.

Indeed, Lizzie leaned against the doorway. On the other side of it was the day-shift Caretaker. They stood with their arms crossed over their chests, thin-lipped and narrow-eyed, like angry sentries. They didn't speak, but fumbled with their torches. Still, there was no torch for me, it seemed.

"You're late," Lizzie said. Her voice was thick. The other one made a little snorting sound.

"Where's Randall?" I asked, moving closer.

Again the snorting sound.

"Where's Randall, she wants to know. Where's Randall, as if she doesn't know," Lizzie said, looking at me. "You tell *me*. Where's Randall?" Her words ran together.

"I don't know. That's why I asked." Something was wrong, seriously wrong. I heard a child coughing inside, a faraway sound.

"Shouldn't we go in? Shouldn't we get a change-of-shift report?" I asked. "And what about a Gatekeeper? We need a Gatekeeper."

They looked at each other. Lizzie's face was shiny and unwashed, her eyelids swollen over bloodshot eyes. The other's face was without emotion, flat and hard. Her headscarf was loosely tied and tangled with the straps of her torch.

"Is there a flag we can hang?" I asked. "Something to let the Authority know?"

"Let the Authority know what?" Lizzie gave a little laugh, as though I had said something that was just short of funny. "There is no Gatekeeper tonight. Haven't you done enough with the Authority?" Lizzie asked. "Who is going to see a flag? Hang a hundred flags. No one to see them. Fool. No one to see anything here tonight."

She was right. It was just me, the two of them, and the children. Again, the faraway cough, and now the cry of an infant. I wanted to go inside. What if that was Elsa crying? I took a step toward the doorway.

The day-shift Caretaker turned to Lizzie. "I'm going to the barracks. See what I can find out. If I hear anything, I'll be back. I'll try to get some more . . . you know." She ignored me and walked away.

I followed Lizzie into the building and down the hall. She walked in an unsteady way, her hand against the wall, as though afraid she might fall. Her narrow torch beam lit a path straight ahead but made the corners seem darker.

At the supply cupboard, she turned on me. I had to take a step back.

"You!" she said. "You did it, didn't you?"

I took another step back.

She raised her arm as though to slap me. She swung but missed. Off balance, she started to stumble but caught herself on the door frame.

"What's wrong with you?" I asked. "Where's Randall? What's that smell?"

"You're what's wrong. You. They took Randall away. You must have said something, done something. You're not one of us. Not Village-raised."

"What do you mean, they took Randall away. Why? Where did they take him?"

"You should know. You must have said something. Reported something."

"Why would I do that?

Another baby was crying. A shrill, sharp sound like a knife in the air.

"Citizens who report others get rewarded. What's your reward, huh?"

She stumbled into the rocking chair.

I said firmly, "I reported no one. I said nothing. What's that smell?"

"Shut up, special friend of Joan. Special home-raised know-nothing. Just shut up."

She was making no sense, answering no questions. I took a deep breath. I had to take care of Elsa. Elsa and the other children.

"Lizzie, I'm very sorry about Randall. We have to work now, or it will only get worse," I said.

"Go ahead. Do useless stuff, waste-of-time stuff. Those babies won't even be here tomorrow." She pulled a container of something out of her pocket, took the lid off, and took a drink of whatever it was. There was that smell again.

"What do you mean?"

"Just what I said. They won't be here tomorrow." She drank some more from the container and dragged the back of her hand over her mouth. "Relocating them. All of them. That's what I heard." She stumbled into the supply cupboard and sat down hard on the rocking chair.

My heart jumped. "Relocating them? Relocating them?" The words came out as though squeezed through thick fog. I felt like my throat was swelling shut.

"That's what I heard." She paused and looked up at me. "Baby Six goes, too. Or maybe they'll just recycle her. You never know."

The container she was holding fell and the little liquid that was left spilled onto the floor, making a dark puddle. Lizzie leaned over, ran her fingers across the puddle, and then licked them.

"They can't do that!"

"Fool," she said. "You are so stupid." She leaned her head back against the rocking chair and closed her eyes. "They can do whatever they want. Have whatever they want. Don't you get it yet?"

She hiccupped and her eyes seemed to wander, searching the darkness beyond. "But I got some. Some of their good stuff. Don't ask me how." She hiccupped.

The day-shift Caretaker appeared out of the darkness of the corridor. She bent over and tried to whisper to Lizzie but her words had no softness to them and came out at near full volume. "I got some more. Here." She held a container out to Lizzie, then took another one out of her pocket, sat down against the wall, and started to drink from it.

I pushed past them and started taking diapers and nourishment bottles from the shelves. I left with my arms full of supplies but then realized I had no light, no torch. I let the diapers fall to the floor, piling up over my shoes and ankles, and clutched the nourishment bottles tight to my chest.

A baby began to cry.

I cried, too.

Oh, dear sweet Jesus. Save what you think you are going to lose.

CHAPTER FORTY-EIGHT

I don't know how long I stood there, leaning against the cold wall. A heartbeat, a minute, a lifetime? Time froze in the dark.

The baby still whimpered, a bleating, breathless cry, wearing out and then stopping. But there was another sound now. Raspy, rattling, coming from the supply cupboard.

I forced myself to look inside. Two torches fanned light onto the gray ceiling and cast shadows over Lizzie and the other. I could see them both asleep, snoring. Lizzie sprawled in the rocker, legs spread, head thrown back, mouth open. The other one lay curled on her side, one hand holding an empty container.

All I thought about in that moment were Elsa and David. If the children were relocated, would I be relocated, too, or would I be separated from Elsa forever? What about David? I had no answers, only questions.

I touched Lizzie's shoulder. She didn't wake. I took the empty container out of the other's hand. I held it near my nose, trying to figure out what had been in it. It smelled like Lizzie's breath had smelled earlier.

With shaking hands, I slid Lizzie's torch slowly over her headscarf. I barely breathed. My pulse throbbed in my temples. My heart was beating so loudly that I thought it would wake her up. I put on the torch. *I had light.* Quickly I gathered up the diapers from the corridor floor and hurried to the nursery, my arms full of everything I needed to keep busy, keep moving, *to think.*

I moved from crib to crib, removing wet diapers, cleaning tiny round bottoms, propping bottles into small, searching mouths. I kissed the head of each baby and swaddled their blankets around their shoulders and legs. I was aware of feeling as if I were saying good-bye to each precious bundle. Elsa was last so I could hold her as she ate. Awake and watchful when I approached, she reached one tiny hand up to me, fingers spread like pink flower petals, the most beautiful hand I had ever seen. A shiver ran across my skin, along my arms and legs and the back of my neck with urgency I had never felt before. *They would not take Elsa.*

Holding her, I quickly made rounds through the other sleeping rooms. First the girls. All was quiet. The smell of girls. Sanitizing solution. Quietness. Then the boys. One was awake, sitting up, facing the doorway, small and still. It was the same child I had taken to the washing-up area the night before.

"Hello," he whispered. What a shy, wistful voice he had. "You came back."

"Yes, I did."

"I was hoping you would." He sat still as a statue, hands folded in his lap.

I knelt beside him. He looked at Elsa and smiled.

"She's pretty."

I nodded.

"You're the only one I ever knew that could break a rule."

We were both quiet for a moment. Elsa sucked on her bottle, her eyes wide open, looking at me.

He spoke again in that same shy voice. "You must be really important."

"Why?"

"Like I said, you broke a rule."

"Maybe I broke the rule for you because *you're* important."

"Me?" he said.

"Yes, you." He smiled shyly when I said that.

He reminded me of the drawings in *The Little Prince,* with his pale hair spiky and on end. Elsa had finished her bottle and was asleep in my arms. I reached out and ran my hand over his hair, smoothing it down.

"Is it true?" he asked at last.

"Is what true?"

"Moving. The big boys were whispering about it. Is it true?"

"I don't know."

"Are they moving you with us?" he asked.

"I don't know," I answered.

He lay down on his side and pulled his blanket up over himself. So vulnerable but still able to hope. I tucked the blanket tightly over his shoulders. He kept his eyes closed.

Even the children had heard the rumor. Even they had accepted it as inevitable. I tightened my arms around Elsa.

Back at the supply cupboard, Lizzie and her friend still slept. I grabbed an extra diaper and I walked to the main doorway. Still no Gatekeeper. I let my torch sweep across the packed earth, over the toy energy boards lined up along the fence, the pink and blue entry flags, the bus-boxes parked along the fence and straight ahead toward the Central Stage. I stood with Elsa in this doorway of the Village. Somewhere across the dark open space was David.

I had to get to him. The corridor behind me was empty. No one could see me, no one could stop me from passing through the door. Holding Elsa, I stepped out of the Village and breathed in the night air.

I wouldn't follow the required path. If I did, Gatekeepers along the way would stop me. No, not the required path. Not this time. I would walk straight across, through the forbidden area, past the pompous stage of the Authority, straight to David.

I switched off my torch. Walking quickly, Elsa against my shoulder, my hand against her soft, silky hair, I took a step, and another, and another, each one taking me farther from the Village, deeper into the blackness and closer to David.

The stars sparkled. So many! What giant hand had scattered them across the sky? The moon, low on the horizon, was a curved sliver like the tip of a fingernail; a small cloud slid over it, then out of sight.

The stage loomed ahead, forbidding. Grass had grown close to it, where Citizens weren't permitted to stand. I walked on the grass and felt the cool dampness through my shoes and around my ankles. How slippery and soft it felt!

Then, the largeness of the stage, now to my right, overwhelmed me. Might there be guards protecting it? I walked faster, expecting any moment to be stopped by an Enforcer in a black uniform.

Finally, when the stage was well behind me, it no longer looked as threatening.

In no time I could see the lean silhouette of David at the gate to our Compound. He peered my way, alert, vigilant, doing his job.

"It's me," I whispered.

It's me. It's me. It's me. A rhythm to my footsteps and my words.

"Emmeline?"

And then I was in his arms, arms big enough to hold both Elsa and me.

"What are you doing? Why are you here? Is this Elsa?"

His questions were rapid, words against my cheek, against my ear.

With blinding clarity I knew what I was doing, why I had broken so many rules. If there was to be a relocation, it would be *my* relocation, *my* choice.

"We have to be like them, the ones who slipped away."

He looked at me, his eyes wide with alarm. He stepped backward.

"What are you thinking? How can we do that? Do you have any idea what the Authority might—"

"What they might do? I know what they're going to do, what they can do, what they've already done. I know they're going to relocate the children. And I'm done living like this. Done."

As he shook his head, his hair fell across his forehead. Elsa stirred in my arms, her knees pushed against my chest, and I shifted her to my other shoulder. I felt wet drool against my neck.

"We don't have much time. We have to hurry."

He looked at me with that same alarm. "What about Randall? And Lizzie?"

"They took him away." Like he was a nothing. Like he didn't even matter. "And Lizzie and the other Caretaker drank something and now they're asleep."

"Drank something?" He shook his head again.

"It smelled funny. It made them sleep really deeply. We have to go before they wake up."

I ran toward our Living Space. Elsa bounced lightly against my shoulder.

I heard a thud and knew, without looking, that David had thrown his clipboard to the ground. All that mattered was escaping with Elsa and taking what Mother had saved. She had hidden these things for a reason. She may have hoped to use them again, make those recipes, display that picture of us, read the New Testament, follow the map to a new home, all of it. The coin. The knife. The matches. I don't know. It only mattered that she saved them. She couldn't use them anymore, but I could.

David followed me into our space. He was breathing hard. I could almost smell his fear.

I told him: "Take everything out of the mat. Put everything in this diaper and roll it up. We're taking all of it with us."

"Taking it where?"

"The other side of the fence. Come on. Hurry up."

"Emmeline, are you crazy? What about all of the Gatekeepers? What about Lizzie and the Authority?"

"I told you . . ." I paused and could feel my jaw tightening, my shoulders squaring. "There is no Gatekeeper. Not tonight. Randall's gone. We'll stay off the path and cut through the stage area. If Lizzie's awake, we'll deal with her. End of discussion."

"But—"

"Please, David. Please. Take everything out of the mat." How could I make him see how important it was for us to leave?

He began to reach into the mat but I could see his hands were shaking. I paced back and forth, willing him to hurry, hurry.

He stopped and stood up straight, rigid.

"We're not doing this," he said.

"Yes, we are!"

"Stop and think, Emmeline! We don't know what's out there. We only know what's here. We know how to deal with what's here. It might be dangerous out there. Animals. Shadow people. And how will we eat? Where will we sleep? Besides, we'll never get away with it."

Elsa stirred, opened her eyes briefly, and then closed them again.

I told him, "There is nothing out there more dangerous than what's in here. This is the most dangerous, evil place on Earth. Mother is gone. And Father and George? If they're dead, it's because of the Republic and their monitoring and eavesdropping and rewards for reporting on our own neighbors. And if they're alive and have somehow gotten away from here then they can help us." My brain ran with the thought, however improbable it may have been. "Maybe that's it, David, maybe Father telling me about those grain bags and an escape plan was a hint, a clue! What if they are out there, just waiting for all of us to join them?"

David just shook his head. He looked sad for me. "It wasn't a clue, Emmeline. Your Father and George had no grand plan and they aren't out there living with the shadow people and waiting for us. They're dead. Deep inside you know that."

His words hurt, but at that moment I realized that David had fallen into his own trap. In trying to temper my hope he'd inadvertently admitted that life had absolutely no value to the Authorities. If they could kill my Father and George without so much as a second thought, then what else were they capable of?

I saw this realization flicker in David's eyes—the understanding that he had lost his own argument. He put his hands on both sides of my face, forcing me to look at him.

"I won't let you do this."

"You can't stop me."

I pulled away from his touch. His hands fell to his sides.

"David, I have to do this. I have to save Elsa. If they take her, my life is over anyway. Don't you see that I have nothing to lose? Don't you understand?"

He stood immobile, pale as I had ever seen him. "What about my parents? You'd leave them behind? You'd ask me to leave them behind?"

"They'll figure it out. They can follow later if they want—your father will obviously know how we got out. We can't save everybody. But I *will* save Elsa. We're wasting time. Finish with the mat. Come on!"

He stood, rigid, tense.

"David, don't make me choose. Please, don't make me choose."

"Choose?"

"I'm leaving with Elsa. If you don't come . . . I'll still . . ."

"You would leave me?" His voice was trembling.

"Yes, David, I would. I don't want to, but I would. Don't make me."

Elsa whimpered softly but didn't awaken.

I went to the mat and, still holding Elsa, started to reach into it with my free hand. David watched as I struggled with it. Then he stepped forward, and put his foot on it. I pushed on his leg and he took a step backward, away from me. Away from Elsa.

"David, please." I didn't want to waste another minute, another second. I didn't know how much time we had. What if Lizzie or the other one woke up? What if a replacement Gatekeeper was sent to the Village? "Please, David, please let me get the things out of the mat."

"No."

"Let. Me. Empty. The. Mat."

He shook his head and stared at me, unblinking. I took a step toward him and touched his lips, stroked his cheek with one finger, traced his face like it was a memory, a thing of value. He blinked. A simple, slow blink, like a deep breath, like a sigh. He took my hand to his lips and kissed it slowly before letting it fall to my side. Then he began to empty the mat: the coin, the knife, the map, the picture, *The Little Prince*, the New Testament, the recipe cards, the feather, and finally the matches. I handed him the extra diaper. He put everything on it and tied it into a lumpy ball, then asked me one more time if I was sure.

I nodded and walked outside, rolling the empty mat and tucking it under my free arm.

He followed.

Dear sweet Jesus, he followed.

CHAPTER FORTY-NINE

In darkness, with only the light of the moon and the stars, we went across the common ground of our Compound, through the gate and across the energy bicycle path. Our footsteps sounded so loud in the silence of the night. Who might hear us?

We scurried across the forbidden Social Update Meeting area, toward the stage. That dreadful, hateful stage. I knew it needed to be destroyed. I flipped the empty mat against a wooden support post.

David instinctively knew what to do next. He untied the diaper and took out the matches. "A diversion." When he said that, I felt closer to him than ever. We were in this together. He struck the match and the small flame revealed firmness in his face. He put the match to my mat and the fire grew, merging with the mat and dancing in the night air.

We moved on, faster and faster, closer to the Village. Elsa began to cry and I put my finger in her mouth so she could suck on it. That seemed to calm her and the warmth of her mouth on my finger tightened our bond and firmed my resolve. Nothing was going to stop me.

We paused at the entrance to the Village. Behind us, the fire at the stage was crackling and growing larger by the second. The corridor ahead of us was empty except for the ghostly light of the other torch still visible from the supply cupboard. I led the way with David close behind me. We paused at the door to the cupboard. They were still asleep and it didn't look like they had moved at all since I'd left. I handed David the torch off my head and stepped into the cupboard. I wanted to get the other torch.

I moved toward the other Caretaker. Lizzie moaned and leaned her head over the side of her chair. I froze, half bent over, my heart racing, watching her, waiting. But she didn't wake up. Slowly, ever so slowly and carefully, I slipped the other torch off the head of the Caretaker sprawled on the floor and put it on my head.

I took some nourishment bottles off the shelf and passed them to David, along with a few diapers, and left the supply cupboard. He shoved them into the diaper with Mother's treasures. Instead of turning back to the entrance, I went toward the sleeping rooms of the older children. There was one more thing I had to do. No time to discuss it with David, no time to explain. A child had hope. I couldn't destroy that.

David followed me to the bedside of the boy who reminded me of the Little Prince. He woke and sat up as soon as I touched his shoulder. He smiled when he saw it was me. David was looking at the little boy, puzzled, and then back at me.

"This young man is my friend," I whispered to David. And then I leaned down to the child. "Would you like to break a rule with me?"

He nodded, eyes wide.

"Quick," I said, "put on your shoes." He bent immediately and slipped his shoes on. So quickly he obeyed! Without hesitation, fully trusting. Trusting me because I had broken a rule for him. I laid his thin blanket across his back and shoulders.

"Carry your clothes and follow me," I said, and he did. Soon we were all outside. I turned off my torch. The fire at the stage was growing. Flames stretched into the air and embers licked the sky. The smell of smoke was strong. I thought I heard someone shout. We had to hurry.

The moon, that great curved sliver, hung low in the sky. We ran to the parked bus-boxes and stopped, looking for the hole. David pointed. There it was. Our gateway to freedom. It was smaller than I had expected, but John had somehow managed to slip through it. So would we.

The stage was fully engulfed in flames now; I heard more shouting and the sound of people running. Gunfire. Why gunfire? From where? By whom?

In an instant, David stepped in front of me and pushed the diaper holding our supplies and Mother's treasures through the hole to the other side. Then he motioned for the boy to go through.

He did as he was asked, slipping through the hole quickly and easily. David took Elsa from my arms and passed her gently through to the boy. He held her carefully, as though he understood that he was holding the entire reason we were attempting this escape, breaking all of these rules.

David motioned with his head for me to go through next. I wanted to be last, to be the final sentry, but David motioned firmly again, so I knelt and began to crawl through the hole. The sharp, cold metal fence ripped my clothes and scratched my skin. The cement base was hard and rough against my knees and elbows. The smell of dirt was close to my face, filling my nose. Crawling like this, moving forward inch by inch, felt like a dangerous eternity. The boy reached down and patted my head, urging me forward. Finally I was through and the boy handed Elsa back to me. I held her close and took the boy's small hand in mine as we looked back across the fence to David.

He was standing with his back to us watching the chaos, watching the fire, which was now casting an eerie orange glow against the black sky. "David," I called out, my voice revealing more urgency than I had intended. "It's your turn. C'mon!"

But he didn't move. He just watched the fire. Crackling. Dancing. Growing.

"David, please!"

It felt like an eternity that we all stood there. Me, Elsa, and the boy on one side of the fence, David on the other. We were probably ten feet apart, but it might as well have been miles. My heart dropped in my chest. I had been prepared to do this alone, but once David had agreed to come I'd realized just how foolish I'd been. How would I survive without him? How would I keep Elsa alive? But now, with him ignoring my cries and time running short, I forgot about the relief I'd felt and instead focused on the one thing, the *only* thing, that really mattered: I had to get Elsa away from this place. Far, far away. And now, with or without David, that is exactly what I intended to do.

I clenched the boy's hand and turned to leave.

"Wait! I'm coming!" It was David. Sweet Jesus, David was coming.

As he crawled through the fence I thought I saw something, someone, beyond it, near the bus-box that obscured the hole. A day-shift Transport Team member? The day-shift Gatekeeper starting duty early, sent by the Authority since Randall was absent? Then more shadows of people running, shouting.

The fire was spreading closer to the Children's Village.

All of those children at risk. The babies. I knew right away that I would have to go back. I had to save more. If I didn't, then I would be no better than the Republic. But I *was* better. I respected life; they destroyed it.

David was now on the other side with me, the boy, and Elsa. They were safe. I had to go back. I turned to David. "Take Elsa and the boy and run." Then I got down on my hands and knees and began to crawl.

David pulled on my shirt so hard it stopped me dead in my tracks.

"What are you doing? Are you crazy?"

"The fire," I gasped, looking up at him. "It's moving toward the Village. Toward the children. And it's my fault. My fault and I have to save them."

"No, it's not. Stand over here and look. That's why I stayed on the other side for so long—I had to make sure my eyes weren't playing tricks on me." He took several steps to the right. "Look closely. It's not moving toward the Village. It's moving toward the Authority's supply building."

I got up and went to where he was standing. I squinted and stared, concentrating hard. He was right. The stage was fully engulfed in flames and soon the supply building would be as well. The children were safe for now and, with all the chaos we'd created, no relocations could possibly occur in the near future. We had bought them time. It wasn't much, but it was a start. I leaned against him in gratitude for a brief second.

But now we had to move. We had to get as far away as we could, as fast as possible. The ground sloped away from the fence, a long, slippery hill sloping down into shadows. At the bottom of the hill, far below, the sound of running water, splashing over rocks.

David started down the slope but stopped after just a couple of steps. With one hand, he took the energy cell off his thigh and tossed it into the darkness.

"Take yours off, too," he whispered. "They might be able to track us if we have these on."

I threw mine and heard it hit against a rock. Something scurried through the underbrush.

Together, David carrying Elsa and the few supplies, me holding the hand of the boy, we ran down the hill toward the sound of the water.

Around us, trees. Great, majestic trees. Leaves rustling. Soft, soothing sounds.

Tall grass, touching our ankles. Damp and cool. Unfamiliar.

Behind us, fire and chaos.

Ahead, freedom. And the unknown.

AFTERWORD

Effective execution of Agenda 21 will require a profound re-orientation of all human society, unlike anything the world has ever experienced—a major shift in the priorities of both governments and individuals and an unprecedented redeployment of human and financial resources. This shift will demand that a concern for the environmental consequences of every human action be integrated into individual and collective decision-making at every level.

—DAN SITARZ, *Agenda 21:*
The Earth Summit Strategy to Save Our Planet

The reason that this novel exists is because of a woman named Harriet Parke. Harriet paid attention to the radio and television segments that I, and others, did on Agenda 21 and could not believe what she was hearing. Alarmed, she started to do her own homework, her own research. When it became clear to her that Agenda 21 was as evil as she'd feared, she knew she had to do something about it.

So she started to write a novel.

Harriet, like so many members of my team, is a "storyteller." She realizes that many people don't want to read a long story in a newspaper or watch a two-hour documentary about a topic like Agenda 21—but they might read a novel. And, if they do, then maybe they'll read this, the Afterword, and learn a whole bunch of new facts. And, if they do that, then maybe they'll make the same decision as Harriet and help spread the word.

If your eyes are now open to the reality of Agenda 21, then I ask that you please pass this story on to a friend—maybe even someone who would otherwise never read about some obscure UN program. Don't tell them about this Afterword. Don't even tell them that Agenda 21 is a real initiative. Let them go through the discovery process themselves. In other words, lead them to water, but don't force them to drink.

If you help activate your friends, family, and neighbors, then I have complete confidence that they will not only educate themselves, but they will, in turn, activate others. Once that happens, we will have a force that is far stronger than any international bureaucracy.

THE BASICS

Now, let me state the obvious: this novel is fiction.

But let me also state the controversial: it may not stay that way. In fact, if the United Nations, in partnership with radical environmental activists and naïve local governments, get their way, then the themes explored in this novel may start to look very familiar, very quickly.

Before all of the accusations begin about me promoting some kind of conspiracy theory, let me be clear: this novel plays out the ideas and concepts contained in the real Agenda 21 to their extreme ends. I do not really believe, for example, that people will be reciting pledges in honor of squirrels any time soon—but when animals and nature are valued more highly than human life, all kinds of absurd things begin to enter the realm of possibility.

Like most plans with evil, world-changing intentions, Agenda 21 doesn't exactly advertise itself that way. Those who are behind it know that they would never get the support they need if they simply stated their true objectives. So instead they couch their ideas in all kinds of flowery language that makes it sound as though their only goal is to leave a better, healthier planet to our children—and who doesn't want that?

Once you cut through all of the propaganda, you're left with nine basic principles that Agenda 21 intends to pursue:

1. Move citizens off private land and into high-density urban housing.
2. Create vast wilderness spaces inhabited by large carnivores.
3. Reduce traffic congestion and slash fuel use by eliminating cars and creating "walkable" cities.
4. Support chosen private businesses with public funds to be used for "sustainable development."
5. Make policy decisions that favor the greater good over individuals.
6. Drastically reduce the use of power, water, and anything that creates "carbon pollution."
7. Use bureaucracies to make sweeping decisions outside of democratic processes.
8. Increase taxes, fees, and regulations.
9. Implement policies meant to incentivize a reduced population (i.e., "one-child" type laws).

But before we get to the endgame, let's go back to the beginning. To understand where Agenda 21 is meant to take us, you first have to understand where it came from and who is behind it.

THE HISTORY

In 1972, Stockholm, Sweden, hosted the original UN Earth Summit. This summit resulted in the "Stockholm Declaration," an action plan containing twenty-six principles and seven proclamations—the final of which made it clear exactly how large and transformative their plan really was:

> [*Achieving our environmental goals*] *will demand the acceptance of responsibility by citizens and communities and by enterprises and institutions at every level, all sharing equitably in common efforts.*

Words like "equitably" should always ring alarm bells, even when the underlying idea—protecting the environment—is hard to argue with. Remember, when we're talking about the world, a country like the United States is in the top 1 percent. "Equitable" means something very different to developing countries than it does to Americans. Whereas we might believe that increasing our gas mileage, using dimmer switches on our lights, or programming our thermostats is doing our fair share, the rest of the world strongly disagrees. They don't want our conservation, they want our money. Our technology. Our land and our natural resources.

To be completely fair, I've read the full Stockholm Declaration and it's fairly benign. Sure, it's filled with a lot of socialist nonsense, but given the summits and declarations that would soon follow, Stockholm turned out to be the least of our worries. But, of course, progressives think long-term. They understand that major change can come in small increments. To them Stockholm wasn't a failure at all, it was just a starting point.

The following year, the United Nations Environment Programme (UNEP) met for the first time and developed a lengthy document that advanced the findings of the Stockholm Declaration. Most notable about this meeting was that it was led by Maurice Strong, UNEP's Executive Director. Strong, a multi-billionaire who has taken up environmentalism as a cause, once warned: "Frankly, we may get to the point where the only way of saving the world will be for industrial civilization to collapse."

Maurice Strong surfaces many times along the road to Agenda 21, but that quote is really the key to understanding everything that Agenda 21 and its affiliated plans are all about. In fact, if more environmentalists admitted, as Strong did, that the only way to achieve their goals would be for the industrialized world to collapse, we might finally be able to have an honest debate.

In 1976, the United Nations Conference on Human Settlements met in Vancouver and determined that humans were simply producing too many children. "World population growth trends," they wrote, "indicate that numbers of mankind in the next 25 years would double . . ."

The fact that they were incredibly wrong (world population actually increased 48 percent over the next 25 years) is really beside the point. Those projections were never about accuracy, they were about fearmongering. If people believed that they were destroying the Earth because they were having too many children then they might be willing to do something drastic about it.

The "Vancouver Declaration" released at this conference focused on what has become a familiar theme to environmentalists: justice and equity.

> Recognizing also that the establishment of a just and equitable world economic order through necessary changes in the areas of international trade, monetary systems, industrialization, transfer of resources, transfer of technology, and the consumption of world resources, is essential for socio-economic development and improvement of human settlement, particularly in developing countries.

So now we understand that "equitable" is not just an empty catchphrase; it means that the wealthy countries (i.e., America) must do whatever is necessary, including transferring their resources (i.e., money and technology) to developing countries. More important, the Vancouver Declaration was one of the first to really target land use as a cause of the world's problems. In fact, a close reading of the following excerpt makes it clear that this was more of a declaration of war on capitalism than it was a declaration about human settlements:

> [Land] cannot be treated as an ordinary asset, controlled by individuals and subject to pressures and inefficiencies of the market. Private land ownership is also a principal instrument of accumulation and concentration of wealth and therefore contributes to social injustice.

Inefficiencies of the market. Concentration of wealth. Social injustice. These terms should send shivers down the spines of anyone who cares about capitalism and true individual freedoms.

Unfortunately, these anti–free market, anti-American views of the world continued to grow and fester over the years after Vancouver. There were more meetings, more summits, more declarations and action plans and pronouncements—but all of it was really just a preview of the main event: the 1992 Earth Summit in Rio de Janeiro, the very place where Agenda 21 was first unveiled.

WHAT IS AGENDA 21?

Let's start with the way the UN itself defines the Agenda 21 program right on the cover of the publication:

> Agenda 21 is a comprehensive plan of action to be taken globally, nationally and locally by organizations of the United Nations System, Governments, and Major Groups in every area in which human impacts on the environment.

That last part is essential to understand as a strong case can be made that almost *everything* a human being does impacts the environment in some way. From what we eat, to how we get around, to where and how we build our homes, to how we heat and cool those homes—it all "impacts on the environment" in some way.

And that's exactly the way the UN wants it.

At its core, Agenda 21 is all about control. Control over land, natural resources and, ultimately, entire populations. It seeks to control the air (via regulations on carbon emissions), ground (via regulations on "sustainable development") and sea (via environmental regulations). In that way, Agenda 21 is a lot like a war plan. As all good generals know, once you take control of the skies and seas, the ground war can begin—and there is very little that the enemy can do to stop you.

Unsurprisingly, the language and objectives of Agenda 21 are the culmination of every Marxist/progressive fantasy developed over the last hundred years. From education to transportation to food and water, there is literally no area of life that Agenda 21 does not attempt to regulate and control in some way.

Agenda 21 also does not try to hide the fact that achieving its goals will require major sacrifice. In fact, all of that talk about "equality" from previous meetings gave way to a very stark assessment that was included right in the Agenda 21 Preamble:

The developmental and environmental objectives of Agenda 21 will require a substantial flow of new and additional financial resources to developing countries in order to cover the incremental costs for the actions they have to undertake to deal with global environmental problems and to accelerate sustainable development.

It's clear from that excerpt that the true objectives of this plan is to redistribute wealth on a global scale. If developing countries are going to receive a "substantial flow" of resources then it's natural to ask where those resources are coming from. The answer, of course, is that the money will come from the developed world—America, Canada, Western Europe, Australia, etc. And while those behind the scheme claim that these resources will help bring the Third World up to the First, the reality is that it is designed to work the other way around.

APPLYING AGENDA 21

Agenda 21 is extraordinarily wide-ranging and complex and therefore should be read in its entirety to fully understand how it attempts to reach into nearly every part of life. However, there are a couple of key areas worth pointing out here because they specifically relate to our story.

Land Use

The idea that private land ownership is evil and results in concentration of wealth and social injustice has not gone away. In fact, it is a central theme of Agenda 21 (although the planners smartened up and were not quite as overt about it as they were in the Vancouver Declaration).

> *Objective 7.28. The objective is to provide for the land requirements of human settlement development through environmentally sound physical planning and land use so as to ensure access to land to all households and, where appropriate, the encouragement of communally and collectively owned and managed land. Particular attention should be paid to the needs of women and indigenous people for economic and cultural reasons.*

In other words, everyone must have access to land. That, of course, is impossible, which is why the phrase "communally and collectively owned and managed" is used. According to those behind the plan, land, as a "finite resource," cannot be left in the hands of private owners.

In our story this idea is played out to its extreme end. If there are no private owners of land, or if large populations must be moved so that land can be reforested or rewilded,* then where does everyone go?

Sustainable Development

Another key concept of Agenda 21 is something called "sustainable development." Like most progressive ideas, it sounds nice, but the concept is pretty insidious. The idea is that Mother Earth will only have a chance to survive if we shrink the economy, put land into government hands, and highly regulate the use of our natural resources.

"Our Common Future," a report issued by the UN World Commission on Environment and Development in 1987, five years before the Rio conference, attempted to define the term:

Sustainable development is development that meets the needs of the present without compromising the ability of future generations to meet their own needs.

If you think about that definition, you start to realize something: if you can't do anything that might "compromise" the ability of future generations to meet their (unknown) needs, then there's really not all that much you can do. Want to cut down some trees to clear the way for a new home? Sorry, those trees help cleanse the air of CO_2—future generations need them. Want to put up a fence around your yard? Sorry, that might prevent the free flow of wild animals and have unintended consequences on the future. Want to keep your home at 68

---

* Rewilding may sound like a made-up term, but unfortunately it's very real. The idea is to return large tracts (millions of acres) of North American land to pristine condition and restore predator habitats like those with wolves, jaguars, black bears, and coyotes. The Rewilding Institute (rewilding.org) is a major developer and promoter of these ideas.

degrees in the summer? Sorry, that will pull too much energy from the grid. And on and on it goes.

There are countless ways in which the government could implement the objectives of Agenda 21. Some, like "rewilding," would be far too radical to implement all at once, so the objectives are instead broken down into smaller goals. Once public opinion on a matter has softened enough (see my book *The Overton Window* for a primer on exactly how that happens), the government is able to push farther and introduce new ideas that, years earlier, would've immediately been rejected by the public.

In the meantime there are plenty of smaller ways that government and associated private groups can impact our lives and promote the core objectives of Agenda 21. For example, so-called smart meters are being installed at an increasing rate in homes around the country. These meters give the government—and, in some cases, non-elected bureaucrats—the power to monitor individual home energy usage. If the grid is under duress then officials can change a home's temperature, or shut off their air-conditioning altogether. *It's all for the greater good.*

Regulation is another area where the government can easily begin to promote some of these objectives on a national level. C.A.F.E. fuel-economy standards, for example, force automakers to change the way they build cars. Price, features, and sometimes even safety (cars with better fuel economies are often lighter and don't hold up as well in major accidents) are all sacrificed in order to meet a standard that may or may not have a meaningful impact on anything. Ford Motor Co., for example, is switching from steel to aluminum next year in its F-150 tucks, despite knowing that lives will likely be sacrificed to fuel-economy standards.

The Precautionary Approach

This principle can essentially be defined as "guilty until proven innocent." More specifically, it means that in a situation where something might cause harm to a person or to the environment, the burden of proof is on the person contemplating the action.

This approach is referenced in Agenda 21, Chapter 22.5(c), in regard to the storage or disposal of radioactive waste near the "marine environment":

> [M]aking, in the process of consideration, appropriate use of the concept of the precautionary approach . . .

Why is this a big deal? Because it turns our entire legal system on its head in favor of an international standard. Think about it like this: if you dump a cup of coffee into the ocean and our government were to prosecute you, they would have to prove, using scientific evidence, that you had willfully damaged the environment. However, using the precautionary approach, it would be up to you to prove that no damage was possible.

By turning the entire system around, all kinds of prosecutions that may have been too expensive or complex to consider now become possible. Companies, and possibly individuals, around the world would be forced to spend time and money defending any action that some national or international regulator took issue with. It's a profound change that would have far-reaching impacts on nearly every area of life, not the least of which being that all of the expenses related to these prosecutions would have to be passed along to consumers.

ALL POLITICS ARE LOCAL

One of the things that really differentiates Agenda 21 from other major environmental programs is its heavy reliance on local governments. One of the primary groups facilitating this effort is the International Council of Local Environmental Initiatives (ICLEI).

Headquartered in Bonn, Germany, ICLEI offers training and support to municipalities that want to enact Agenda 21's programs. This large but relatively unknown network has managed to raise private funds (George Soros's Open Society Institute gave ICLEI a $2.1 million grant in 1997) and has subsequently embedded itself into cities and counties all across the country.

According to the ICLEI USA website:

ICLEI USA was launched in 1995 and has grown from a handful of local governments participating in a pilot project to a solid network of more than 600 cities, towns and counties actively striving to achieve tangible reductions in greenhouse gas emissions and create more sustainable communities. ICLEI USA is the domestic leader on climate protection and adaptation, and sustainable development at the local government level.

Austin, Texas, is one of the hundreds of local governments that have seemingly been mesmerized by ICLEI propaganda. Prior to a council vote on some Agenda 21–friendly initiatives, John Bush, a member of "Texans for Accountable Government" (TAG), delivered a succinct presentation on ICLEI and Agenda 21 that attempted to appeal to a traditional Texas value—land ownership. He said:

Among the stated objectives of Agenda 21 is the "re-wilding of America" under the Wildlands Project. This project would remove human beings from over half of the land in America and deem these areas core wilderness zones. Regardless of where your family farm once was, human beings will not be allowed to set foot in these areas. There would also be highly controlled and monitored buffer zones around these areas where travel would be severely limited.

Bush's short argument against the proposal was immediately followed by a unanimous 7–0 vote adopting the plans.

And Austin is far from the only city to have gone down this path.

Syracuse, New York, is laying out Agenda 21 plans to control local property and make urban "sprawl" a thing of the past through the "Onondaga County Sustainable Development Plan." Much of the language used in this plan (i.e., "Sustainable development today pays dividends well into the future") seemingly comes directly from Agenda 21.

Despite being functionally bankrupt, California refuses to drop plans for an enormously expensive high-speed-rail project. This project is the brainchild of a sustainable growth group called America 2050. (One contributor to America 2050 is the "Surdna Foundation," a group whose "[E]nvironmental work is grounded in an understanding of the interplay between the environment, the economy, and social equity."

California is also hoping to make detached housing a thing of the past. A recent piece in the *Wall Street Journal* ("California Declares War on Suburbia") explained how the Golden State wants half its population to move into Agenda 21–style high-density urban housing:

> *The Southern California Association of Governments wants to require more than one-half of the new housing in Los Angeles County and five other Southern California counties to be concentrated in dense, so-called transit villages, with much of it at an even higher 30 or more units per acre . . . The campaign against suburbia is the result of laws passed in 2006 (the Global Warming Solutions Act) to reduce greenhouse gas emissions and in 2008 (the Sustainable Communities and Climate Protection Act) on urban planning. The latter law, as the* Los Angeles Times *aptly characterized it, was intended to "control suburban sprawl, build homes closer to downtown and reduce commuter driving, thus decreasing climate-changing greenhouse gas emissions." In short, to discourage automobile use.*

A similar issue is discussed by Stanley Kurtz in his book *Spreading the Wealth: How Obama Is Robbing the Suburbs to Pay for the Cities*:

President Obama is not a fan of America's suburbs. Indeed, he intends to abolish them . . . Obama is a longtime supporter of "regionalism," the idea that the suburbs should be folded into the cities, merging schools, housing, transportation, and above all taxation. To this end, the president has already put programs in place designed to push the country toward a sweeping social transformation in a possible second term. The goal: income equalization via a massive redistribution of suburban tax money to the cities.

The city of Hailey, Idaho, has set a goal of reducing their carbon emissions by 50 percent (over 2001 levels) by the year 2050. Would the mayor of small-town Hailey (population 7,960) ever have considered slashing his town's economy in half without the guidance and advocacy of the ICLEI? How many other small towns are considering the same kind of drastic actions?

Speaking of carbon emissions, Barack Obama has targeted the coal industry with Agenda 21–style regulations. Prior to the 2008 election he gave an interview to the *San Francisco Chronicle* detailing his overall approach to coal:

So if somebody wants to build a coal-powered plant, they can; it's just that it will bankrupt them because they're going to be charged a huge sum for all that greenhouse gas that's being emitted. . . .

Phil Kerpin recently wrote a story for FoxNews.com that revealed just how effective this strategy has been:

[T]he U.S. Energy Information Administration reported a shocking drop in power sector coal consumption in the first quarter of 2012. Coal-fired power plants are now generating just 36 percent of U.S. electricity, versus 44.6 percent just one year ago. It's the result of an unprecedented regulatory assault on coal leaving us all much poorer.

WATCH YOUR LANGUAGE

Towns and cities across the country are beginning to use the language of Agenda 21—in some cases without even knowing it. The Planning Board of Kingwood, New Jersey, recently recommended the following change to the town's Land Development Ordinance:

> *The Township Committee's desire to preserve and enhance the undeveloped rural lands situated along the Route 12 Corridor in such a manner that will maintain and reinforce the Township's rural character and existing scenic views and vistas. . . .*

The preservation of "existing scenic views and vistas" is classic Agenda 21–speak and can be found in many other city land-use statements. Consider Scandia, Minnesota's statement, which is also soaked in Agenda 21 clichés:

> *The Guidelines will be used by the City to review new developments proposed under the "Open Space Conservation Subdivisions" language of the Zoning Ordinance. The existing ordinance language allowed for a density bonus as an incentive to encourage projects that demonstrate* "Preservation of priority scenic views as identified by the City, especially as viewed from public roads and property."

Countless other cities and towns are using the same kind of vocabulary in legislation and proposals: Tacoma, WA; Torrey Pines, CA; Charleston, SC; Rancho Palos Verdes, CA; Dacula, GA; Hemet, CA; Oakland, CA; etc. Others, like Davis, CA, list almost every Agenda 21 goal in their city plan. Many of the biggest enthusiasts of these concepts undoubtedly have no idea about their socialist origins.

WHAT YOU CAN DO

There is good news. Since Agenda 21 relies so heavily on local governments for its acceptance and implementation, individuals have successfully been able to halt its progress.

The key is education. People who educate themselves on the real objectives of Agenda 21 usually turn into serious critics of it. But while awareness about Agenda 21 seems to have increased significantly in recent years, there is still much work to be done. Many local officials— even well-meaning ones—are completely naïve as to what, and who, they are really up against.

One of the best and most surprising advocates *against* Agenda 21 is a woman from California named Rosa Koire. Koire is a liberal Democrat who understands that Agenda 21 will destroy America as we know it. She travels the country giving speeches to both sides of the aisle, presenting her case against ICLEI and Agenda 21. Her website is included in the list below and is definitely worth a read if you're interested in helping spread the truth.

RESOURCES & EDUCATION

1972 Stockholm Declaration: http://www.unep.org/Documents.Multilingual/
    Default.asp?documentid=97&articleid=1503

1973 UNEP Report: http://www.unep.org/resources/.../73_06_GC1_report_%20K
    7309025.pdf

1976 Vancouver Declaration: http://www.unhabitat.org/downloads/docs/924
    _21239_The_Vancouver_Declaration.pdf

1987 UN Report: "Our Common Future": http://conspect.nl/pdf/Our_Common
    _Future-Brundtland_Report_1987.pdf

Full Agenda 21 Publication: http://www.un.org/esa/dsd/agenda21/index.shtml

1992 Rio Declaration: http://www.un.org/documents/ga/conf151/aconf15126
    -1annex1.htm

ICLEI USA website: http://www.icleiusa.org

ICLEI "U.S. Mayor's Climate Protection Agreement": http://www.iclei.org/documents/USA/documents/CCP/Climate_Action_Handbook-0906.pdf

Rosa Koire's website: http://www.DemocratsAgainstUNAgenda21.com

The American Policy Center offers a one-page primer on Agenda 21: http://americanpolicy.org/sustainable-development/agenda-21-in-one-easy-lesson.html

The 9/12 Project counts Agenda 21 education among its objectives: http://the912-project.com

Online (Facebook) groups:

Wake Up Call To Agenda 21: http://www.facebook.com/groups/185234981487143/

Resist UN Agenda 21: http://www.facebook.com/groups/183101898406874/

Stopping UN Agenda 21: http://www.facebook.com/pages/Stopping-Agenda-21-and-sustainable-development/200953626623622

* * *

Finally, since those who speak about Agenda 21 are constantly marginalized as radicals or conspiracy theorists, I wanted to include a link to the official 2012 GOP platform, which formalizes the party's opposition to the plan:

> *We strongly reject the U.N. Agenda 21 as erosive of American sovereignty, and we oppose any form of U.N. Global Tax.*

The complete GOP platform can be found at: http://www.gop.com/2012-republican-platform_exceptionalism

ACKNOWLEDGMENTS

Glenn

Special thanks to . . .

The listeners, readers and TheBlaze TV viewers—you are changing the world by changing minds. You humble and inspire me every single day.

My partners at Mercury Radio Arts and TheBlaze. You are the storytellers of this generation. Never stop dreaming.

My incredible wife and family, who support me in all things at all times. And very special congratulations to my amazing daughter, Hannah, who was recently "paired" with her new husband, Tim. Hannah, because you helped find this needle of a novel among the haystack we are going to wake people up and ensure that your marriage is full of all the love, hope and joy that those in this novel never got to experience.

Everyone at Simon & Schuster, Premiere Radio, Clear Channel, NEP, MLB Advanced Media and all of the other world-class companies we've partnered with—your hard work behind the scenes has always been one of the secrets to our success.

Harriett

Grateful appreciation goes to:

My family, the most loyal cheerleaders in the world;

Carlow University's supportive fiction writing division of Madwomen In The Attic, mentored by the amazing Evelyn Pierce;

Editors Emily Bestler and Kevin Balfe; Sarah Cypher and Elayne Masters;

and last, but certainly not least, Glenn Beck, for his inspiration and support.